No Way Out

To Jon,
Never Mind
the Bollocks!

Barry

Dec '16

No Way Out

*Those who enter here are told to leave their
dreams behind,*
*You may never go to sleep again, but you don't
mind.*
It's a place that I could write a book about
*When they let you in, you'll find there's no way
out.*
Elvis Costello – *The World of Broken Hearts*

Den Barry

Acknowledgments

The completion of this book would not have been possible without contributions from a variety of people so, in time-honoured fashion and in no particular order, I would like to express my gratitude to;

David Worth for his excellent cover design. I contacted David out of the blue one day when I first saw his fantastic work. He had no notion as to who I was and I hadn't even half-finished the first draft of this book at the time so – like me - he had little clue as to where I was going. He wasn't fazed by being tapped up by a clueless, unknown first time author. Not only did he agree to do the artwork, he offered it for free as he shared my 'Do-It-Yourself' ethic. He is a rare beast, being a talented man with a big heart and an open mind. David is also a punk rock fan so in my opinion has pretty much the full package. In my opinion, everyone should check out his work (on Facebook via www.facebook.com/punkrockcartoon or on Twitter @punkrocktoons and on his website www.punkrocktoons.com).

Clare Christian and Karen Day who provided much advice on self publishing and the content of the book respectively. Clare and Karen have given me so much excellent guidance and have commented so positively. The best bits of the book are where I heeded their advice and the weaker parts are inevitably where I chose to ignore them. I am grateful for their help and I offer apologies for the times when I should have paid more attention to their undoubted expertise. I am also grateful to Rebecca Emin for her practical assistance with formatting for both the paperback and E-book versions of this novel.

Karen Jackson for her support in putting some huge things behind me and for helping me look towards a brighter, more positive future. Karen is a courageous, wise and intelligent woman; she is also my lawyer so I should maybe stop writing these words about her now in case she charges me for the time she has spent reading them.

Ruth Anstee-Tricker for her proof reading skills and for her time, which no doubt would have been better spent with her husband and son...and teaching English to her students of course. Thankfully she knows her way around a verb, an adverb and an adjective. She knows where to place an apostrophe, when to leave one out and is comfortable with a smattering of hyphens. I won't mention her knowledge of the colon as that would just be puerile. Ruth helped me no end, and for that I am grateful.

I would also like to thank my son Danny Barry and my friend Tony Panons for taking the time to read my final draft before publication and for their sense-checking and helpful comments on the story, my punctuation and a couple of unusual tangents. Also I am grateful to all of the members of the Portsmouth Creative Writing Group led by Conor Patrick for their helpful input in earlier drafts.

Gratitude also should go to JW (AKA John Warne, AKA Frank Limon) for his web design skills, patience and persistence. In his words I am his "...*worst client ever*" which is fair comment given the amount of time he has had to wait for information, comments and agreement on various proofs he has designed for me. I should add at this point, in my defence, that I am also his ONLY client to date, although I am sure this will change imminently. I would also like to acknowledge JW's endurance in numerous beer drinking sessions over the years and for sitting beside me on the middle-aged-male scrapheap with such good humour. Jane and I have spent many hours getting rat-arsed in the company of JW and his lovely wife Lizzie and we never fail to arrive home without a warm glow inside and aching face muscles from the laughter. Friendships such as these are rare and serve as food for the soul.

At this point I should also take time to acknowledge the friendship and company afforded to me at various times by; Paul Hazzard, Don & Tracey Curtis, Leon Tricker, Helen Hudson, Andy Frazer, Andy & Sally Cornish, Bill Gaynor, Mark Rogers, Steve Lithgow, Johnny Parkes, Graham Fletcher, Ian Farr, Patrick Pugh, Vince Gibbs, Graham Toddy Todd, Ian Hunt, my son Sam Barry, my daughter Jo Barry, my family, my brothers Kevin & Mike and my parents; all of whom have helped me laugh during the more challenging times of my life as well as periodically feigned interest in the forthcoming novel. They have also promised to buy a copy of this book if I mention them in the acknowledgements...

Finally, I owe a few words of gratitude to my long-suffering wife Jane for her unswerving support, encouragement and for keeping my life and soul together. She has spent countless hours reading numerous drafts of this book in the bath whilst trying to unwind from tough days in the office. She stood by me during difficult times; she gave me hope and still holds my hand in the dark. On the bleakest of days she makes me smile, makes me tea and provides the perfect running commentary every time I step out of the house to literally prevent me from falling on my face. She's one in a million and I would be lost without her. Most of all, she makes me feel significant when I am feeling anything but. I like to think it's a two-way thing of course as I look after our menagerie of cats and dogs who would all have been taken into care by now if left to her alone. She has also finally learned to clap on "2 and 4" under my expert tutelage. It's time however, for her now to enjoy a relaxing bath without me badgering her to re-read another re-drafted chapter...and maybe she'll even get a glass of wine and her back scrubbed occasionally by way of payback. This book is dedicated to her.

Den Barry

Yeah well, I say what I mean;
I say what comes to my mind,
I never get around to things;
I live a straight, straight line.
You know me I'm acting dumb.
You know the scene, very humdrum...

Chapter 1

"It's Geri Halliwell."

"Eh?"

"Look, there! It's Geri Halliwell."

"Get lost."

"It's Geri Halliwell I tell you."

"You mean Mollie Sugden right?"

"Mollie WHO? Where *exactly* are you looking? No, it's GERI HALLIWELL!"

"No, it's not Geri-fucking-Halliwell, it's MOLLIE FUCKING S-U-G-D-E-N!"

Mike and Sid had argued for over twenty minutes and could, in fact, argue like this for hours if the mood took them. Sitting in the mismatched armchairs in Mike's non-descript lounge, they had been gazing out of the window at the rain for what seemed an eternity. Mike had started the current debate having ventured aloud that the water dripping and running down the outside of the double glazing had formed into a shape that closely resembled the face of the former-union-flag-dress-wearing, former-flame-haired, former Spice Girl.

Sid closely studied the watery shapes forming as rivulets of rain that ran down and across the glass, yet refused to budge in his own assessment.

"You can even see her Mrs. Slocombe beehive kinda hair-do" he insisted, "Just like she had in Grace Brother's heyday...LOOK!"

With his voice raised, he jabbed his long nicotine stained index finger repeatedly on the window, making a "tub-tub-tub" sound as it pointed out the late character actress' likeness formed in water droplets outside.

Leaning forward, Mike squinted at the patterns that had been forming and tilted his head to one side like a puzzled dog vacantly confused on seeing its own reflection. He seemed intent on disproving his friend's view once and for all when the wind briefly changed direction, a deluge of rainwater hit the outside of the glass and the shape of Geri/Mollie was gone.

"Aw bollocks. We didn't even see her famous pussy...hur-hur!" muttered Sid, somewhat seedily and leaning back, he took another long puff on the joint the two had been passing between them, "What now?" he asked emptily, he leant over the arm of his chair and, not looking but with his left arm outstretched, passed the joint to Mike. Reclining back in his soft black leather armchair, Mike took what was left of the weed they had been smoking, being mindful not to allow any small glowing embers to drop onto the polished floorboards or his favourite chair. He pulled on the joint and with narrowing eyes, looked at his best friend.

"Where did you say you got this gear again Sid? It's *VERY* good." Mike exhaled a huge final lungful of grey-blue smoke which rolled slowly across the raindrop covered window. He stubbed out the burning roach, singeing the end of his thumb as he did so and winced.

"I got it from Twitchy Tel in the White Hart..." Sid mumbled, "...you like?"

"I do indeed, I bloody do!" said Mike before changing his satisfied tone to one more resembling puzzlement, "...but who the hell is *Twitchy Tel*?"

"Oh you know, Terry Morris, the guy with the nervous tic who wears the grubby red Harrington and always sits in the corner of the White Hart...T-W-I-T-C-H-Y" Sid explained again, this time cruelly demonstrating the involuntary mannerisms that afforded Tel his nickname.

Mike, none the wiser, smiled and sat back once again. He closed his eyes and sighed.

"Do you know what Sid? At this precise moment, I feel just about as relaxed as I've been since I got the letter." Mike smiled for the first time in days. And all this despite the fact he seemingly had no idea who 'Twitchy Tel' actually was

Sid said nothing; he was relieved that Mike had quickly forgiven him for not mentioning his chance meeting with Mike's "Ex-Wife-From-Hell" and didn't want to re-open that particular subject. It was always tricky mentioning her and, given that he hadn't spoken in detail about what had *actually* transpired between the two of them when he bumped into her recently, Sid decided that keeping silent on the matter was the better part of cowardice on this occasion.

From between the rainclouds, a momentary shard of sunlight gently rested on Mike's brow and warmed him. After a few moments, he opened his eyes again to watch Sid who had started to hum a tune out loud and gently strum a couple of chords on his beloved vintage Gibson Hummingbird acoustic guitar. Sid often did this after a smoke.

"Are you working on something new Sid?"

asked Mike, still with his eyes closed.

"Nah, just drifting along in another place mate, cradled safely in the bosom of a mystical High Priestess..." Sid's voice trailed off as he continued playing. Mike smirked at his friend, he always dismissed this kind of talk as pretentious hippy bollocks, yet Sid was certainly away somewhere else, his fingers dancing along the mother-of-pearl inlaid fret board.

Mike looked on through red and puffy half-closed eyes and drifted away momentarily himself. They were both quietly enjoying the gentle but unusual percussive rhythm of Sid's guitar playing,

'Tap-tap-tippety-tap-tap' it went and, with eyes closed, they independently nodded along.

'Tap-Tap-Tippety-Tippety-Tap' it continued.

'TAP-TAP-TAP' it developed into something more urgent.

'TAP-TAP-BLOODY-WELL-TAP-TAP-TAP' and suddenly as the knocking coming from the front door grew in its intensity and was joined by a female voice shouting through the letterbox, they both found themselves standing up, trying to unscramble their senses.

"It's OK, it's Amy," said Mike with no real sense of relief in his trembling voice at all. "I'll let her in, you put *that* somewhere out of sight." He passed the ashtray to Sid, straightened his t-shirt, ran his fingers through his cropped spiky blonde hair and dusted some imaginary detritus from the front of his jeans. He disappeared from the room and went to the door to greet his sister.

Sid looked at the ashtray, did a full three-hundred-and-sixty degree turn searching for somewhere clever to hide it, and opted to simply slide it under the brown Dralon armchair he had been sitting in. He opened the window, sat down, smoothed his own hair back with both hands and picked up his guitar again. He was busy focusing on getting his 'non-stoned' facial expression right when Amy walked in, closely followed by a nervous looking Mike.

As she came in it quickly appeared that Amy wasn't at all happy. She walked into the room bedraggled and carrying a soggy newspaper which had served – somewhat unsuccessfully - as the only protective barrier between her and the worst the spring weather could throw at someone caught out by the British climate.

Amy dropped the soggy newspaper onto the glass-topped coffee table where it made a wet 'Schh-lupp' sound. Water, like blood slowly oozing from a corpse, drained from the newspaper onto the table as it quietly surrendered its life in Amy's defence. Sid pulled a face of faux disgust as he lifted the remains of the *Guardian* from the previous Thursday and slid it unceremoniously into the waste paper basket. Sid's stoned idyll was then abruptly shattered.

"What the *ACTUAL FUCK* are you pair of fucking clowns up to?" she screamed, "I've been knocking on your fucking door for fucking ages waiting for some fucking moron to open the fucking thing!". Amy slumped down into the leather armchair recently vacated by Mike and started to sob "...and I've just heard your news from Candy of all people, not from *you* Mike, from *FUCKING CANDY*!"

"Man, that girl can swear!" Sid quietly exclaimed to himself, momentarily proud in the knowledge that his years of teaching had rubbed off so beautifully on his best mate's little sister. "Could do with a little more variety but...Man...I mean, fucking hell that was awesome!" He turned to Mike and went on, "Do you remember how we used to wile away boring rainy weekends teaching Amy all the swear words we picked up at school and youth club? We bloody creased up when she used the words we taught her, usually incorrectly I might add..." he nodded at Amy who stared back at him, her mouth wide open as he continued. "...and how she would always get caught by adults but she never told on us, did you Amy? So we used to take full advantage..."

"Shut up Sid, can't you see..." Mike tried, unsuccessfully, to interrupt as Sid faced Amy.

"...And nowadays you're *so* very mild mannered and sweet so your potty mouth only appears when you've had a couple of proseccos. But it's *still* highly amusing!" Smiling broadly, Sid tapped a Camel filter out of the soft pack he had taken from his shirt pocket and lit it, somewhat flashily, with his Zippo lighter.

Mike looked at his friend disdainfully, he was such a cliché.

"*SHUT UP SID!*" he barked, as he pulled a tatty throw from the back of the sofa and gently placed it around his sister, at the same time surreptitiously mopping up the rain water dripping from her onto the soft black nappa leather of his chair.

"Now what do you mean by '*my news*' Amy? What has Candy been saying to you now? I can assure you nothing important is happening Amy...honestly! I just got this letter from Maddie out of the blue that's all." Mike nervously chattered on, appearing to know exactly what Amy was alluding to. Amy struggled to fight back her tears and Mike carried on trying to mask the awkwardness in the room,

14

"This is so unlike you, you're always the more grown up one of us Amy, regardless of the fact that you are so much younger than me. You're the steady one, the one I lean on in times of drama, and we know there have been a few of those over the years, eh?" Mike was nodding at his sister and Sid in turn, smiling unconvincingly.

Sid rolled his eyes; Amy sobbed and tried to catch her breath. She cleared her throat and started to speak, her voice trembling,

"This Maddie thing, I know I'm not supposed to mention anything about her and Liam bu..." Amy suddenly stopped speaking, stopped crying and sat bolt upright. Remaining rigid for a moment, her eyes darted left and right in their sockets. She took a deep breath, opened her eyes wide and started swearing again.

"Are you two fuckwit losers smoking fucking pot?" she exclaimed. Before either Mike or Sid could respond by pointing out that no one called it 'pot' anymore, she aimed an accusatory index finger at her brother's face and quizzed; "Are you completely out of your tiny fucking mind?"

"Actually, he *IS* out of his mind..." ventured Sid, looking ever so slightly pleased with the comic intent and timing of his answer, "...all thanks to some of the best home grown skunk money can buy, *hur-hur!*" He sat back, relaxed and smugly triumphant, enjoying the sensation for just long enough not to spot Amy lean across the arm of the chair and aim a blow to the back of his head.

The slap landed on its target and caused a momentary lull in Sid's ability to think even remotely straight. This lapse was just long enough for Amy to land a second and then a third blow on the now increasingly bewildered Sid's head.

15

Before Mike could protest or intervene, he felt the first of two slaps himself, one either side of *his* head. "Of all the childish, juvenile and immature things you could be doing of a weekend...*THIS HAS TO TAKE THE FUCKING BISCUIT*!" Amy screeched, now standing and angrily waving her arms around.

"Mmm...biscuit" thought Sid momentarily, but rather than point out that he was beginning to experience the inevitable post-weed munchies and therefore the hilarity of what she had just said; or indeed that she had used three different words in her telling off that meant exactly the same thing; or indeed say anything of any consequence at all; Sid just looked back at Amy, shrugged his shoulders and smiled dimly.

"What-EV-err!" he eventually said, in a mock California accent, before relaxing back in his chair once again.

Amy, seemingly re-energised by Sid's apparent contempt, wagged her finger at him and continued her rant;

"Don't talk to me like that you fucking idiot, what are you doing to my half-wit loser of a brother?" They both looked at Mike who by now was thinking along similar, biscuit related, lines to Sid. Mike looked back at them both and politely enquired,

"Tea and biccies anyone?" He stood up and walked out of the room, still vigorously rubbing the side of his head as he went.

"Listen Amy..." Sid mumbled as he leant forward, pulled the ashtray out from under his armchair and put out his cigarette before sitting back again. He tapped another Camel from the pack and, again with *way* too much style for Amy's liking, he lit it. "...he's had a couple of pretty rough days OK? Maybe you could just cool it a little?" he held his arms out, and with the palms of his hands open upwards, trying to reinforce his words with a "*Y'know?*" sort of gesture.

"You're such a cliché sometimes Graham, such a fucking cliché. He looks like he hasn't shaved for days, is probably wearing dirty clothes and to cap it all he's now off his head on drugs!" said Amy as she too sat down again, exasperated.

Sid was always taken up a little short when someone used his real name. He was given the nickname when he was fifteen years of age as he looked a little like the Sex Pistol's bass player. There were few people still in his life that knew his real name, let alone used it after all these years. He may not have looked much like Sid Vicious any more, but the moniker was his now so it mattered very little. Amy tended to use it from time to time when she was telling Sid off, a little like a mother using a child's full name, and he would show nothing more than irritation when she did so. She continued unabated;

"He's a responsible adult with a responsible career and all of that *Sid*, what would happen if his students – or worse still the other staff at Highdown College - knew about this? "Mr. Mike Powell, Senior Lecturer and Erstwhile Stoner" said Amy, in a deep radio announcer's style voice, "I can just see the sign on his office door now," she said, making the rectangular shape of an imaginary sign in the air with her hands as she said so, "He'd be out on his arse in five minutes flat."

"*He* may be on his way out already Amy..." said Mike, walking back into the room carrying a heavily laden tea-tray. "...not too sure I want to go back after the break...or ever. And anyway, I haven't got my own office...well, not yet. I'm still in the old open-plan room with the rest of the Humanities Team, so technically it would have to be a v-e-r-y l-o-n-g sign on my desk. Plus Tim smokes a bit of weed with Tania from time to time and he's more senior than I am. It's a very middle class thing these days; the Principal probably does it too."

Amy pulled an 'OK, smart-arse' kind of face at her brother but he continued without seeming to notice,

"Anyway, I know this isn't exactly the end of the world or anything but it does mean I am rethinking stuff about my life," he said, "So I'm just glad Reading Week has started and I can get my shit together and contemplate the future. I'm going to see the doc at the end of the week too."

Mike carefully placed the tray on the coffee table. It was piled high with two small plates of biscuits; an assortment of crisps and snacks in bags; three mugs; a sugar bowl; a jug of milk; a pot of tea covered with a tea-cosy in the style of a terrorist balaclava (a recent present from Sid); and a Fortnum & Mason silver tea strainer (a birthday present from Amy).

"How *on earth* did you not drop anything?" said Amy, forgetting her bad mood momentarily whilst simultaneously remaining oblivious to how impressed she sounded.

"I did," said Mike, going out of the door and returning a moment later with an already open packet of digestives and a bag of cheese straws. "There..." he said dryly, "...now, shall I be Mum?" and he started to pour three mugs of tea.

Sid always seemed slightly taken aback that his otherwise slightly slovenly best friend had never broken the habit of making tea in a pot and serving it from a tray with a small milk jug and sugar-lumps out of a sugar bowl. It had become something that Mike was known for doing, it was his *thing*...and something of a tradition.

This habit had been instilled in him by Sid's late Mum – foster Mum actually – Anita, when they were young and whilst she was dying of cancer. Sid was sure Mike only did it at first to please her when he visited them during her illness. Whenever he let himself in the back door of Sid's house as a teenager Mike would start by yelling;

"Hi Anita! Alright Sid? I'm here and I'm putting the kettle on!"

She would respond in dulcet Irish tones, "Hiya! Don't forget to scald the pot properly first Michael, you know I can tell when you haven't!"

Sid would join his friend in the kitchen as Mike would inevitably respond to Sid's foster mother with a; "Yeah, yeah, yeah, I know!" pretending to be both dismissive of Anita's orders and slightly rude towards her. He would then pull a face in her direction from the kitchen and smile knowingly at Sid.

Anita would pause for a few moments and then, as people of her generation often did, she would reply, "And if the wind changes direction, you blaggard, your face will *stay* like that!"

Sid and Mike would never cease to be both amazed and impressed. They were always awestruck at the power of a woman who, despite her failing health, could *still* see through walls or out of the back of her head – as all mothers in the 1970s could of course - and they would both laugh, uncontrollably. It was an altogether familiar routine at the time. Sid sometimes found it a little patronising on Anita's behalf, especially when Anita got close to the end. Sometimes he wanted it to stop as it was nothing more than a thin veneer masking the sadness in the only home in which he had been happy since his parents' death. But Anita seemed to enjoy it so, for her sake, he wouldn't ask Mike to stop.

Since she died, however, Sid never failed to feel anything but a warm glow when Mike made tea. Although ordinarily preferring coffee, Sid just loved tea at Mike's. When all around them were impatiently dunking tea bags in and out of mugs, squeezing and re-dunking if the colour wasn't right, Mike would single-handedly try to buck the trend. This could accurately be described as 'Hand Crafted' and wasn't similar in any way to the ubiquitous 'Hand Crafted Tea & Coffee' sold in pubs and cafés, Sid hated all that nonsense.

Mike always used loose leaf tea in a pot and poured it into bone china mugs through a strainer. He always used freshly boiled water; he warmed the pot beforehand, just as Anita had taught him all those years before; and most importantly, he always allotted sufficient time to allow the beverage to brew correctly. As a consequence, a cup of tea at Mike's – although seeming slightly ritualistic and occasionally annoying when one was impatiently thirsty – was always a treat. This was especially true when he had been shopping for suitable sweet and crunchy things to accompany the tea. This, incidentally, always happened when the pair enjoyed an occasional smoke.

Sid, however, wasn't hanging around today as he had work to do. He slurped his tea quickly, way too quickly judging by the look of disdain on Mike's face and selected a handful of biscuits,

20

nuts and a couple of cheese straws.

"Gotta split guys," he said, stuffing two Jaffa cakes in his mouth and sliding an arm into his beaten up leather biker jacket.

"I'm gonna be in the studio all evening and probably most of the night," he mumbled, through the mouthful of chocolate-covered sponge and orange jelly. "Mmm, these are *lovely* by the way...I once had a raspberry version of these when I was on holiday somewhere Mediterranean or Greek...Corfu I think it was...maybe?...Well somewhere out that way...real nice they were but nothing like a *proper* Jaffa Cake...these were a great invention weren't they?"

Mike and Amy sat silently and watched as Sid rotated slowly on the spot where he had been standing, dropping flaky cheese straw crumbs from the food in his left hand in a ring shape on the wooden floor whilst wrestling with his jacket in order to get it to relinquish its second sleeve to his flailing right arm. As he walked out of the room and down the hall he called out some instructions;

"If Candy, or *anyone*, calls, I'm working and probably going to be unavailable for a bit...maybe even a few days...just tell her, or *anyone* else, to leave a message on my voicemail...if I have any coverage at the studio...and take care mate, look after yourself ok? Cheers!" The front door slammed shut and all was quiet.

"I wish you would try to stop him driving when he's had a smoke, he'll kill himself or an innocent person one day..." said Amy after a few moments had silently passed, "...and how would you feel *then*? You'd think his parents dying in a car crash would have served as an example to

21

him, but I don't reckon it even registers."

Mike said nothing, he wanted to give his friend the usual backing he was afforded following criticism but he realised he couldn't offer a strong enough defence on such an occasion, so chose to remain silent. Mike was always reluctant to lecture Sid, they had been friends since childhood, a rarity amongst men these days, and although they frequently fell out of trees as children, they never fell out with each other.

Mike went to the window; it had stopped raining at last and the sun seemed to have elbowed itself between the clouds to put in an appearance. Mike was just in time to see Sid pull the roof down on his red 1978 Alfa Spider and get to work trying to start it up. The car was neck-twistingly beautiful but, especially in the rain, just about as reliable as Sid himself. In the small space behind the seats Mike could make out the tools of Sid's trade. A black and grey rectangular flight case with the word *'Fender'* emblazoned in the corner and home to his 1966 sunburst Telecaster. Next to it was the fatter, hourglass shaped dark brown case that protected his pride and joy, a 1958 Les Paul Standard. This was also in sunburst; Sid was nothing if not consistent when it came to such things.

"Why does he insist on leaving those things in his car when we all know the doors can be opened with any small and pointed object?" Mike said, exasperated, knowing that the Gibson in particular was worth almost as much as Mike's entire Victorian terraced house.

"I've told him time and again to leave them at the studio or out of sight, or keep them in a fucking bank vault for Christ's sake...he could even leave them here with his acoustic, at least they'd be safe."

As Sid's Alfa spluttered into life - on the fourth turn of the ignition and with a cough and a cloud of oily blue smoke from the exhaust - Mike turned his attention back to his sister. Although she was drying out a little and enjoying a pile of biscuits with Mike's delicious tea, Amy was clearly still waiting for an explanation as to why Candy had heard the news that Maddie had been in touch before she had.

"So, Candy..." enquired Amy, more calmly this time, "...why *her*?"

"She stayed over the other night," offered Mike and then, realising he had explained nothing, he went on; "Sid was here and she had been repeatedly calling him, like she does, you know? Anyway, she eventually turned up, a little drunk and promptly fell asleep on the sofa..." Mike gestured towards the sofa with a nod of his head in case Amy didn't understand the concept of what 'the sofa' meant "...and so I just covered her up and left her there. I'd heard from Maddie that afternoon and was telling Sid about what she'd said about Liam in the letter. Candy must have been a little more sober and a little less asleep than I thou...." Mike trailed off, noticing that the damp patches on his beloved leather recliner had increased in size, "...er...thought."

He went on stoically; "Listen, maybe the situation isn't as serious as you think, you know how flaky Maddie used to be, especially when it comes to matters about our son...I haven't seen her *or* Liam for thirteen years after all...and anyway look, you're still *very* wet. You need to get out of those things and go home...er...I mean....maybe go home and get out of those wet

23

things. I'll drive you back and tell you on the way, or better still we can meet up this evening and I'll tell you all about it then. You can help me see what's to be done...if anything is to be done at all. We can get something at the White Hart if you want, it's 'International Nite, All-You-Can-Eat' on a Monday...on me...what do you say?"

"OK" said Amy, not wishing to pressure Mike any more than she already had. The offer of her brother buying dinner *was* appealing given the extent of her overdraft and empty purse so Amy withdrew from needling him further. "But I'm getting the bus home. I've got a return ticket anyway and like your daft mate, *you* are in no condition to drive either. Can I just have a jumper or something I can put on instead of this though?" She pulled at her own wet cardigan, "I'm bloody freezing."

Mike grabbed a zip-up fleece from the hook on the back of the pine door and threw it to Amy. She deftly caught it in her left hand, seemingly without looking, whilst simultaneously finishing her cup of tea with the other.

Amy put her mug down and turned her back on her brother. She took her wet top off and slipped into the warm dry fleece, zipped it up and turned back to face Mike. She stood on her tip-toes and kissed him on the forehead. She smiled and collected a small handful of assorted nibbles for her journey, packing them into her pockets. Mike winced slightly as his favourite *North Face* top's pockets became akin to a kangaroo's pouch with handfuls of crispy snacks in place of a joey. He wanted to protest...but for the second time since Amy arrived earlier, he chose to say nothing.

"I'll call you when I get home....late-*errs!*" she said seemingly back to her best breezy self and, with a slam of the front door, Mike was alone.

Mike sat down on the arm of the sofa and started to contemplate the turn his life might take now he had heard from Maddie after all this time. As he did so, he picked up a Jaffa cake and held it aloft for a few moments before popping it in his mouth. Whilst enjoying the delicious sensation it gave him, Mike couldn't help but also wonder how a raspberry one might taste.

I am an island, entire of myself,
And when I get old, older than today,
I'll never need anybody's help in any way.
I'm gonna take your money, count your loss
when I'm gone,
I'm alright Jack, I'm looking after number one.

Chapter 2

As Sid drove in the direction of Surrey and TinCan Studios, his mobile rang continuously. Craning his neck so as not to take his eyes off the road for more than a moment, he could just about make out that it was Candy's name and number on the display. He let it ring, choosing instead to turn up the CD player to drown out the ringtone.

Sid had never been bothered to give his friends, colleagues or acquaintances different ringtones on his mobile. Mike had a different ringtone for *everyone* on his mobile phone contacts list and so he knew who was calling without looking. Sid thought this was just Mike trying to be clever and slightly rebellious, although he also knew it was the kind of 'list-thing' that they both secretly liked. Mike was known to use ringtones that weren't altogether flattering for some people, especially ex-girlfriends. Sid recalled that Amy had once asked Mike about him ever worrying if his girlfriend at the time should find out that she had *Personality Crisis* by The New York Dolls as her ringtone. He had simply replied by explaining that, as far as she was concerned, she believed that her ringtone was *Foxy Lady* by Jimi Hendrix and that she wouldn't discover the truth as, logically, she was

26

always elsewhere when she called him.

Sid rolled his eyes, begrudgingly recognising that he had missed a trick in not copying Mike's methods. It would be easier to identify the individual caller quickly and it might even be more pleasant to have his drive interrupted by a tune than by the shudder he experienced when he realised it was Candy calling again. As he mused on which song he would have chosen for Candy's ringtone, he turned the CD player up to its loudest setting and planted his foot into the threadbare carpeted floor of the Alfa.

'*Just Fade Away*' HA-HA!" Sid laughed aloud. Stiff Little Fingers were his kind of band and the tune was just cruel enough to use as a ringtone for Candy. "Bloody perfect!" he said to himself, smiling broadly as the Alfa sped through the twists and turns of the leafy Surrey country lanes.

On his journey to work, Sid was listening to the new record (he still called them records) by Johnny Ronson and his band The Electric Shavers. '*Pure Noise*' was The Shavers' third studio album and a bit of a commercial success. Their first two albums had both been well received yet had achieved only what one would call 'cult' status. This was a euphemism – in Sid's mind at least - for being liked by music journalist wankers who wanted to appear supremely knowledgeable to their editors and readers alike but were in fact nothing more than music snobs of the highest order. This was ironic, considering Sid was of a similar ilk. It was true; he had played with some of the greatest and most influential bands and artists of a generation and would use the stories of such work to impress people, especially if there was a chance of him getting laid. Yet despite this, he would still anonymously whore his talents to all comers when asked to play session work, even recording tracks for wannabe winners of the dreaded TV show '*Pop Factor*'. He'd inherited his jazz musician parents' musical abilities and exploited his talents to the full.

Sid liked the new Shavers' album a lot and had played it repeatedly for over a week now. This hadn't happened with an album he hadn't appeared on for some time. New CDs usually made one play through in Sid's car if they were any good. Many more were merely skipped through, track by track, for a few seconds on each song before being ejected and unceremoniously dumped in the passenger footwell. This record was different; it was *very* good.

Sid had known Johnny since the latter was plain old John McShane, son of the local baker in town, close to where he and Mike grew up. Sid, Mike and John were all at the same school for a couple of years, although John was slightly younger than they were. John was always; well, sort of 'interesting' as a boy. Before punk rock came along, he refused to wear his hair long when all the other boys did. He listened to psychedelic rock and American garage bands rather than the glam or pop the other boys were in to...much like Graham Stevens and Michael Powell (as they were then) and John got picked on as a result of this apparent 'weirdness'. Graham and Michael would often stick up for him, saving his lunch money or helping him avoid having his cropped head being flushed down the fifth-year toilets on a number of occasions. One day, John's parents split up – just as Graham became Sid and Michael became Mike - and he went to live with his mum in London.

Sid and John's paths crossed again a number

of years later when Sid was invited to play one of his early sessions at TinCan, an up-and-coming studio where he was starting to become the first choice player for all things 'Alternative' or Rock'. Sid became a regular contributor over the ensuing years and his reputation – and that of TinCan – steadily grew in parallel.

On this particular occasion, he had been invited to come and play *'all the difficult bits'* on a debut album for the next big thing coming out of the capital. When he arrived he was met by the studio boss Malcolm who was a weasel-like, sly, wheeler-dealer of a man. Malcolm was standing with a thin, blonde-haired and rather white, androgynous character known as 'Johnny Ronson'. The moment Sid walked over and held out his hand to be shaken, the pale wannabe rock god gasped somewhat enthusiastically and threw his arms around Sid, hugging him tightly.

Sid smiled to himself as he did whenever this particular memory came back to him. Although he hadn't instantly recognised Johnny, it was great seeing him again. During their free time between recording album tracks they re-acquainted themselves over a crate of Red Stripe, a couple of bottles of tequila and some great Afghan black. Over the course of the next few days they also created an eponymously titled debut album that topped every indie, rock and alternative chart known in Europe. It briefly crossed-over into the lower reaches of the mainstream chart too giving Johnny Ronson a modicum of success. The two continued to collaborate whenever Johnny was in the country. Sid refused to replace the existing guitarist and join the band himself, much to Johnny's dismay. He did, however, agree to tour with them once, on the European leg of their sell out (albeit of minor underground venues) first tour. This ensured that until their guitarist had mastered all of the complicated riffs Sid had played on their debut album, the bands' fans would never know he was still having lessons.

The new album was great, or so Sid thought. This was surprising to him though, knowing as he did that most of it had been recorded in the States without him and that he had only contributed by helping remix a few of the tracks back in the UK prior to its release. Gone were the days of laying down his own guitar tracks and then recording the numerous over-dubs and keyboard work that he would charge separately for. It had been both a lot of fun and very lucrative for Sid, as was most of his studio work becoming by this time. It had also afforded him a little notoriety amongst the music critics and served to promote his undoubted talents to other promoters, talent scouts and management companies.

Sid swung the Alfa through the gates and along the concrete drive up to TinCan. The studio was in a converted stable block and outbuildings, once part of a rambling country estate in a quiet, uninhabited part of Surrey. It was almost derelict when Malcolm, an electronics engineering student who had dropped-out of his second year at Cambridge on a scholarship claiming it to be "too posh" for him, took them over. Malcolm had – as legend had it - relieved the buildings from their previous owner to settle a gambling debt in the early 1970s.

To his credit, Malcolm *had* creatively converted the buildings into a comfortable, well equipped and now quite sought after, studio set up. It was christened 'TinCan' as a nod to the high corrugated iron roof the stables had for the first year of the studios' existence and the terrible noise that was made by rain that blighted many an early recording session. The replacement roof was the first major investment after Malcolm had built the 32 track desk himself. He had spent time and money on continually improving upon TinCan's facilities ever since. The studios had become Malcolm's life, choosing as he had to remain faithful to it and it alone and not to the succession of wives and girlfriends that seemed to come and then go again, with alarming regularity.

As a consequence, Sid had a begrudging respect for Malcolm. He knew he could get work from a variety of places these days but TinCan felt somehow like home. He had become increasingly successful at the same time as TinCan had and he knew that Malcolm had played a significant part in that success. Malcolm was, however, a difficult man who never wanted to pay the full going rate for anything and who would cut corners on everything he could, except for the kit in the studio. Sid recalled many a session that ended with a near punch-up as Malcolm tried to dock money from the session players' fees for drinks, food and other expenses that he had 'failed' to inform them were not included, such as strings, leads, plectrums, drumsticks etc.

Moreover, Malcolm had never paid full price for anything in his life, apart from his infidelities. His first marriage resulted in a huge cash settlement to his ex-wife and custody of a daughter, Nancy, or *'Little Miss Expense Account'* as Malcolm often called her. Malcolm had been caught cheating by successive women on numerous occasions since Nancy's mother left. This often led to them fleeing with a sports car, some jewellery or a work of art as payment for - as Malcolm would coldly put it - 'services rendered'. Malcolm was the first person Sid had met who went on to sign pre-nuptial agreements and, it was rumoured, he even had blank ones in a filing cabinet in his office in case he needed one quickly and couldn't contact his lawyer.

Sid drove up to the front door of TinCan and maneuvered the car into a parking space marked 'Artist Parking Only'. He climbed out of the Alfa, stretched for a moment and, with a flight case in each hand, sauntered to the door and pressed the buzzer with his nose.

"Elloww?" enquired a high-pitched crackly female voice "Ooh is it?"

"Alright Miss, it's the Revenue" said Sid in his best comic BBC clipped tones. "Would you mind awfully opening the door like a good girl so we can come in and arrest your nasty boss for tax evasion please?"

"C'mon in Sid, kettle's on," replied the voice and with a long beep, the front door was automatically unlocked and Sid was inside. He walked past the coffee machine, the cold drink machine, the snack machine and, opening the double swing doors with his backside, Sid walked backwards into reception, spun around and deposited his guitar cases on the floor.

"Alright Gorgeous, so how's it going?" asked Sid, as the receptionist turned to him with an empty mug in her hand, "...and how's your dad?" Nancy blew a large pink bubble with the gum she was chewing, allowed it to pop and then gathered it all up with a swirl of her pierced tongue before depositing it back in her mouth again.

"Still a conniving, tight-fisted, low-life little ferret....*love* '*im*!" she added sarcastically, before re-commencing her chewing more furiously than before. Nancy wiggled towards the coffee maker, struggling to walk due to the tightness of the multi-coloured mini dress she was wearing and the near six-inch high Louboutins on her feet.

"When are we going to get out of here forever Sid?" she asked, bending over to fill the mug with steaming coffee, "You've said it yourself, 'Sid and Nancy' has a *luvvely* ring to it so *puleeease*, take me away from all this shit!" She turned to face him and caught him slowly looking her up and down. Although caught clearly drooling in Nancy's direction, Sid didn't bat an eye and she feigned a loving but soppy puppy-dog face back at him, which wasn't easy following the three years of continual Botox treatments Nancy had undergone since her first wrinkle appeared, according to her, aged sixteen.

"It *does* have a nice ring to it, sure it does..." Sid said, still thinking ringtones ('*Trouble*' by Elvis Presley for Nancy obviously) "...but it would probably end tragically, you know, with me stabbing you to death in a hotel room in New York and ending up in Rikers. That is of course if your dad hadn't already tracked us down and forcibly removed my bollocks with his Rottweiler." Sid pulled a pained face and Nancy laughed.

"Ha! We'd look great on them t-shirts though, wouldn't we? Both forever young and gorgeous!" she said, blowing another huge gum bubble and fixing her bright crimson hair with her free hand. The familiar routine was suddenly interrupted by a loud voice from behind Sid,

"You're late lad, I'm gonna find me a guitar player with a fahckin' watch one of these days!" growled Malcolm, coming through the double doors. "Car trouble again was it?" he enquired, nodding towards the front door and the Alfa outside, which was in all likelihood still wheezing and reeking of petrol and burnt oil when Malcolm walked past it. "Would've thought you could've bought yourself a decent fahckin' ride by now, with all the fahckin' money I pay you" he continued.

If the car ever needed a ringtone of its own, Adam and the Ants *'Car Trouble'* would be at the top of the list thought Sid, albeit briefly, the effects of the cannabis now wearing away pretty quickly.

"Let's get to work shall we?" enquired Malcolm and he strode off in the direction of the studio control room, taking the mug of coffee from the still outstretched hand of his daughter as he went.

"AND GET THAT FAHCKIN 'ORRIBLE STUFF OUT OF YER MOUTH!" yelled Malcolm, quickly adding, rather sarcastically, *"Sweeet-heaaarrt!"* and throwing Nancy a thin smile before walking through the studio door. Sarcasm seemed to run in the family.

Nancy dutifully picked a waste paper basket from under the reception desk and spat her bubble gum into it, turning to the door through which her father exited and sticking out her studded tongue theatrically. She smoothed her mini-dress down over her gym-toned body and dropped back into the leather receptionist's chair. She crossed her long slim legs and picked up a copy of 'Rolling Stone'.

"*'What a Waste'* by the Blockheads," Sid said quietly to himself. Nancy looked up, momentarily confused, she tried – and failed - to furrow her brow. Sid smiled at her, shrugged his shoulders and picked up his flight cases. "...And definitely

'*Charmless Man*' *by Blur*'" he said under his breath. He turned towards the door and dutifully followed Malcolm.

Hey what'cha talking about? I hope you know,
Something you've thought about, it doesn't show,
You've got so much to say, I wonder why,
Is what you're saying just another lie?
I hear you talking; it seems to me you ain't said
nothing yet
Talk is cheap.

Chapter 3

"It's WAY more common for women to suffer low mood or depression than it is for men..." said Debs (*Protest Song* – Anti Flag), piling another forkful of Hungarian Goulash and rice (dish number 4) into her mouth "...I read this report..." she continued with her mouth full, "...One in four women as opposed to one in TEN men in fact. Although men are more than three times more likely to commit suicide than women, especially between the ages of thirty to sixty." Debs knew these facts as she was someone who continually returned to college or university to study one qualification after another, rather than unleash her 'under' qualified self on the world and forge any kind of career. She stopped chewing momentarily, rocked the wobbly table a couple of times and pulled a face.

They were sat at a corner table in the White Hart, the place they had quite recently considered to have become their *local*. It was a dark and shabby looking bar, but cosy too. The friends had long believed that to look this *shabby-chic* was in fact a very expensive exercise in interior design and planning. There was an array of mismatched wooden chairs and tables that had scratches and

36

stained tops and threadbare cushions; the walls were adorned with a variety of mirrors advertising such diverse brands as White Horse Whisky and Metaxa; metal signs advertising "Erinmore Flake" and something called "Ashton's Artisan Blend"; and a 1970's style poster for Peter Stuyvesant cigarettes. Each wall had the obligatory wall-light with candle-shaped bulbs, each in turn with an individual tassel covered, grubby shade. At the far end of the bar there were old nicotine stained copies of Constable's *'Hay Wain'* and *'Dedham Vale'*, as well as some ubiquitous horse brasses.

The reality was, however, that the mismatched furniture had been randomly collected over many years and had clearly just seen better days; the décor and accessories were variously presented to Nigel, the landlord, by sales reps and the brewery over previous decades and never replaced; and the signs were picked up by Nigel at trade fairs and holidays over a similar period. The paint on the walls and ceiling had yellowed during the days when smoking was allowed in pubs and, since the ban, had served as a reminder - to those who knew it before – that the White Hart once had a reputation as a simple *'Drinkers Pub'*. As with many town centre pubs, the White Hart had learned to survive the smoking ban by both serving food and by erecting a gazebo in the tiny pub garden and calling it a 'covered smoking area'. The heavy-drinking, overweight and chain-smoking Nigel, originally fearful that his days at the pub were nearing an end, considered the new clientele this had attracted something of a coup on his behalf.

"Yeah?" said Candy (*I Want Candy* – Bow Wow Wow), toying with the remains of her Irish Stew (dish number 2) and pushing it around her

37

plate, rocking the table back and forth as she pushed the piece of cold turnip to one side and put her fork down. "But I read that women are more likely to suffer with phobias, anxiety and stuff like OCD too."

"I read all that Men versus Women stuff too!" exclaimed H (*Someone's Gonna Get Their Head Kicked in Tonite* - The Rezillos) joining Debs and Candy at the wobbly table, holding a bowl of Mexican chili and rice (dish number 1). "And they're more likely to have trouble reading maps, driving and parking...as well as the PMT - don't forget the PMT. I reckon that's what drives most of those men to kill themselves." H swung his leg over the backwards facing chair next to the girls' table and sat astride it like a cowboy in a 1960's western. He leant his big tattooed arms on the back of the chair, still cradling his bowl, and smiled broadly at Debs and Candy.

"Shut up *Henry!*" the girls said in bored unison. H glowered at them momentarily and then smiled again; happy in the knowledge that at will, he could piss them off sufficiently that they would break his golden rule and call him by his real name. He picked up a JLB Ale beer mat, inspected it briefly and folded it in half before sliding it under the base of one of the table legs. He leaned back slightly and tried to rock the table again, nodding sagely and smiling with satisfaction as the table refused to budge.

"I'll let you have that one...but seriously, no more eh? You'll make me angry and..." he raised a single eyebrow and paused for dramatic effect, "...you wouldn't like me when I'm angry." H pulled a face that he thought looked like The Hulk but in truth more accurately resembled a badly constipated Dr Bruce Banner. He balanced his spoon on the edge of his bowl, picked up his pint glass and downed almost three quarters of the contents in a single gulp and belched loudly, winking at the girls as he did so.

Debs smiled weakly "Men DO tend to be much more likely than women to be dependent upon alcohol and recreational drugs though. I think it's something to do with them being immature, unintelligent, feeble-minded and socially awkward...or something like that," she said, smiling at H again, but in more of a "I win *again*...you twat" kind of way.

Candy picked up her fork again and looked at H, "We are talking about..." she looked furtively around the bar of the White Hart to see if anyone was listening who shouldn't be, "...*Mike,*" she continued, in more of a whisper, jabbing her fork towards the quizzical look on H's face but thankfully missing by some distance. "He's *really* depressed this time, his doctor has prescribed him with pills and everything, reckons he should go to counselling, all that stuff". Candy relayed to her friends the details of what she had overheard whilst at Mike's, the content of the letter and how it had affected Mike. By the time she finished her story Candy was talking so quietly and hissing so much that H and Debs had to crane their necks and lean in closer to her so as to not miss anything. They were concentrating so much, in fact, that they didn't see Mike and Amy walk in behind them.

"HI ALL!" said Amy loudly enough to make the three sit up rather too quickly to look guilt-free, "Who are we plotting to kill *this* week then? Or are we just discussing stuff that doesn't concern us?" Amy turned to Candy and looked her square in the eye. "I think it was Eliot who said that gossip is like smoke that comes from dirty tobacco pipes; proving nothing but the bad taste of the smoker."

"Not sure I know what you mean Amy...*Good Evening* by the way!" Candy said, lowering her eyes to her cold stew and putting her fork down yet again, this time looking rather more defeated than sated by dish number two.

"You know *exactly* what I mean; the look on your faces tells me everything I need to know. You're talking about my sappy brother aren't you?" said Amy, scanning the three friends' expressions somewhat too forensically for their comfort. "What gives you the right anyway?" she continued, returning her attention to Candy.

"I overheard him telling Sid all about it the other night...and he sounded SO sad...and it doesn't sound good...and we were just...y'know...concerned about him...th-th-that's all," stuttered Candy, again picking up her fork and contritely returning to her Irish stew manoeuvers.

"Well he doesn't need it ok? What Mike needs at the moment is understanding, empathy and he needs a little space in which to breathe..." said Amy, sounding a little like she was making a grand announcement to the rest of the White Hart diners "...oh and put that damn fork DOWN for heaven's sake!"

"Correction!" uttered Mike sternly, holding his open hand up in a *'Please Stop!'* fashion. He then commenced to speak in a way that, when others did it, annoyed him immensely. "What Mike needs is threefold;

One – for you to realise that Mike is, in fact, actually here in the room and as a consequence can hear everything being said about him;

Two – Mike needs something delicious to eat but, failing that, he needs at least to see what five *truly international treats* Nigel has lined up for him this evening and;

Three – Mike needs a *BLOODY DRINK*!"

"*Four* – Mike needs to practice what he preaches and stop talking about himself in the third person," added H sarcastically before he stood up and moved to the bar. He drained his glass and waved it in the air to attract the attention of a member of staff who was gathering empties and generally tidying tables at the far end of the room. She looked over, smiled and, expertly picking up four glasses in each hand, returned to her position behind the bar.

"Usual?" H enquired, looking at Mike. Mike nodded and sat down, "And you?" H looked at Amy, eyebrows raised.

"Gin and tonic please H, and make it a house double seeing as you're buying," she sat between Candy and Mike, nudging Candy slightly, encouraging her both to move up and surreptitiously also to behave.

"How's your love life then Candy? Still bordering on the tragic?" asked Amy, still somewhat aggressively. "Been on any more *first* dates?"

Candy glowered at Amy, "Not since I saw you last," she offered, "I've been busy." She pulled a face at Amy as if to say "Enough, ok?" and returned to her plate of rapidly congealing Irish Stew.

"What? Not even a one-night-stand to report on? Nothing at all?" Amy pressed. H winced from his position at the bar across the table towards Debs at the uncomfortable direction the conversation was headed. Debs' face coloured slightly but she said nothing, even though she knew it was a cheap shot from Amy. H turned to the member of staff who had approached him from behind the bar. Staring at her chest, but making out he was reading her name badge he enquired;

"Hi N-a-t-a-s-h-a, would you be so kind as to get my friends here a house double G and T, with ice and a slice of course, and a pint glass full of Nigel's best room temperature, cloudy and flat-foaming ale please? Whilst you are *at it* – ooh err - I will also have a pint of your ice cold, premium lager...unless you are thinking of taking me home later, in which case I'll have a weaker lager with a top so as not to adversely affect my performance. Oh, and I'll have your number too if you' be so kind my lovely." He winked at Natasha and turned to face his friends whilst she served him.

Natasha looked at the group sitting across from the bar, feigned sticking her fingers down her throat and started preparing the drinks. H said, tapping the side of his nose and then pointing a finger over his shoulder, "I think I might be in here."

Moments later, Natasha returned and placed the gin and a small bottle of tonic, together with a pint of JLB on the counter. She then picked up the pint of lager she had poured and roughly slammed it in front of H, slopping the over-sized foamy head down the side of the glass and onto the bar. "That'll be nine-seventy-five please," she said curtly.

"Thanks gorgeous..." said H, handing Natasha a ten pound note. "...and one for yourself of course." He looked at the pool of lager on the bar and inspected the glass, immediately recognising the signs that he was going home alone tonight, as usual. Meanwhile, Natasha looked at the note in her hand, looked at the group where H was delivering the drinks, shrugged her shoulders and walked away.

The group sat, not speaking, each of them sipping their drinks and waiting for someone else to break the silence. All around them was the hustle and bustle of a busy early evening trade, whilst they sat without a word between them. The White Hart always did well on weeknights due largely to the All-You-Can-Eat 'Nites' format dreamt up by Nigel to encourage customers to visit the establishment straight from work. It was his way of replacing the custom he lost following the smoking ban. Like many (but not all) pubs, the smoking ban had changed the White Hart for the better, well in most customers' eyes at least.

Nigel wouldn't readily agree. These days, therefore, the week in the White Hart went thus;

Monday	International Nite
Tuesday	Burger Nite
Wednesday	Curry Nite
Thursday	Seafood Nite

The 'Nite' theme continued into the weekend, albeit with less of an emphasis on food, as Friday was dubbed 'Karaoke Nite' and then there was usually a live act on a Saturday, billed as 'Music Nite' of course. On a Sunday, customers were either treated to a general knowledge pub quiz ('Quiz Nite') or encouraged to play traditional and not-so-traditional pub games ('Games Nite', naturally).

Mike eventually broke the silence, "Well this IS fun. I wonder what culinary delights we have in store for us to-N-I-T-E" he spelled the last four

43

letters out aloud and the group chuckled, instantly enjoying the running joke they shared every week *and* the feeling of relief that the awkward silence had finally been broken.

Mike looked up at the hand-written menu on the pub chalk board which read;

The White Hart

<u>**INTERNATIONAL NITE**</u>

<u>**ALL – YOU – CAN - EAT**</u>

Mexican Chili
Irish Stew
Moroccan Lamb
Hungarian Goulash
Asian Lentil Curry (v)

<u>All of the above served
with rice/various breads/salad and/or chips.</u>

<u>Customers/Diners please note:</u>
*Some/all items may contain nuts and/or
some/all items may have been prepared in an
environment where nuts are/have been present.*

*Please order/pay at the bar where you will
be given cutlery
and a plate/bowl, then please help yourself
to food/accompaniments as required.*

*Simply return to the servery/bar and help
yourself as frequently as you want/like
afterwards.*

*Please leave your plate/bowl on the
servery/bar
when finished.*

<u>Thanks/Merci/Danke/Gracias/Shukran</u>

The group often couldn't help but wonder why each menu item needed a nation's name as a prefix. They had concluded that it was some kind of emphasis on the 'International' presuming Nigel was fearful of being prosecuted under Trades Description legislation if it was discovered that all of his food in fact came from the local cash and carry store and was cooked by a succession of pub-chefs earning a touch above minimum wage, rather than being lovingly prepared by chefs that the White Hart had flown in at great expense from exotic foreign locations to work in its three-star hygiene-rated kitchen.

In addition to this, they also marveled/wondered at the judicious/generous use of the forward slash on his black/chalk board menus, which they found amusing/irritating in equal measure.

As Mike pondered the menu, his mobile phone rang (*'King Rocker'* - Generation X);

"Hi Sid," said Mike, clearly knowing who it was immediately.

"Hi mate," Sid said, somewhat furtively, "You alone?"

"Yeah, I'm alone..." lied Mike whilst smiling knowingly to his friends, "...what's up mate?"

"Did I leave my gear at yours earlier? It's just that there are a couple of guys here I want to...er...*loosen up* a little if you catch my drift? They're pretty fucking square mate I can tell ya...I mentioned skinning up and they looked at me like I wanted them to go for a naked dip in the river with me. Ha! I reckon they'd even think a roach has something to do with fishing...bloody kids these days have easier access to better recreational drugs than we *ever* did and...anyway, I digress. I was hoping to improve things no end here but can't locate the weed."

"Nah, haven't seen it," said Mike, pausing for a moment to recall the state of the coffee table before he left home. There were various crisp packets, crumbs, three bowls, tea pot and dirty mugs but there was no sign of Sid's hand-painted stash tin there, well, not in his mind's eye at any rate. "You sure it's not on the floor of your car with the rest of your crap?"

Mike picked up his beer and took a long gulp, inspected the light shining through the amber coloured ale before slowly lowering the glass again to the table. As he did so, Candy leant across Amy and grabbed the phone out of Mike's hand. Holding it to her ear, she sat bolt upright and looked back at Mike, daring him to say or do *anything*.

On the other end of the line, Sid was busy visualising the old tobacco tin, with its hand-painted JLB Ale logo on the lid. In his mind's eye it was just visible in the passenger foot well of the Alfa. The head of the person pictured in the logo was peeking out between an empty brown McDonald's bag, a three week old copy of the *New Musical Express* and a Coke Zero bottle.

"I'll go and have another gander, you're probably right mate," he said, feeling a little more relaxed about how the session was going to turn out after all. He went on, "Are you going to the pub tonight? Remember what I said if you run into Candy? Ok? Mike?...OK?" Sid was clearly unaware of the fact that Mike could no longer hear him or of the colour Candy's face was turning at the other end of the phone. He continued, "I mean, fuck me, she's been calling me non-stop this afternoon...non-fucking-stop. I mean, you'd think a girl would get the message by now wouldn't you? WOULDN'T YOU MIKE?"

There was no answer as the phone went dead but somewhere in Surrey Sid was re-energised. He shrugged his shoulders at Mike's apparent reticence and switched his phone back to 'silent' mode. As he slid it back into his jean's pocket, Sid made his way out of the studio to look around the floor of the Alfa, outside in the car park.

Back in the White Hart meanwhile, Mike was staring open-mouthed at his phone which now sitting in the bottom of his pint, lifeless as the screen darkened to black. The friends fell silent again too, all except for the sound of Candy quietly sniffing and dabbing tears from her eyes.

Catch me if you can, when I come your way,
Catch me if you can, I'm falling like the rain.
Everyday I see you, but you're so far away,
Every way I love you, don't you know I love you
so.
I would never ever let you go,
I am yours...

Chapter 4

"WILL YOU STOP IT H? STOP IT *PU-LEEEEEASE*!" said Candy, pulling harder at H's arm, which was still holding the long-haired man by the throat, up against the wall.

"Yeah, let go mate, I meant nothing by it, honest!" whined the man, his hair partly covering his eyes and his toes barely touching the ground. "I wasn't talking about you, or *her*, or ANYONE here!" he continued, with a degree of panic seemingly setting in as he struggled to breathe. A small crowd had gathered at this point, waiting for the inevitable fight, rare on a Monday in town but a completely free – not to be found on Sky TV - spectator sport nonetheless. Candy suddenly thought of another way out of this. She pulled at H again and in a high-pitched and somewhat melodramatic tone this time said,

"*C'mon H, 'e ain't werrrf it!*"

Seeing the knowing smile on her face and getting the point immediately, H finally relaxed his grip on his prey. The long-haired man seized the opportunity and instantly fled, leaving the small crowd to disperse in a mood of anti-climax and H sniggering like a naughty schoolboy. Regaining his composure for a moment H shouted after the long-haired man,

"I should've slapped you into the middle of next fucking week!" The man, who had covered the distance to the end of the street like the proverbial scalded cat, stopped momentarily and turned back towards H and Candy, waving a 'V' sign with each of his hands he shouted back, "Fuck you AND your wife!" before turning and disappearing around a corner somewhere near the Post Office. H and Candy looked at each other and burst out laughing.

"Shall we go then, *Wife*?" asked H, grinning broadly and turning towards Candy, holding out his arm.

"Ooh yes, *Husband*. And may I say, you are SO masterful and yet merciful this evening," replied a faux-impressed Candy. Taking his arm and linking it with hers they walked towards home. She was in a better mood now than earlier when she had her run-in with Amy and been humiliated by Sid. H was simply thinking *"If only"* at the thought of being married to Candy. Candy was simultaneously thinking *"Not likely"* to exactly the same thing.

H had always defended Candy and, as a consequence, wasn't Sid's greatest fan.

Although clearly fond of H too, Candy had seen him in violent situations before. Too many times he had pounded some undeserving – and admittedly sometimes deserving – person to a pulp in front of her. Candy had only learned to deal with this behaviour effectively in adulthood. In years gone by H would often frighten his friends with the level of aggression he could display and could only be dragged out of a fight by a passing police officer or three. These days his friends, and Candy especially, could invariably appeal to his better nature. Although he *had* mellowed there was still little that H enjoyed more than occasionally giving someone what he called a *'little slap'*. Most of the time he managed to let off steam these days by teaching other men how to beat up strangers; or improve their physique; or how to box, in the gym he owned.

H had grown up in a house where he was one of four boys who, due to their mother's drinking and the poverty they endured, competed physically for everything. The brothers would listen from the top of the stairs to their largely absent father who would occasionally resurface from the bookies, another woman's house or prison to take whatever money he could from the boys' mother before beating her soundly and leaving once again. This was a pattern that would repeat itself two or three times a year until the brothers reached their teens and were capable of standing up to him physically. One day they were able to frighten the old man away and they never saw him again. H rarely spoke of his family; he'd lost touch with his brothers soon after leaving school and last saw his mother, inadvertently, when she appeared on an episode of *Trisha* about alcoholism in the late 1990's. He never told his friends.

As a consequence, H had gotten into fights on a regular basis since before Candy and the others met him at school and he had continued to do so, albeit less often these days. He used to joke that it was the only thing he was ever any good at...and he was *very* good at it. Whilst in their teens he would often single-handedly come to the aid of the others, fending off aggressors from other schools or rival gangs. He would also warn off unwanted admirers for the girls. H had an unpredictable nature as a younger man, sometimes threatening someone with a pummelling for swearing in front of the woman he was with or in front of children. It was, as a consequence, a skill that had endowed him with a reputation for trouble, as well as a police record. His friends often remarked that he would only ever get work if he was self employed as few others would take him on with his history.

These days, out of the gym at least, H used his physical prowess more sparingly and sometimes even for comic effect. He limited his latent violent streak to defending the honour of his female friends from wandering hands or any unwanted advances and attention from drunken long-haired men in the pub. It also came in handy when attending demonstrations or rallies, as he often did, due to the fact that bashing the odd right-wing skinhead extremist was now acceptable to most *and* pretty much legal he had learned. H absolutely *loved* bashing a right-winger as it was the only time his friends wholeheartedly approved of his violent nature and favourite pastime.

As their breath made small clouds of mist before them, H and Candy slowly made their way along the High Street towards Candy's parents' house, on the edge of the town centre. It was where the shops, offices and bars became less frequent and in turn, the gardens and drive-ways of the houses that replaced them became larger.

"S'funny this, you living back with your mum and dad," ventured H, arms still linked with Candy's as they walked together, "it's like we've gone back in time and I'm walking you home from youth club, remember?" Candy smiled; they were much simpler times of course so she recalled them with affection and warmth.

"Yeah," she softly agreed, with a hint of sadness and nostalgia in her quiet voice as she stared backwards nearly thirty years in time rather than into the middle distance.

The group of friends would meet at the church hall every Friday evening, play table tennis, pool and listen to Sid and Mike arguing over which of their newly purchased punk records would get first play on the youth club imitation teak stereogram. The boys would take it in turns to play whichever single their weekly allowances had afforded them – endlessly – throughout the evening. Sid and Mike would dash to the Rumbelows shop that stayed open until six on a Friday on their way to the youth club. There they would buy the latest punk rock singles, from *any* punk band it seemed.

The group would congregate outside the club until it opened at seven o'clock, smoking Player's Number 10. They would listen to Sid and Mike with their Siouxie or Undertones or Buzzcocks singles, noisily debating the merits of each and which should risk the scratchy needle on the club record player first. The only Friday this debate wouldn't happen was when The Clash had a new release...then there was no contest, other than that between the vocal merits of Joe versus Mick of course. The alternate sound of punk music or Sid and Mike arguing at times seemed to be the sonic backdrop to much of the groups' teenage years.

As they passed the Golden Town Chinese takeaway Candy spoke, this time with a much less melancholy tone and more animated than before,

"If you weren't battering someone along the road, you'd get a portion of battered chicken and sweet and sour sauce from here instead I seem to remember..." she said with a big smile on her face "...dunking those massive chicken balls into that cup of bright orange gloop, burning your fingers and dripping it down your chin, shirt and everything!" she laughed loudly and H immediately felt a warm stab of affection that cut through the cold night air. As far as H was concerned, Candy could light up a room when she smiled but when she laughed, well, there was no feeling that could quite match it.

"Well that *was* before the advent of kebab shops, and McDonalds had barely reached London let alone this one-horse town! Anyway, you were more of a pancake roll kinda girl weren't you? And they were MASSIVE in those days, weren't they?" H laughed too and held his hands up in a fisherman's 'you should-have-seen-the-size-of-the-one-that-got-away' fashion. "Not like now, now you get three or four tiddly little things in a bag with a tiny pot of red stuff to dip 'em in, and they don't really taste of anything much. In those days though, they were a meal on their own!"

"Christ, we're going to end up doing the whole *'and Wagon Wheels aren't as BIG as they were when we were kids'* routine in a moment!" said Candy and smiling at him, she took H by the arm once again. "What about the Mike situation then H? What do *you* reckon?" she asked, changing the subject and hoping H wouldn't notice.

H paused for a moment, shrugged his shoulders and replied in his usual blunt manner; "Fuck it and fuck *her*!" he said. Then, apparently in an effort to explain his forthright conclusions, H continued;

"He can have his life back now, he can stop fretting over the situation and WE can forget about walking on bloody eggshells around him when it's a birthday, Christmas, Father's Day and all that crap. He never has to think about *any* of that shit again AND he can do what he wants with the extra hundred quid or so a week he's gonna be left with...job's a good 'un I reckon. Anyway, we should all have the chance to say goodbye and good riddance to the bad rubbish in our lives every so often and Mike's got the chance now hasn't he? To my mind that's pretty cool...isn't it? Sid has probably said as much to him already though and *for once* in my life, I'd agree with the jerk."

And resisting the pressing urge to add that *Wagon Wheels* used to be the size of your face and that they have, therefore, reduced in size considerably and that *Spangles* should be brought back for good measure, H simply smiled back at Candy and they walked on.

Thought of you as my mountain top,
Thought of you as my peak,
Thought of you as everything I've had but
couldn't keep...

Chapter 5

"If you wanna upgrade it to a £39 per month two year contract I can get you the new iPhone sir," said the implausibly young and spotty assistant in the phone shop whose name badge read *'Troy'*. What was it that made *anyone* who worked *anywhere* these days have to wear a name badge pondered Mike. And for heaven's sake, what kind of parent these days calls their kid *Troy*?

Mike drifted off for a moment; this was one of the subjects he and Sid could toss backwards and forwards for *hours*. Why was it that kids these days all seemed to have ever stranger names? During his time in teaching he had noticed a transition from the traditional Stephen, Paul, James, Tracy and Julie to those named after TV stars – which teachers secretly laughed at in the staff room – such as Tiffany, Bianca and Kylie. Then there was the more recent craze of 'surnames-for-first-names', so we had Harrison, Riley, Austin, Brandon, Carrington and Trent. This was accompanied by a rise in traditional English names, so kids sounded like East-End villains. At one point, Mike had classrooms full of Berts, 'Arrys, Reggies and Ronnies. To an uninitiated supply teacher reading the class register; it must have felt like doing the roll-call in B-wing at Parkhurst.

This trend, however, was now slowly being

superseded by something more ridiculous than ever as far as Sid and Mike were concerned. There was now a marked increase in kids names that seem completely made up. Names that grated on the friends were those such as Teo, Tamrah, Jayden/Jaiden, Bryce and Skyler. Mike had always struggled to understand this. Parents would often try to explain them away as being 'Navaho' or 'Hebrew' or some other bullshit. Mike and Sid knew better, these names weren't some indigenous name plucked from a history book, the parents were just indulgent wankers. Mike had even had the dubious honour of teaching a young woman named Delilah for a term a little over a year before. Delilah had no second or family name by all accounts. When asked "Delilah *what*?" by the lecturer she would respond simply by saying "No, we don't use *that* any more, it's *just* Delilah now," dismissively. Mike would bite his tongue rather than give in to natural temptation and ask her "*Why, why, why?*" (or just tell her to fuck off). She left Highdowns in the end to attend a performing arts college for the 'Artistically Gifted' and Mike and Sid used to joke about the inevitability of Sid being made to back her up on a television talent show at some point in the future.

Now Mike would pride himself in being liberal enough to, somewhat reluctantly, understand how kids became known as Summer, River, Rain, Keanu or Skye and could get – still grudgingly – how parents would simply mess with the spelling of names which gave the world Jaymie, Debz, Hydee and Jimi. He could do this, he thought, as these were simply the children of hippies and should be pitied. He could even forgive the naming of Zowie Bowie or Dweezil and Moon-Unit Zappa as these were the children of *his*, somewhat eccentric, heroes and had been exposed to enough ridicule and endured weird enough upbringings already without need for his personal castigation. Mike went out with a woman once who had a young daughter called Harmony, which was ironic as the kid screamed continually for the two months he was seeing her mum. Where would it end Mike wondered, kids called after objects such as Table, Shed, Ladder, or even after fruit like Apple or Peaches or...er...yes, ok then.

It was Tuesday morning of what the management team at Highdowns College euphemistically called 'Reading Week' when the students could spend a week away from college researching their project work or catching up on outstanding essays and reports in their own time. In reality, it was actually half-term week and the freedom that Reading Week allowed was useful to mature students with young children and the subsequent childcare issues many would experience if they studied full-time. It also allowed those without responsibilities such as children to sleep until the afternoon, eat *Rice Krispies* or *Pot Noodles* and watch *Countdown* to their hearts' content.

For teaching staff like Mike and Tim, Reading Week had endless possibilities such as short holidays, catching up on marking or, in some cases, detoxing from the huge amounts of caffeine, nicotine and alcohol they had imbibed during term-time. For Mike it was an opportunity to take stock of his situation and, well, to go with Amy to try to replace his now sadly defunct mobile telephone.

He wouldn't admit it, but Mike hated not having a decent phone. He understood very little about mobile technology – he was after all a specialist in humanities rather than any science or technology based subject – but old mobiles were embarrassing, especially if his students caught a glimpse of him using one. He simply could not allow *that* to happen. Mike had managed to dry out his soggy SIM card when he got home and was able to use it in a ten-year old Nokia house brick, they called it a 6320 in the shop but Mike knew better. It might have had a battery life longer than anything ever used in a drumming fluffy rabbit toy yet this telephone clearly had to be replaced without delay. Mike couldn't use different ringtones and individual pictures to let him know which of his friends were calling and he couldn't swap the images on his display as the mood took him. For some unknown reason, although unimportant in the grand scheme of things, this was *very* important to Mike.

"You can do everything you currently do, but quicker and you have unlimited download capability...." Troy trailed off when he realised Mike wasn't really taking it all in. "...and you can have it in one of four colours that really make a statement about *you* sir...*SIR*?"

Amy pulled at Mike's shirt sleeve and he came to momentarily, "Oh, yes....er...blue?" he enquired in a somewhat detached manner before retreating into his alternate world.

"Not just *any* blue, it's a blue unlike anything you've *ever* seen in your life sir!" replied Troy. Apparently blue was a good choice. With this statement not exactly ringing in Mike's ears, the enthused Troy disappeared through a door behind him, returning with a white box and some paperwork a few seconds later. As he started to open the packaging he paused and looked up at

Mike, who still looked as if he existed somewhere else rather than in a quiet phone shop.

"Would Sir like to open the package himself? It's the only time he'll ever get the chance to touch this device for the *first* time, and that privilege should go to the new owner, don't you think?" Troy looked at Mike as if he were handing him a pair of surgical scissors and the umbilical cord of a new-born child.

Mike vacantly took hold of the package and whilst he pulled at the cellophane covering the virgin snow-white box, Troy continued, "Would you be interested today in this weeks' special of two years insurance for the price of one? You pay nothing for a month anyway and then we just add the fee to your monthly contract. Just in case this one gets damaged like your old one...how *did* you say your old phone one got broken again sir?"

"It was, shall we say, collateral damage in a very one-sided fire-fight," interrupted Amy dryly.

"Wow! Are you in active service sir? Iraq? Afghanistan?" asked Troy, stopping what he was doing for a moment and looking at Mike with a new and growing sense of wonder and admiration. Before Mike could put him straight, Troy carried on grasping at the wrong end of the stick as he looked at Amy and said, with his head tilted slightly, "You must be SO proud!"

Mike looked dumbly at his sister. Amy tilted her head in a similar fashion to the wide eyed assistant and replied "Proud? That doesn't *nearly* cover it!" and smiled, grabbing hold of Mike's right hand and squeezing it. She looked up at Mike, he looked at her, then looked at the still awe-struck Troy, then back at Amy and finally back to Troy again.

"What th..." he started to splutter when he

60

was interrupted with a *don't-talk-to-the-face-talk-to-the-hand* gesture from the young man, "Wait!" said the triumphant Troy, "I'm going to give you my staff discount for this phone sir and that means that it's fully insured for anything *including* acts of terrorism, acts of war or even against acts of God Himself." From the momentous tone of his voice, Mike felt to put Troy straight at this point would be even more cruel than staying quiet, as well as the fact that at least his new device would be insured against both insurgent attacks and from pissed off women. He decided that discretion would therefore be preferable under the circumstances and said nothing but for a weak "Thanks." Mike quickly signed the contract being offered by Troy before leaving the store with Amy and his new phone.

The lift in spirits afforded him by his new purchase and the fun provided by Troy was short-lived. Amy and Mike chatted lightly on their way back to Mike's house and giggled at his heroics in the field of warfare but, by the time they arrived he was again quiet and reflective. They went inside, Mike flopped into his black chair and Amy went into the kitchen to put the kettle on.

"You want tea then or what? I've got some tea bags!" called out Amy, accompanied by the sound of cupboards being opened and closed, drawers sliding open and mugs and cutlery generally being assembled on the worktop.

Mike reluctantly responded with a "Yeah, ok!"

Amy knew his tone; Mike had always criticised Amy for her 'slapdash attitude' - as he called it - towards making tea, always preferring to brew his own. She would drop tea bags into cold mugs, put the milk on top and simply add hot water when it boiled. Mike understood that if water was to make the perfect cup of tea it needed to be just off a rolling boil to infuse correctly. Using a cold china mug with added cold milk prior to the hot water meeting the tea meant it was nowhere near the right temperature to brew sufficiently. Amy would also commit the cardinal sin of leaving a spoon in each of the mugs whilst the tea 'brewed' which was utter madness in Mike's eyes. The metal spoon, being a conductor, would further reduce the temperature of the water in which it sat. Finally, she would impatiently dunk, stir, bash, squeeze, mash and re-dunk the tea bag continually until it surrendered enough colour to make the mug of tea *look* acceptable, thus rendering the brewing process a completely irrelevant exercise. Mike hated Amy's tea and snapping out of his dark mood for a moment called out to his sister,

"Do you need a hand? Do you want me to make a pot?"

Nothing.

"Amy?"

Again nothing.

Mike raised his voice, "AMY? I said do you need any help? Shall I...?"

At that moment Amy walked into the room carrying Mike's wooden tray, which in turn carried a teapot already hidden by its balaclava cosy, two mugs, sugar bowl and milk jug. She looked at her bemused brother who was unable to disguise his shock. She gently placed the tray onto the glass topped coffee table, being careful not to spill the milk jug which was full to the brim and she turned to her brother, beaming.

"I even warmed the pot, so it's all *just-as-it-should-be*! You are *SO* anal when it comes to tea sometimes! I know *exactly* what you were thinking and the look on your face now is bloody priceless. I made this with exactly the right mix of love, care, attention to detail and autism that you demand ok? You are SO far up the 'tea-obsessive-spectrum' aren't you? It's completely unreal!" She laughed loudly and Mike self-consciously smiled back at her. Amy poured two mugs of tea through the stainless steel strainer and they sat silently for a few moments, sipping. Before too long though, she asked the inevitable question,

"When are you going to tell me all about it then? It was going to be last night – thanks for dinner by the way – then I thought you might say more at the shops; how long can you avoid an explanation Mike?"

Mike said nothing but stood up and went to the bookshelf where he picked up a light-blue envelope and handed it to Amy. He sat down again and slowly transported another perfect cube of sugar from the bowl into his tea, stirred it and sat back. He watched Amy intently whilst she opened the envelope and started to read the letter she pulled from it.

She then appeared to read it again, seemingly unsure if she had fully taken it all in first time around.

Dear Michael,

Bet this is a bit of a surprise?! I've been meaning to write this for a long time but somehow never managed to get my head together long enough to manage it until now. I bumped into Sid in London a little while back. It was lovely to see him but it sort of got me thinking and he made me feel a bit guilty about a load of stuff so I thought I would get in touch. I hope you're ok and the teaching is going good and I hope you are happy and all that?

Anyway, to the point of this letter, I am pretty sure you will be ok with this, it's just that I am with someone steady at long last! Actually I have been for a little while now and it's going really great. His name is Clive and he is real kind to me and Liam. I think this is really going to last and I am ready for that...reckon you never thought it would happen eh?

Anyway I want to thank you for always getting the child support money to me, it's come in handy over the years

I can tell you but Clive says you should stop paying now. I will let the CSA know that we have agreed this so they don't hassle you. Clive is taking care of us and wants us to get married and wants to adopt Liam as his son and all that.

I've got reasons why I never let you see Liam when I left and I feel a little bit guilty about it all so want you to know everything is good now. I hope there's no hard feelings ok? I always knew you were a good bloke and a reliable straight guy so I knew you would do right by us. Liam needed that. Clive is sort of like you in a way and I really care about him so I think it's best to give it a proper go. He thinks I should cut my ties with you so we can be a proper family and stand a decent chance, so that's what I'm doing.

Hope you have a good life, take care of yourself,

Mads (& Liam) x

Amy looked at Mike, dumbfounded. He in turn stared at the wall. She looked back at the page in her hand again and scanned the letter for more information or a better explanation. Then she re-

read aloud the part that said,

"...I've got reasons why I never let you see Liam when I left and I feel a little bit guilty about it all so want you to know everything is good now. I hope there's no hard feelings ok?"

She paused, red faced and unable to adequately express herself. This was a rarity for Amy. She gripped the paper in her hand, knuckles whitening and finally exclaimed, loudly,

"Did Sid not tell you about seeing her? Did this all come out of the blue? Mike? What the *FUCK* does the stupid cow mean by this bit? What is she up to?" She repeated the last bit of the paragraph aloud, again.

"...I hope there's no hard feelings ok?

Amy looked angrily and quizzically back at Mike. Unable to furnish answers herself she awaited a response from him.

Mike said nothing.

He couldn't explain how he felt; he couldn't explain why Sid had said nothing or tell his sister what Maddie was up to and he was unable to describe how it now felt like all the lights in his life had been switched to a dimmer setting.

Mike couldn't explain these things in any way at all...he was too busy crying.

I kept the faith and I kept voting,
Not for the iron fist but for the helping hand.
For theirs is a land with a wall around it
And mine is a faith in my fellow man.
Theirs is a land of hope and glory
Mine is the green field and the factory floor....

Chapter 6

As Tim (*Happy Together* – The Jam) pulled a length of gaffer tape across the reinforced cardboard, securing it to the back of the white-painted "4x2" he looked lovingly at his girlfriend. Tania (*Happy Together* – The Jam) was stood at the dining table, painting the words "NOT IN MY NAME, STOP THE WAR" on the white cotton sheeting they had bought from the Oxfam shop in town for this very purpose. While Tania took great care over the spelling as, after all, they didn't want a repeat of the "STOP LIVE ANIMAL EXPERTS" banner fiasco from a few years back, Tim couldn't help but notice she was sticking her tongue out of the side of her mouth in the cutest way. The couple had long ago been christened *Titan* (*Ti*-m *Tan*-ia) by their friends because they had partly morphed into one another during the many years they had been together. Tim stared blissfully at Tania until his train of thought was suddenly and rudely interrupted by Debs;

"Are you done with the gaffer tape Tim? I need to seal off the top corners of the banner so we can get the poles in without them coming straight out when we're marching."

"Yeah...here!" he threw the silver roll of tape to Debs who caught it and set about expertly securing the top corners of the sheeting in turn by rolling them around one of the broomstick-poles and taping each of them down.

"There!" she said, "All done". Debs was pretty good at the banner making process being a veteran of countless demonstrations over the years. She had been a protector of everything from the Aardvark to the Zebra in her time as well as campaigning on more trivial matters like world peace. She stood for women's rights and against slavery; for equal pay and the living wage and against welfare cuts and bankers' bonuses. She wanted to start dismantling nuclear weapons whilst simultaneously stopping anyone else from dismantling the NHS. Basically, she had a myriad of causes and a pretty packed calendar standing up for each and every one of them.

This wasn't the first time Debs was planning to drag members of her group of friends out on a march; she attended demonstrations on a regular basis. Often her friends were willing participants yet sometimes she would persuade them to attend against their will, all in support of her latest crusade. In the past this had been an opportunity both for H to break a few noses (all in a good cause of course) and Candy to seek out Mister Right (or 'Mister Right-On' as H would call it). Debs had the ability to be a bit preachy at times yet she always seemed so well informed that she tended to impress everyone with her knowledge and earnest nature. She was also fearless in the face of authority, having been arrested many times whilst on 'active service' as H described it. Debs would treat this as a badge of honour. This coming weekend the friends were preparing for a 'Stop the War' demo ahead of the Anti-Fascism demo planned for a few weeks hence. It was the turn of Tim and Tania to tag along and lend their voices. They had visited Debs to help her get her banners and placards ready for the event. It was the last day of their holiday before returning to work after the demo weekend, following a ten day break in the Canaries.

With a satisfied flourish, Tania finished her banner by painting a broken-cross, peace sign inside both of the "O's" in her slogan. She put her tongue and her paintbrush away and stepped back to admire her handiwork.

"It's a bit 1980's CND isn't it?" remarked Tim, frowning slightly and not quite filtering the comment as much as Tania seemingly would have preferred. He looked at the woman he adored and she glowered back at him. Quickly realising his clumsiness he triumphantly added, "...yeah...kinda retro...I *really* like it!" Smiling once again, Tania turned to Debs who was stacking the placard Tim had been making with another five she had already prepared in the corner of her student flat;

"It's nice using our last day of holiday doing something so *worthwhile* Debs, but is there anything more you need? I mean, we'll be at the demo but is there anything else you could do with in the meantime? What about supplies for the day? We're off to the farmers' market first thing Saturday before we join you in the Town Square..."

"No, we don't need pickles, jams, any fresh vegetables or handmade sausages to start the revolution thanks," said Debs sarcastically. "Everything's set now; we just need to get everyone we can persuade to come to meet up at the muster point outside the Civic Offices by 10 o'clock. Can you round up a few people for us?

Mike, Amy and Candy maybe? H too? He loves a good demo." While doing the familiar roll-call, Debs was also mentally adding up the numbers.

"If he's got someone to bash up he'll be there, but a peace march? I reckon we'll struggle to get H along if the gym's busy..." said Tim cynically, "...maybe the others though."

"Yeah, be great if we can persuade some of the men to come along, eh Debs?" said Tania eagerly. "We can use what we've been given to persuade them!" she looked herself up and down – much to Tim's chagrin – as if to emphasise her unique feminine powers.

"Listen Tania, as women we don't need power over *men*, just power over *ourselves*, to paraphrase Mary Wollstonecraft, so let's just see who we can bring along. We need numbers people...*NUMBERS!...O*k?" finished Debs emphatically.

"We'll certainly do what we can," offered Tania more meekly than before. "Won't we Tim?"

"Oh...er...yeah of course we will sweetie," he muttered, somewhat unconvincingly, he turned to reassure Debs once more "Leave it to us."

Debs clicked the button of the kettle on the work-top to the 'On' position and turned to her friends, still with her most serious face on.

"Look, while you're both here, I ought to give you the goss...er, the heads-up on what's been happening whilst you were away. Have you heard about what happened to Mike yet?

In hushed tones, and over a mug of very weak ginseng and blueberry tea, Debs regaled them with details of her conversation with Candy a few days earlier.

"This is all on the *QT* of course; you can't say anything in front of Mike or Amy ok? And

NOTHING at work at the mo either Tim, ok? I saw how Amy reacted in the pub the other night when she caught us talking about it and she wasn't best pleased I can tell you. I haven't seen her like that in I don't know how long, so let's not have it spread around the staff room at college ok? Anyway, Mike's been to see his doctor and has another appointment today. He seemed ok when I saw him but I reckon it hasn't fully hit him yet. Now he'll get signed off work and prescribed something to take away the pain, poor bastard, they can't do much more than that these days, what with the cuts in the PCT budget and all that. There's no NHS money for community mental health services anymore, not these days. Bloody Tories have a lot to answer for. There'll be no counselling or help like that, not unless he pays for it. Do you know if Highdowns offer anything to staff Tim? Some employers do, anyway, I really feel for him you know? It was completely out of the blue so it side-swiped him, know what I mean? He could have been such a positive role model for that boy you know. Boys need positive male role models, especially since the break down of the nuclear family, there are so many absent fathers these days, and it's at the root of gang culture and everything like that, yeah?"

Tim and Tania listened as Debs continued rarely pausing for breath. They sipped their herbal tea and said nothing except for the odd "*Aww*" and "*Aah*" in sympathy for their friend, and to punctuate Debs' monologue.

"So when you see him don't expect too much from him, I mean, he may be drugged up on all sorts by the weekend or if not, he'll be elsewhere emotionally. You know Wittgenstein or someone once said, *"The world of the happy is quite another than the world of the unhappy"*. It's so unfair, Mike's like, the *best* isn't he? Such a sweet and bright guy and all that...and Maddie? What's *her* game for heaven's sake? Whatever her plans are she should remember that the ends very rarely justify the means. And, well, I don't know why he ever got tucked up with her in the first place, Mad by name mad by nature I reckon. I tell you what though, I'd swing for her if I saw her now and you know I abhor violence of any kind."

Debs often preached like this. She could talk on any given subject, seemingly for hours, whilst quoting great thinkers at will along the way. This was a result of years of study bankrolled by her absent – wealthy – parents, so her friends believed. She would also occasionally justify the violence she so abhorred. Whether it be her personally aiming an imaginary slap at Maddie's face or H punching out a couple of neo-fascists on a march before the police could intervene, the ends sometimes *could* justify the means.

It's not too hard to cry, in these crying times,
I'll take a broken heart, and take it home in parts
But I will never fade.

Chapter 7

"Sorry to keep you waiting Mr Powell, everyone seems to be coming down with something this week! Now, how have you been since I last saw you?"

It was a familiar greeting from Dr Baker (*Down at the Doctors* – Dr Feelgood). Mike wondered how things would seem if everyone answered her with an "I'm fine how are you Doc?" like they must do whenever she meets the same people outside of her surgery or her friends socially. Very few people ever answer a "How are you/How do you do?" with an "Oh, my bunion/backache/flatulence/acne is giving me Hell" response do they? Surely not all of her friends answered *truthfully* when she bumped into them at the shops or when they met for dinner?

Mike had never had a female GP before Andrea Baker, always having preferred treatment from another – usually *much* older – male doctor. He preferred what Amy called an 'old-school doctor' who was gentle, smelled faintly of pipe tobacco and liniment and spoke with Oxbridge gravitas. Mike didn't want *female* or *young* in a GP however, a year ago his previous GP retired and the practice amalgamated with two other local surgeries in the newly built Health Centre. This left Mike with little choice but to sign up with - *the newly qualified, female and young* - Dr A.

73

Baker.

If getting a quick doctors' appointment with your own GP wasn't difficult enough in the 21st century NHS, getting one with a part-time GP was next to impossible. Yet this week Mike had won the NHS equivalent of the National Lottery by getting two appointments with Dr Baker inside five days. Mike had already made a mental note to stop choosing Lotto numbers in the future...after all, he would never be as lucky as he had been this week ever again.

Answering his GP's question, Mike started to ramble, barely coherently, whilst his shaking left hand rubbed his chin.

"Pretty much the same as last week Doctor. I'm still not sleeping; I can't concentrate or think about anything but my son and I cry at the drop of a hat. I'm still feeling SO angry, so very VERY angry with *her* but I am helpless you see? I'm not at work this week but I don't know how I'll handle next week as I'm due back Monday...I've never felt this low before, I've never known such all-consuming gloom...I don't know what I...I mean..." Mike's voice quietly trailed away as the tears started to roll down his face.

Mike was still taken aback as to how easily the tears came and how difficult it was to stop them once they had started. He could recall situations in the past where tears would have been a natural expression of his feelings, or even expected, given some circumstances. He had been to the funeral of a close friend whose life had been extinguished far too young; he had lost a couple of work colleagues over the years; various pets since childhood and a number of older relatives and yet was able to control his emotions when all around him struggled to do the same. As a younger man

74

he went through difficult and unexpected relationship break-ups. He didn't react badly whilst watching sad films, on reading sad stories or hearing tragic tales and, although always getting a tingle down his spine on hearing Mick Jones singing the final lines of 'Stay Free', he didn't shed tears to emotionally charged songs either.

So what was new? Was it something to do with his age? He had no palpable or existing relationship with his son and no emotional tie on any level with Maddie. He could not understand why this had affected him in such a way that he couldn't sleep, concentrate or socialise with his friends easily. Mike was even starting to experience panic and anxiety and to fear his own future as at present, it appeared pretty bleak.

Andrea Baker held out a box of tissues and, with a sympathetic look on her face, said;

"The last thing you need concern yourself with at the moment is work. I'll sign you off for a bit so you can work out a way forwards, a way to lift your mood and reduce your anxiety. Shall we say a couple of weeks to start with? I can make it longer if you want, or we can see how you are in a few weeks."

Mike paused and his tears slowed. He replayed his GPs statement over in his head. Blimey, '...to start with...' well that was pretty easy, a couple of weeks off work and he'd be right as rain of course, exactly what he needed. He could go away, or spend time with Sid or Amy, or Sid and Amy, perfect.

"Do you think you need me to prescribe you something too?" enquired Dr Baker as she typed a few words onto the computer and then re-read the words as they appeared on her screen.

"I can give you something to augment the production of serotonin and rebalance the neurotransmitter chemicals in your brain. They'll take a few weeks to start working and I would usually recommend taking them for at least six months, but I can see you again in a few weeks and monitor your mood, what do you think?" said Dr Baker in an alarmingly matter-of-fact way.

"I'm not sure I really want to be taking medication if I'm honest Doctor. I mean, what about driving while I'm popping pills or returning to work or..." he trailed off again, thinking a few months feeling numb could have it's upside.

"The pills I'm recommending don't affect you like that Mr Powell. There are some side effects, all detailed on the box, but nothing to stop you leading a full and normal life, whatever *normal* means. They may just help lighten your mood," reassured a smiling Doctor Baker, before adding another sentence or two to Mike's file. She went on,

"I'm also going to put you down for a preliminary assessment for a series of group CBT sessions with an organisation called "Talk It Over". It's paid for by the NHS but places are limited, so there may be a bit of a wait before you hear anything. Someone will call you on the telephone and assess your needs and then you'll either be referred for the course or I will be informed as to what else might be suitable for you. CBT, or Cognitive Behavioural Therapy, is a treatment that is proven to work for people experiencing low mood. It focuses on problem solving and helping you learn little ways to help lift your own mood. You could become your own specialist in time, with practice, what do you think?" She didn't wait for an answer, choosing to leave the question hanging in the air between them. She went on;

"Do you perhaps have the where-with-all to get some private counselling or coaching in the meantime? I can recommend a couple of people locally but there's little or no NHS provision these days, so you would be expected to pay. They can be quite effective though so it's worth a thought".

The printer on her desk spat out a prescription and Dr Baker signed it and handed it to Mike together with a page from her notepad on which she had scrawled a couple of names and telephone numbers. Mike could barely make out the numbers let alone the names but thanked her meekly and stood up to leave. As he did so, Dr Baker offered another suggestion to add to those Mike was already digesting;

"I'm no counsellor but maybe it would be helpful to get in touch with your ex-partner and tell her how you feel. It wouldn't be any tougher than what you've achieved in coming to see me about this and you said yourself that you've never really pursued the matter. Well maybe now is the time to put up a bit of a fight for your son? I know it's none of my business and I am sure you'll recover from this over time, but it couldn't do any more harm now, could it? Maybe your friend could shed more light on how to reach her perhaps? Don't forget to make another appointment to see me in a few weeks too, ok?"

And with her words ringing in his ears and having made a further appointment on his way out, Mike left the surgery. He headed to the pharmacy to pick up the pills he would probably never take and whilst on his way, he called Sid.

Should I kiss the viper's fang?
Or herald loud the death of Man?
I'm sinking in the quicksand of my thoughts,
And I ain't got the power anymore...

Chapter 8

"Look man it was flamin' weeks ago, she was just kinda *there* you know? I didn't think she was ever gonna get in touch...I'd pretty much forgotten all about it until you got the letter to be honest, so thought I'd keep *schtum*. Look, I had been working. I was tired and was having a few drinks with some session guys, just to unwind. I looked up and she was there, sitting with some guy wearing a scarf round his neck and a tweed jacket...a fucking tweed jacket I tell ya...Well, what I mean is, HE was wearing the scarf and tweed jacket, not her...I can't actually remember what she was wearing like..."

"I DON'T GIVE A SHIT WHAT SHE WAS WEARING! SHE COULD'VE BEEN WEARING A FUCKING GORILLA SUIT FOR ALL I CARE!" yelled Mike interrupting Sid; he paced back and forth, seemingly about to explode. He tried again, starting more calmly this time and trying to control the rage that was welling up inside him. He grappled with the words in his head and tried again;

"So, Sid...mate...*PLEASE*...tell me where you were and how this happened....and WHY THE FUCKING FUCK YOU'VE NEGLECTED TO EXPLAIN ANY OF THIS OR MENTION IT TO ME BEFORE NOW, EVEN WHEN I SHOWED YOU THE SHITTING LETTER?" exploded Mike, again failing to maintain the volume of his question below eleven.

Sid recounted how he had bumped into Maddie and a man called Clive in some wine bar in Kilburn. He explained that he had spent a couple of *very* long days in a studio where he had been helping an Essex-Girl Pop Factor contestant record a Grand Final showstopper, a cover of the R.E.M number '*Shiny Happy People*'. He had told a couple of the other guys he was working with – Jimmy and Steve – that he wanted to get away for a few hours to unwind and they took him to this bar they knew. Mike did his level best to not scream at Sid to leave out the superfluous details and cut to the 'bumping into' Maddie bit...which Sid finally did.

"I was in a kinda world of my own, being as I was in natural early-evening daylight for the first time in over twenty hours like, when I suddenly saw someone I thought I knew. I was looking at her, like you do, not really with it but thinking that she was familiar and maybe a cast member on the show or an old conquest or something when she smiled back at me. It was a sort of nervous smile but kinda *dangerous* too, know what I mean? Anyway, I got a chill down my neck...then it hit me...fuck...it was *her*! The bloke she was with, you know the Clive guy with the tweed jacket an' all, he was looking at me too by this stage, wasn't keen on me staring at his bird I reckoned, so he wasn't smiling. He looked pretty sappy so I just thought to myself, 'Fuck me this could be fun' and I went over to wind them up a bit, yeah?"

Mike was purple in the face. "What. Did. She. SAY?" he yelled the last word, hoping Sid would finally expand.

Sid continued with his tale;

"Ok, ok. She sort of awkwardly said 'Hi' and introduced Clive as her *'partner'* and then asked how I was after all this time....and I told her. I asked if she had been in town long and she said she lived there now, with Clive and Liam. That's when I thought I should give her some shit, you know, 'cos of the way she's treated you over the years an' all...anyway, I told her straight that she should be letting you know about Liam, or let you see Liam or if she was with someone else now she should be getting *them* to pay his keep/support/maintenance or whatever you call it instead of making you pay with no access rights. All that stuff really, I stuck up for you mate, I really did." Sid sat back and looked pleased with himself. Mike was less impressed.

"So what *then*? She just agreed and said she'd write to me and make it all better did she? Or she'd make it all go away? She knew a way of saving me some cash did she? Something like that? Sid, WHAT DID SHE SAY?" pressed Mike, now hitting eleven on the sarcasm scale too.

"Well, that's the funny bit...you'll love this. Clive, her fella, tries interrupting 'but I thought Liam's father was...but Madeline, you said....am I not right in thinking....love?' and she sits there and stops him every time he opens his gob! She says something about *'not bothering'* him about Liam's dad and *'it was complicated'* but all the time looks well fucking sheepish I tell you, an' I don't reckon it was because he called her *'Madeline'* either...huh huh!" Sid said, sneering triumphantly. "Look, she's obviously been spinning him a line or two for however long they've been together about you not caring about Liam or whatever and all the time she's still been

80

pocketing your monthly cash, the bitch!" Sid folded his arms and added, rather superfluously, "There!"

"I suppose that's an easy way to not have to answer any more questions about me," said Mike, in a tone that was a little too close to 'complete understanding' for Sid's liking. "I guess she's always looked for the easiest, trouble free road hasn't she?" Mike paused for a moment then, with a dawning sense of realisation continued,

"Hang on though, that means Liam thinks I've never cared or wanted to be there for him; he doesn't know that I always wanted to be a part of his life; that I was always hoping that one day I might....that I would like to...for FUCK'S SAKE SID...HE DOESN'T KNOW JACK-SHIT ABOUT ME!"

In his mind's eye Mike was inspecting the contents of the red record case in his wardrobe. He could see all of the letters and cards he'd written to Liam and kept and was feeling pain and regret at not trying harder to get them to Liam over the years. What a wasted opportunity. Yet Sid tried to put things into context for his friend;

"Listen, I didn't know she was going to write to you ok? I didn't know she was going to do *this*, but do you know what? I reckon it's turned out for the best. You're better off now, without her being a drain on your resources. Whatever Liam did or didn't go through during his earlier years, he's well over it now isn't he? It's been flippin' ages Mike. Anyway listen, if I'd known what you were going to be like when you called me and asked me to come over tonight, well I wouldn't have answered". Sid sounded slightly hurt, but continued to elucidate;

"I came over 'cos you said you 'needed some

answers to some difficult questions'. I presumed you were speaking metaphorically or metaphysically...or *meta-what-ever-ly* and wanted some of *this,*" and he produced a metal tin out of his jacket and a packet of rolling papers and waved them towards Mike;

"Shall I try to help you get some perspective? I've got some of Twitchy Tel's finest? You can't sit here listening to Elvis Costello records for the rest of your life can you? I mean, he's great and does *'heartbreak and loss'* pretty well I grant you but, man, he can be a right miserable fucker too. I'll skin-up shall I?"

Mike sat down. With his head now in his hands he looked at Sid, utterly defeated.

"Your answer to everything eh? A quick smoke? Off to oblivion and the world of blissful ignorance? No thanks Sid, I'm not smoking any more of that crap..." he ventured "...and do you know what? Its *boring* Sid and it makes *you* boring when you smoke it, it really does. I can't believe you would be this disloyal to me and not call when you saw her, or tell me when you came home, or say more when I got the letter, or get an address from her or *anything*. That's what a *real* friend would do Sid, it's what I would have done for you. And do you know what else? I'm getting my shit together as of *NOW!*"

Mike, having something of a Damascene moment, stood up and marched purposefully out of the room, slamming the door behind him.

Sid said nothing. Listening to the sound of doors opening and closing, drawers being turned out, water running and the odd bit of cursing, he just shrugged. He rolled his eyes and then opened the hand-painted tobacco tin in his hand, deciding to get *his* shit together too. Pulling a small plastic bag from it he looked up and scoured the room for something suitable to rest on whilst he rolled himself a smoke. Spying the record collection in Mike's cabinet he smiled to himself and walked over to it. Opening the glass door that protected Mike's sacred vinyl, he slowly pulled a familiar record sleeve from the collection within and inspected it slowly. The red, blue and yellow Gene Greif designed sleeve had been a part of his life since 1978 when the album was first released. Sid carefully slid the kohl-black record from the sleeve and, holding it only by its outer edges between his two palms he blew gently across each of its surfaces with reverence.

"Side one first of course..." he whispered "...like I'm back in the day." Sid chuckled at the thought of listening to *"Give 'Em Enough Rope"* whilst rolling a joint on the record sleeve, it was like he was back in Mike's bedroom as a teenager. As *'Safe European Home'* started, with all its swaggering urgency and crashing guitar chords, he momentarily wondered if he should have chosen a more chilled out recording, but soon he was too busy with the task in hand to mind.

As the last track on side one ended Mike reappeared in the doorway, it appeared that he had shaved and put on some clean clothes. Although wearing odd socks, Mike looked better than he had for a few days thought Sid.

"You took your time mate," said Sid through the haze, "It's *'Last Gang in Town'*...how cool does it still sound? Eh?" Sid took down another lung full of smoke and grinned at his old friend, the marijuana making him feel like they were once more at one and back on the best of terms. "Blimey, at one point when I was skinning up I swear I thought your Mum was gonna walk in on me...how funny's that?"

Still standing in the doorway Mike didn't look amused at all; he simply issued a determined call to arms that put Sid's favourite Joe Strummer in the shade for a moment;

"Yeah, I've heard it all before Sid. *ALL* of it. Now come on, put that out and come with me, we're going to London and we're gonna find her. WE'RE GONNA FIND HER SID!"

The kids in the halls and the pipes in the walls,
Make me noises for company.
Long distance callers make long distance calls
And the silence makes me lonely.

Chapter 9

It had been two weeks since Mike had pulled back the curtains in his house, charged his mobile phone or opened the mail which was piling ever higher on the doormat. He hadn't shaved, had only showered once and his television was radiating heat into his lounge after not having been switched off for days. He had in fact answered the door, just once, to Amy. That was eight days ago.

Amy visited as she had become concerned for her brother's welfare. Mike had, in fact, known that his sister had been calling him a number of times over the preceding days, recognising the ringtone (*'Heroine'* by The Boys) on his phone but hadn't much felt like speaking to her. No-one had heard from Mike in a while, not even Sid. As it happened, Amy hadn't stayed very long on this occasion either. Mike hadn't exactly made her feel welcome, he'd told he was going to *'get away from it all'* for a few days and was busy packing. He told her that he didn't want her to worry about him as he was just taking himself away for some much needed quiet thinking time. This was especially important to him following his fruitless trip to London to find Maddie.

Although unhappy with the situation, Amy decided that she should afford her brother the space he seemed to crave. Mike wasn't, in fact, going anywhere at all but just wanted to be left alone. The reality was that he was simply shutting the world out whilst he tried to deal with the crippling emptiness he still felt.

Thus far, however, his plan wasn't working.

Whilst he was awake, which was most of the time, Mike moved from distraught and crying uncontrollably to numb and completely listless. He didn't have the energy or inclination to do anything other than eat or watch television. He had tried listening to some music – his usual place for solace was in a classic album or five – but he found it didn't transport him far enough away from his thoughts in the way he was used to, or needed in this particular moment. In fact the opposite was worryingly true. It seemed every song he heard reminded him of his heartbreak, every song was written about his situation, every song a cruel reminder of how life was now destined to be.

In watching television however, he was distracted enough so as to drown out his painful thoughts. He told himself this was just to escape the pain and loss he was experiencing. Mike soon found he could watch *anything* on the television to take his mind away from his contemplations. Daytime TV was so awful he couldn't understand how his students could talk so animatedly about spending endless hours in front of *Jeremy Kyle* or some *Loose Women* when they all appeared to be mind-numbing in the extreme. Yet here he was, living vicariously through the home buyers appearing on *Homes Under the Hammer* or the bargain hunters on *Bargain Hunt*. The welcome distraction to be found in ten-year-old repeats of comedy current affairs' shows on *Dave* was unfathomable.

There was no real relief in these shows of

course and they were ironically having a negative effect on Mike's situation. An unintended effect of course and clearly unbeknown to the undoubtedly talented broadcasters involved in their development. The less Mike did, the slower he became and the less inclined he felt to do anything at all. His lack of energy discouraged him from any form of activity other than eating and thinking and over-eating and over-thinking. He was spiralling into a deeper and darker place than ever before and was becoming increasingly isolated. There were times when Mike couldn't visualise a future for himself, everything simply looked black. This worried him.

Mike had always been the sort of person who was able to see into an imagined future and how his life might pan out. In the past he would be able to see himself growing old; travelling to places he hadn't yet seen; seeing bands he hadn't yet heard of; meeting a woman he could share his life with; and spending time in retirement after a successful teaching career. Most of all, at some point in the future, Mike would always see himself and Liam becoming good friends.

Now all Mike saw was black storm clouds and nothing else. Very little made sense to him and there was no joy in his usual pastimes anymore. His favourite pastime, going to gigs, was no longer fun. Rather than the teenage experiences and adventures that he still talked about years later, seeing a band was now an uncomfortable, boisterous affair where younger people would just continually bump into him. Where idiots who were dancing would slowly force him away from the vantage point he had spent ages seeking out so that they could swing their arms about wildly and with abandon. They were places where the only pair of six-foot-five inch tall people in the audience would apparently seek him out, just to obstruct his view. Whereas he had in his teenage past, happily enjoyed a can of Watney's Pale Ale whilst watching a band, he was now forced to drink pints of creamy smooth 'bitter' from a flimsy plastic cup and pay over four pounds for the privilege. That was of course if he could get to the bar at all.

Mike asked himself if this was what depression, or 'low mood' as Doctor Baker had insisted on calling it, looked like for everyone who experienced it. Wasn't this just him turning into something of a grumpy old man rather than depression? He had experience of his lottery numbers repeatedly failing to come up on a Saturday evening so was what he felt now the same thing or just further along the same spectrum? Mike had seen his toast fall buttered-side-down on the carpet, was this similar to losing a son? And what about losing a job, was it better or worse than losing your train ticket? Losing a bet or losing a limb, where *exactly* did 'low mood' become *full on* depression?

He also found himself asking if the world would miss him if he was no longer in it. He always felt he knew the answer to this. Amy and Sid at least would mourn him, surely? He wondered if their grief should be enough to stop the darkest and most final of contemplations. Would CBT help stop these thoughts Mike pondered, and how? Surely it was as simple as the power of positive thinking? Mike had been on the training courses and sat through interminable sessions where the finance team, teaching staff and IT support workers would all sit together and ponder such things.

After torturing himself, repeatedly ruminating on such matters, Mike also played over and over again his and Sid's recent trip to London to find Maddie. He wanted to re-trace their steps and replay their actions in order to identify where they might have gone wrong.

It had been a relatively bad-tempered trip and Mike regretted that much at least. Sid was pretty stoned when they set off and so wouldn't see the seriousness of the situation. Mike was still angry that Sid hadn't informed him immediately the original meeting had happened. Mike thought that, if Sid has asked the right questions he might have been able to provide some better clues as to how Mike might locate Liam. He might have even called Mike from the bar and given him the chance to directly talk to Maddie to find a solution to the situation that *he* wanted rather than just allow her to dictate terms. Instead, his apparent disloyalty had cut Mike to the core and, in truth, this was hurting Mike almost as much as the loss of the son he had never been able to get to know. Through the years, Sid was always on Mike's mind – if not also his sofa – and Mike thought he mattered to Sid just as much. Sid simply said he was *'looking at the bigger picture for a change'* and that, as Mike was always telling him he should do this, he should be grateful for Sid helping to get Maddie to cut herself loose at long last so he could get on with his life.

Mike and Sid sat in near silence in the bar opposite the floodlit church on Kilburn High Road for hours. It was a pretty nondescript place considering Sid's *Pop Factor* mates had seen fit to drag him there rather than any of the decent places they could have chosen nearer the Maida Vale studio where they had been working. There were neon lights of blue and red, two indoor waterfalls made up of water running down large sheets of glass, there were six-foot high twigs stood in oversized grey stone vases and shiny granite as far as the eye could see. There was a bar serving over-priced wine and small bottles of expensive foreign beer – there was nothing available on draught at all - and more noticeably, not a single ounce of atmosphere to be found anywhere amidst the bland, cold minimalism that surrounded them..

Thankfully, Mike hadn't much felt like talking to Sid as the tuneless music in the bar was deafening for much of their visit. Needless to say, there was no sight of Maddie or a man in a tweed jacket called Clive or anybody resembling either of them. Mike had asked each of the eastern–European bar staff if they knew the couple at all. They indicated that they did not but pointed to a man called Jacek, who was sat in the corner and was apparently the owner of the bar. Mike introduced himself and asked if the couple were known to Jacek as regulars in his establishment. Again the answer was negative and the bar owner pointed out some regular customers who might possibly have more information.

Mike left his name and number with Jacek in case he thought of something later and went to speak with the locals he had identified. When asked, however, these strangers replied in a similar fashion. After nearly four hours of door watching whilst Mike drank diet cola and Sid nursed a few bottles of something that looked like Polish Budweiser, the trail stayed cold, their drinks warmed up and the defeated pair left for home.

Sid had quipped at this point – *a la PG*

Wodehouse – that he could tell that Mike, if not actually disgruntled, was far from being gruntled. Rather than lighten the mood as it had been intended, it simply guaranteed that the trip home was as silent as the drive up had been, six long hours earlier.

Within a day of the trip to London Mike was having trouble sleeping. Each night he lay in bed, or latterly on the recliner in front of the television as he didn't have the energy required to physically move himself into his bedroom, and simply went over things again and again. He wondered what would have happened if he had fought for the right to see Liam when the couple first separated. He could even have fought for custody of his son due to Maddie's unpredictable nature and state of mind. He might have tried harder to locate Maddie so he could at least have sent a card on his son's birthday or at Christmas. Instead, Mike wrote letters to his son about his life, family and career and placed them inside birthday and Christmas cards, sometimes including a photograph or two, and put them all in an old red-vinyl LP case he kept in his wardrobe. He didn't know why he did this, or what else to do with them, but it seemed to fulfil a major role in his coping mechanism in dealing with the situation, the complete compartmentalisation of the subject.

Mike just wanted to be able to wish Liam luck on his first day at school or support him when he went up to secondary level. Mike thought about never being able to offer advice to his son about his subject choices before he went on to study for his GCSEs, realising this would be soon; never helping him with choosing a college and later a university; he knew he could have offered guidance on Liam's future career options. Mike thought about never being there to offer advice on girls or meeting the woman he eventually chose to be his wife. But what if Liam had turned out to be gay? Would Mike have been ok with that? He liked to think he would have been, he was pretty liberal and wasn't easily shocked by the young people at college, so of course he would have been cool with having a gay son. Mike knew, however, that it had all just slipped from his reach and yet all he wanted, all he *yearned for*, was to be a father to the son he had never really known.

When contemplating these things, Mike instinctively appreciated that the life he had made for himself was, in reality, pretty good. His wide circle of friends meant that – when he felt like it - he enjoyed a decent social life. He was in reasonably good health for a man of his age too. Although currently single and having a failed marriage behind him, Mike still went on dates with women from time to time and sometimes these would lead to more. He had a career that was both demanding yet satisfying, it was also quite well paid. His career choice provided longer than average holidays during which time he could have fun spending his hard-earned disposable income on pretty much whatever he liked. Mike had a great family and, although he didn't see them too frequently, they had great times when they occasionally got together. Closer to home, he did have a talented artist for a sister whom he adored and who loved him back. As an artist, Amy was always destined to be poor and Mike considered himself fortunate to able to help her financially so that she could follow her dreams. His life, in short, should have been giving him tremendous pleasure. Mike felt rich in these terms but simultaneously felt guilty because, although he had so much more than most people to be thankful for, the thing that was screwing him up was not the picture of his life thus far but of what his life was *supposed* to look like.

In his head, Mike played out the role Sid had in his life. It was true that he had always defended his friend in the face of all detractors. It was also true that this had sometimes meant that Mike was vilified – albeit temporarily – alongside Sid who would often prove the critics right by continuing to behave appallingly. Loyalty, however, was a huge part of Mike's personality and a quality in people that he prized greatly. Sid and Amy were two people he had counted on as a child and who had always been there for him. Sure, Sid could press Mike's buttons like no other and would therefore sometimes piss him off with his apparent lack of thought and hedonistic ways, but Mike knew Sid would always be there for him. At any rate, whenever Sid became too much for someone, Mike could talk him around and would invariably improve the situation for all sides. And if Mike was Sid's moral compass, Amy had sometimes played a similar role in Mike's life.

Amy supported Mike when he was down; she encouraged him to be even more in life than he already was; and whilst doing all of this for Mike, Amy also managed to appear to depend upon *him*, a role Mike was thrilled to take on. Whenever he thought of this however, Mike would quickly also realise how great an Auntie his little sister would have been to Liam. This frequent thought was an additional source of regret to Mike. Liam would never experience the love, encouragement and support of his favourite Aunt Amy; he wouldn't experience her taking his side against someone else in an argument and how great that felt; he would never have a day out with her at the funfair, zoo or a shopping trip to buy cool clothes; he wouldn't watch late night horror movies through his fingers with Amy when sleeping over at her place; and worst of all, he would never get a comforting, consoling hug from her when a girl broke his heart.

Inevitably, when contemplating such things, Mike would weep.

Anxiety anxiety, keeps me happy,
Anxiety, anxiety, keeps me happy,
Always stiff, all day long,
Nothing's right, 'til its all wrong,
It makes no sense until I'm tense,
Always laughing at your expense.

Chapter 10

At the appointed time Mike walked into the brightly lit, modern reception area of the new Health Centre. There were a number of people sitting or standing around the room, each one appeared to be completing some survey paperwork on clipboards. No one looked at him as he entered and they seemed to be making as little sound as possible, as per the unwritten rule of waiting areas across Britain. Full of trepidation, Mike introduced himself quietly to the woman at the desk.

"I'm here for the group session for...well...er...is it called CBT? The one for stress and...." He trailed off, unsure as to what to say whilst being acutely aware that any of the strangers in the room would be able to hear him. The only sounds at that point being the hum of a water cooler in the corner and the sound of six or seven ballpoint pens scribbling on six or seven sheets of paper.

"The Mood Club love?" the reception worker replied, rather too loudly and cheerfully for Mike's liking, given that everyone in the room now knew what he was there for. Not waiting for an answer she went on, "Ok, if you could complete this questionnaire please and give it to your therapist when the session starts. Can you bring the pen back to me though please? They disappear all the time and so I'll need *that* back, thanks."

Mike hadn't heard it called a 'Mood Club' until that moment and remarked – silently to himself of course – that it sounded a little bit *American* and therefore, a bit too *American* for his liking. Mike looked at his mobile and quickly decided on a ringtone for the service should he need to call at any point (*The Lunatics Have Taken Over the Asylum* - The Fun Boy Three*).* He took the clipboard and pen the receptionist had given him and turned around, looking for both something to lean on and somewhere he could gauge how many of the strangers around him heard the reason for his visit. It was immediately clear that everyone had heard yet none initially seemed to judge him for it. Mike's perception was that this was possibly due to them all having been subject to the same treatment and that they were all probably therefore members of Mike's CBT group – the Mood Club – for the next six weeks. He smiled weakly and sidled over to a ledge at the end of the reception desk where he started to complete his form.

Mike quickly realised that the questionnaire was simply a way of establishing his baseline mood and emotional position. It asked how he felt about a number of things, on a scale of one-to-ten or in a series of yes/no tick-boxes. It included such things as the frequency of him attending social events during the previous week (1) and the level of difficulty he experienced in doing so (7); his ability to do things such as housework or cooking meals (7). It included a question about the number of times he contemplated or considered ending his life (o)...and if he had, how many times he had attempted to do so. It was worded in such a matter-of-fact way that it appeared to be a simple, relatively mundane question like all of the others. Its very normality was quite shocking to Mike. He had, it was true, wondered who would mourn him if he wasn't around anymore, but he had never seriously contemplated actually *ending* his life. Was he *really* being grouped together with the kind of people who didn't just contemplate suicide but also attempt it, seemingly between one and ten times per week? Did Dr Baker really view him in this way?

The questions in Mike's head remained rhetorical of course and, within a few short minutes, the surveys were being collected by a member of staff. The group was then led in silent, single file to a room some way down a long featureless corridor. They walked into the brightly lit, bland room, shuffled around whilst quietly removing their coats and jackets and took their seats, still in complete silence. After a couple of stragglers had come in and found a spare seat each, one of the staff stood up to address the room;

"So, shall we start with some introductions? Anyone can start...so if you just tell the group who you are and what you want to get from these sessions."

Silence.

"So. Anyone want to go first?"

More silence.

"Come on, anyone at all?"

Again, there was nothing except buttock-clenching silence. A silence so loud Mike would swear he could hear it, that is he would if he

97

hadn't suddenly been struck dumb by the question. Mike always quite enjoyed group meetings, seminars and training sessions. He enjoyed getting away from his students and bouncing a few ideas around with his colleagues. He could be quick witted and would show off a bit in these gatherings. He would say that it was his duty to help break the ice and get people at their ease. Some of his colleagues would suggest it demonstrated more a lack of self-discipline or it was over-compensation for a lack in self-confidence. Mike had been told that his making light of subjects in such sessions was more about him having an aversion to interacting in a group setting. Mike thought this was utter bollocks; he bloody *loved* all this stuff. But not here, not today. Today, Mike stared at his scuffed Dr Marten shoes and said nothing at all.

"So...OK, we can start with me I suppose. So my name is Sally-Anne – with an 'e' - and I am a Cognitive Behavioural Therapy Practitioner and I work for *Talk it Over*. So, to let you know a little about the organisation I guess. So *Talk it Over* is a social-enterprise contracted by the NHS and your local Primary Care Trust to provide support to local patients who are experiencing low mood and/or mild anxiety issues. I, with my colleagues here..." she gestured towards two women sat next to the flipchart on her right-hand side, "...will support your learning and development over the coming six weeks in an attempt to help you all..." she peered at everyone in the room in turn, "...What?" Sally-Anne-with-an-e's abrupt and unexpected question sat in the air for what seemed an eternity and then, without anyone answering she said, "That's right! To help you all lift your mood!" Her voice rising in tone, rather patronisingly, at the end of the sentence.

Sally-Anne smiled. She was clearly satisfied with the responses from the voices in her head, if not from the room, thus far. Mike was already feeling his hackles rise. One of Sid and his soapbox issues was people starting a sentence with the word "So" and 'So-So-Sally-Anne-with-an-e' was already starting to get on his wick.

"This is Gabby and this is Natalie" Sally-Anne introduced her two colleagues, both of whom, like her, appeared young enough to be fresh out of university. They clarified the introductions in turn;

"Hi I'm Gabby...or *Gabs* actually...I prefer Gabs" said the first, looking more at Sally-Anne than the group as if to reinforce an earlier conversation the two might have had. Natalie then stood up and took her turn;

"And yeah, er...hi...I'm, like, er...*Na'er-lee*?" said Sally-Anne's other colleague, her estuary-English accent and a clear upwards vocal inflection at the end of her introductory sentence making her sound like she was asking a question rather than making a statement of fact. It soon seemed that everything she said sounded like a question, which was as annoying to Mike as the silent 'T' in Natalie was. Perhaps she was checking with the group so as to ensure they all knew exactly what a "*Na'er-lee*" actually was?

Mike couldn't help but wonder at the young age of the three course practitioners. He hated when a person was written off by someone else due to their age but found himself wondering what these three young people could possibly teach *him*...an experienced and qualified lecturer nearing fifty years of age. Consequently, he couldn't help but think that their most recent jobs before their current employment were probably in *New Look*, *Next* or *Nando's* during term time. They were so similar to the students he taught at Highdowns and he was increasingly ill at ease with the potential healing power of a CBT course run by such youngsters. Both had held a hand up in turn as their names were called out by Sally-Anne-with-an-e. They appeared somewhat uncomfortable and self-conscious given their roles. This only served to confirm to Mike that they probably felt as uneasy about their level of responsibility as he did. Sally-Anne-with-an-e was different though, she was confidently looking back at the people in front of her, she continued,

"So, now, shall we go from left to right?"

The unfortunate woman who had recklessly chosen to sit in the end seat of the semi-circle of chairs nearest to the therapists was suddenly thrust into the spotlight. The remaining eight members of the group, five men and three more women, moved their gaze from their feet towards her and waited expectantly, each of them also grasping the little time they had left to think of what they would say when their turn in the spotlight inevitably came. She quietly introduced herself but no-one heard her name, her voice trembling inaudibly. When she had finished her incoherent opening gambit, she scribbled something in marker pen on the white rectangular sticker provided with her hand-out and stuck it on the front of her blouse, it read *M-A-U-R-E-E-N*.

"Thank you Maureen," said Sally-Anne, "I know this is tough so we all appreciate you taking the first turn. So next we have...?" she turned to the woman to Maureen's left and raised her *'Angry-Birds'* style inked-in eyebrows. In turn, each of the group quietly introduced themselves and stuck their name stickers on their lapels, shirt fronts and jacket pockets. Mike was struck by the variety in age and appearance of the people in attendance; it really was a wide cross-section of society...although the room seemed to be short of anyone who could pay privately for decent quality one–to-one counselling he thought.

"So, the first principle we need to establish is that these six sessions need to be participatory," Sally-Anne said, rather grandly. "We need to ensure that everyone gets a chance to speak and that everyone contributes in whatever way they can. This way, we will have a meaningful and inclusive experience and will all get positive results from our efforts, ok?" She looked at each and every one of the group in turn, whilst each member of the group, in turn, looked back at their shoes.

The first task of the group was apparently to establish a few ground rules. According to Sally-Anne – and pretty much every training session and textbook Mike had ever come across – when members of such a group established the rules and standards it felt were most appropriate, it would achieve them and would rarely, if ever, transgress them.

"So, given that we all need to contribute, who would like to be the first to suggest a ground rule that they would like the rest of the group to stick to in these meetings?" asked Sally-Anne, somewhat optimistically, given that none of the group was actually making eye contact with her – or anyone else – at the time of asking. She pressed on, "What about arriving on time, or at least calling us on the phone before we start if you are running late?"

The easier option of agreeing with Sally-Anne

rather than speaking aloud was unanimously taken up by the group who all nodded in unison, whilst making positive affirmative sounds under their collective breath.

"Excellent!" said Sally-Anne, happy to have made some headway. She started scribbling on the flipchart before continuing;

"So how long shall we give any stragglers before we say to them that we've started and don't wish to be disturbed? After all, we might have made some progress and, as these sessions are only one hour long, we don't want to spend half of it re-capping for latecomers do we?" It seemed Sally-Anne had a bit of an issue with tardiness...or maybe with re-capping, Mike couldn't really work out which yet. A man whose name badge read *'Bryan'* bravely ventured a thought on the matter,

"What about ten minutes? If someone is ten minutes late we should say they're too late to join the group."

Privately Mike thought this a little harsh but as he moved to say so, *'Maureen'* and *'Fiona'* both nodded and Sally-Anne immediately started to write it next to a number *(1)* at the top of the flipchart. Mike looked back at his feet and remained silent.

"Ok, ten minutes cut off it *IS*!" announced Sally-Anne, "So, what else?" she continued. She was answered merely with more silence and shoe gazing.

"So, anything, anything at all?" Sally-Anne scanned the room and then looked at her two colleagues who, for a moment or two, appeared as dumbstruck as the clients. Na'er-lee suddenly found her voice;

"Well...er, what about...like...somethin' about, like, respect, or somethin' like that...yeah?" she offered, sounding more like one of Mike's sixteen year old General Studies students. She looked back at Sally-Anne, apparently for some vindication of her contribution but Sally-Anne was already looking back at the group with her heavily-inked eyebrows raised even higher than before.

"Great! That's great Nat, thanks! So shall we make that number two?" she asked rhetorically again as she added it to the flipchart next to a large (2). "Now we're getting somewh..."

"Talking over people when they are talking!" blurted out 'Geoff' before Sally-Anne could finish. "No one should talk over anyone else while they are talking!" he very quickly and somewhat needlessly clarified. He sat upright and smiled, looking enormously pleased with himself.

Mike snorted and looked around at the others expectantly. They in turn looked back at him, blankly. No one appeared to be sharing the joke.

"So Mike? Is there something you have to add to the list?" asked Sally-Anne, also seemingly oblivious to the clown-outfit wearing elephant they were all ignoring.

"Well...er...hmm...what about..." as Mike struggled to think of another rule quickly, the door opened and a woman walked into the room.

"Excuse me, *REALLY* sorry I'm late, the friggin' car wouldn't start, then, *Christ* the traffic in town is an absolute bloody nightmare tonight, getting here and finding a parking space was an absolute friggin' nightmare...Oh...'scuse the language". She sat on the one empty seat and slipped her leather jacket off, hanging it on the back of her chair. As she ran her fingers through her bright red spiky hair, Mike noticed that she had been biting her fingernails and what was left

103

of them matched her hair colour. He also saw Bryan look enquiringly at his watch; eyebrows furrowed, and then back at the latecomer. Mike wondered if the new rules already applied, which seemed harsh given this woman's absence whilst the rules were being 'unanimously' adopted. And anyway she seemed, well, sort of *nice* really. She wrote her name on the sticker with a squeak of the marker pen and stuck it to the front of her black t-shirt; it read *C-A-R-O-L*.

Sally-Anne provided a very short re-cap for Carol's benefit, much to Bryan's obvious irritation and then said, "Right! Where were we?" Mike had established Sally-Anne didn't mind the odd re-cap or two so must therefore have a dislike for tardiness. He sensed he was again about to be forced to re-engage his brain when Sally-Anne surprisingly came out with,

"Where were we? Oh yes, that's it, so we were about to have a little chat about the challenges of experiencing low mood, stress and anxiety and how these things manifest themselves in people." Mike exhaled gently, relieved he had dodged the proverbial bullet. Bryan folded his arms and stuck his bottom lip out a little further than it was already on hearing the news that there would be no more rules established today.

After reminding everyone that it was a participatory session and that she wanted everyone to fully engage, Sally-Anne did a quick question and answer session on the symptoms members of the group might be experiencing with their low mood and anxiety.

"So, what kind of challenges or symptoms might someone with low mood have?" She asked.

There was no response. Sally-Anne continued undeterred by the group's reluctance to answer.

"So, what about, perhaps, feeling a sense of withdrawal from formal settings or less formal social gatherings?" she asked.

Mike suppressed the urge to respond with an *"Obvs!"*

The Mood Club silently nodded as one and Na'er-lee dutifully wrote it on the list for Sally-Anne.

"So what else?" asked Sally-Anne, eyebrows raised. The Mood Club was as unanimous in its silence as it was in its obvious discomfort.

"So, a lack of energy? Experiencing lethargy at all? Anyone?" pressed Sally-Anne.

The Mood Club was unsure as to whether she was asking for another challenging symptom or asking how the group felt at *that particular* moment in time, so demonstrated its collective lack of energy by doing and saying nothing.

"So, what about an inability or lack of desire to interact with others generally?" Sally-Anne offered. The Mood Club affirmed its unanimous and unequivocal agreement by making no discernable sound at all and without further enquiry Na'er-lee wrote it on the flipchart. Sally-Anne continued, apparently on something of a roll;

"So, what about sharing your inner-most thoughts, emotions and feelings with a group of complete strangers? How do you feel about *that*? Is *that* difficult?" Sally-Anne ventured with something bordering on an evil grin on her face. As if to use shock tactics to elicit some response, *any* response at all from the group, Sally-Anne peered at each member of the group in turn after this probing. It was a stare that felt like it lasted an hour. The Mood Club remained tight-lipped and simply shuffled in their seats and fixed their gaze anywhere but on the lead practitioner. Mike wondered what kind of pressure it would take for one of them to answer, to scream or to burst into tears. It looked as though it might take a vacation in Guantanamo Bay and a few turns at being water-boarded before any of the group would crack.

Mike wondered if this really was the best approach for his recovery. He quite liked group sessions yet didn't feel able to open up to this group. They were all strangers and all so very different. When he also considered that the three people charged with assisting this recovery looked no better trained or informed than his General Studies students, and the intellectual level at which he was to be challenged, he considered pulling out of the group rather than drag himself through this torture for six weeks.

The session went on to discuss what low-mood was, how it was triggered and how it made someone feel. It all became a bit of a blur for Mike who had started to quietly lament on his situation. By the end of the session the group members were as quiet as they had been at the beginning. It was clear that it would take more than a week to drag them out of their malaise. Sally-Anne outlined what she wanted each of them to do prior to the next time they met.

"So, I need you to look at the inside-back-page of your *hand-outs*..." she waved her copy of the stapled A4 sheets everyone had found on their chairs when they sat down, just in case they didn't know what a '*hand-out*' was. "...and you will find a grid. Got it everyone?" she arched her jet-black eyebrows in expectation.

"So, what we want you to do is to monitor your state of mind during the next seven days.

You need to think about how you feel, mood-wise, and make a note on a scale of one to ten – with one being the lowest and ten the highest – in the boxes provided. So, if you wake up tomorrow and you feel pretty lousy, let's say...three out of ten, you put a '3' in here, ok?" Sally-Anne looked around at the Mood Club and they looked back at her, silently. After this evening, Mike wondered if he would *ever* feel as good as a three again.

"So, when you are happy with that, you can then repeat the exercise throughout the day at various times, noting what you are doing and how you are feeling at that time. When we come back next week we can share some of this information and see if we can spot any patterns or areas where we can start to address your low mood, ok? If we can address what triggers your low mood and spot what you are doing when your mood is better, we can start to recover. Happy with that?"

Mike was wondering if anyone else in Mood Club had spotted how Sally-Anne used the word '*happy*' with no sense of irony at all. Maybe this was subliminal he thought. Also, what if everyone in the Mood Club monitored their mood before and after they had attended to see if the group sessions were adversely affecting them he thought. And maybe, Mike thought, he was just over-thinking.

"Remember everyone that your places on this course are valuable. There is a waiting list and some people weren't able to come along today as the places were filled by you guys," Sally-Anne pointed to each of the group in case they were in any doubt as to who she meant.

"We will all go through this process together and at our own speed, so we can't simply parachute someone else in part-way through. It wouldn't be fair on them to have to catch up and if we end up with empty places, it means someone has dipped out doesn't it?" If Sally-Anne expected someone to answer her this time she had another thing coming, although it sounded more rhetorical than most of her previous unanswered questions had sounded. Mike knew, however, that his conscience would not allow him to stay away now, so he made himself a little commitment to attend....even if it killed him.

"So has anyone got any questions for us? Anyone?" asked Sally-Anne. A woman in her early thirties, whose name badge read *R-U-T-H,* put her hand up as if she were in school and needed the toilet; Sally-Anne nodded to her like a primary school teacher in response,

"Yeah, Sally-Anne, just out of interest really, I've never heard your surname before and I wondered where it originates, I mean, is *Withany* an English name?"

Mike stifled a laugh and looked around the room to see how many of the others were enjoying the moment as much as he was. There wasn't so much as a murmur.

Sally-Anne paused, looked at Mel, looked at the rest of the group and made an executive decision to move on briskly;

"So, please make sure you stick to the schedule and return every week won't you? Look, I've done *SO* much talking I'm going to hand you over to Gabby to complete our first Mood Club meeting by taking you through what we've done thus far, to keep these thoughts upper-most in your minds."

Sally-Anne, appearing to run out of steam, sat down and surrendered to the group. In doing so she confirmed to Mike two things; one was that it might in fact be re-capping that she had something of an aversion to after all and secondly; she *did* know how to correctly use the word '*So*'.

"It's Gabs by the way, *G-A-B-S*?" said Gabs, looking back at Sally-Anne more assertively. Gabs went on to recap on the tortuous hour the Mood Club had just spent together, before wishing everyone a good week and saying good night.

+ + + + + +

When Mike reached home after his first Mood Club, Amy was waiting for him and they went to the White Hart for a drink. As he sat nursing a beer, Mike reflected upon the evening to his sister.

"I can't believe they actually call it '*Mood Club*' Amy, I mean, '*Mood Club*'. It sounds like somewhere you might go to listen to Tony Bennett or Perry Como for fuck's sake. It's like a parody on that comedy show that continually does the *Jazz Club* sketch. Don't they understand it's already a fucking parody! It's not for me; I don't think I can drop out but I can't go back either."

Amy watched her brother whilst he ranted. She was used to seeing him being tense; it was a condition he had claimed as his own many years before. Amy knew that Mike was someone who could command respect and was popular simply because of the fact that he cared *so* much about things that they often worried him. Everyone he knew was aware of the fact that he actually gave a shit about things. His authenticity was his strength, as well as the reason why he sometimes lived on his nerves. Amy touched Mike on the arm;

"You really don't *have* to go back you know? I

appreciate that places are limited and all that but if it's not going to do you any good you should pull out. We can say you aren't well enough or something can't we? I mean, it's about time you put yourself first rather than doing the right thing for everyone else all the time. I know you like *the rules* Mike but for once in your life damn it, just blow the bloody rules, ok?"

Mike smiled at his sister, he loved it when she said things like 'damn it' or 'blow the rules'. He picked up his glass and held it up to her in silent salute before downing the last of his beer.

"I'd better get off now Amy, will I see you on Saturday? Debs has put out another call for everyone to get along to the Civic Hall for a counter-demo you know? I'll think about whether I'll go back to the Mood Club during the week, ok? Meanwhile, we can use next weekend usefully and take on the local Neo-Nazis together!"

"Yeah, I'll see you there and the Mood Club thing? You make sure you DO think about that!" said Amy, who stood up and kissed Mike on the cheek. "Now, you can drop me off home if you want. It'd be the least a brother can do to repay his sister for listening to him whine all evening. And besides, I haven't got the taxi fare!"

Mike smiled, pulled his jacket on and picked up his car keys. He put his arm around his sister and they left the pub.

Just because you're a black boy,
Just because you're a white,
Doesn't mean you've got to hate him,
Doesn't mean you've got to fight.

Chapter 11

"No signal here sweetie? Try further up the Civic Hall steps; you might get something a bit higher up." Tim was shouting instructions to Tania, who was walking around the town square holding her smart phone with outstretched arms in front of her as she did so. "Anything now? Any bars? Er...don't get too close to *them* will you..." His tone wasn't exactly encouraging and Tania threw him a glance that struck him dumb for a few moments.

"What's the other half doing pal?" enquired a smirking H, "Is she trying to join up with the bad guys?" he nodded towards the English Liberation Force membership that had rallied in the town square after their march ended an hour earlier, "...Or has she got an app that assists her search for ley-lines, ancient burial sites or hidden water courses or something?"

Debs, Candy and Amy all smiled knowingly at H. Oblivious to his sarcasm, however, Tim replied to H's question somewhat earnestly;

"She's trying to get a mobile signal so she can go on social media to see what tactics the ELF is planning. Y'know, if they are going to try to get to our counter-demo or whether they're going to march on the Mosque or what. It's all about intelligence these days H, we need to stay one step ahead of the neo-Nazis and their ilk if we're going to fight Fascism" Tim waved his placard as he

111

spoke to H. Not un-coincidentally, it bore the words "Let's Fight Fascism!"

"Well good luck with that friend, there's no bloody signal in the town centre for starters, never has been in fact and if she, or anyone, thinks they can keep up with all this shit via Twatter or Faeces-book or whatever they've got another thing coming." H nodded at the ELF again and continued,

"Also, if this lot of half-witted, meathead wankers has got any strategy at all I'll be fucking amazed. I work with their sort all day. Do you really want to know what '*the elves*' are planning on doing today?" H made air quotation marks as he spoke. "That is, of course, apart from fixing your shoes overnight like good elves and hoping United get a no-score-draw this afternoon? Well this is how you find out!" he said and he squeezed through the barrier-cordon that the police and stewards had set up earlier that morning.

Before anyone could stop him, H calmly strode across the square towards the multitude of shaven-headed ELF marchers. As usual, the ELF had brought a number of their own activists into the town from far and wide. The majority of marchers present on the day were actually just local football fans who had decided to come down to the town centre at lunchtime to see if anything kicked-off with the ELF before returning to the Victoria Park Stadium for their own kick-off at 3 o'clock. Onlookers in the counter-demo crowd watched as H drew a few jeers from the lads at the front of the ELF group who didn't think he would have the bottle to walk right up to them. They were quickly proved wrong and quietened down when he got close to where they stood. H also attracted the notice of a couple of police officers who started to nervously move towards him. By the time the police officers drew closer it became evident that H had already engaged in conversation with members of the ELF – the *Elves* as he tended to call them - and seemed to be in control of matters. He was seen pointing towards the anti-fascist demonstrators on the opposite side of the square and then chatted some more. After the police caught up with him, and a few cautionary words were exchanged, H calmly walked back to his friends, hands still in his jacket pockets. Candy remarked to the others that at that moment, H looked like he owned the town square.

On reaching the counter-demo, H was greeted with a mix of admiration and disdain. Admiration from the younger members of the anti-fascist group, many of whom relished the heightened tension, secretly hoping that a little violence was brewing. The disdain was evident from some of the older anti-fascists who feared the fuelling of confrontational elements among the two crowds. Or maybe they were simply concerned that shoe repairs were going to fall behind whilst the elves were out on the streets, H wasn't sure. Anyway, Candy rubbed his arm affectionately when he squeezed himself back between the barriers. He smiled and looked like the cat that got the cream.

"Well what did you learn *mate*?" asked Tim eagerly, and in somewhat too familiar a tone for H's liking. Tania was now back at Tim's side, having seemingly given up her quest for making contact with the outside world. Together again, Titan looked at H, patiently waiting for him to share the intelligence he had gathered. H was more than happy to oblige;

"Firstly, they reckon they'll listen to their leaders make a few speeches over by the war memorial. This will be followed by a photo opportunity for the local press and is the customary chance for some of the less-intelligent members to make their parents proud of them by getting their ugly mugs in the paper. Then there'll be a couple of verses of '*Jerusalem*' from a PA system in the back of that van there," he pointed to a white mini-bus parked behind the crowd across the square. "Then they reckon they're coming over here to bash the shit out of some Lefties....Oh yes...and one of 'em said something about a hard-fought 3-1 win against City this afternoon!" H looked Tim in the eye, "How's all that sound *MATE*?"

Tim looked ashen and stuttered "R-r-r-really? Do you reckon that's true H? Will that happen?"

"Nah!" said H somewhat predictably, "We'll *never* score three past City."

Everyone, except Tim, laughed.

After normality had resumed, the ELF leadership commenced their usual racist rantings about Johnny Foreigner coming over here and presumably stealing shoe repair jobs from the English; then they went on about Muslims being evil ne'er-do-wells who hated and feared women even more than ELF members did. This was greeted with the inevitable barrage of cheers from the knuckles-dragging-on-the-ground brigade who had turned out to listen on their side of the town square. On the opposite side of the square, Debs called on the growing crowd to start chanting in a bid to disrupt the bile being spouted by the ELF.

"WHOSE STREETS? - *OUR* STREETS!
WHOSE STREETS? - *OUR* STREETS!
NAZI SCUM - OFF OUR STREETS!"

Two weeks after they last turned out at the Stop The War demo with Debs, Amy, Mike and Candy joined in with the chanting once again. This time, in a more self-conscious and less enthusiastic way than Titan and Debs; who waved their clenched fists as well as their homemade banners in time with the refrain from the crowd. H didn't join in at all but simply watched the group of Guardian reading, middle-class professionals, as he saw them, having a battle of wits with an unarmed group. The neo-fascists were, in his eyes, just a special needs section of the community allowed out in public every so often and shouldn't be taunted in this way. They didn't know anything about far-right politics really; they most certainly had no appreciation of the dark history of such things; they were simply looking for a scapegoat during tough economic times and should be educated, or pitied, rather than belittled.

As H amused himself people watching, a sudden and piercing scream from nearby brought him sharply back to his senses. A grey-haired woman who had been standing just where Candy had stood a few moments before, was lying on the ground holding her head and there was blood, an awful lot of blood.

Candy had moments earlier slipped away quietly to pick up a couple of coffees for her and H. She was unaware of what had quickly developed in her absence. The chain of events had started with a member of the fascist group carelessly throwing half a brick he had found. It was loose and simply lying in the block-paved decorative border around the war memorial. With little thought of the possible consequences, the man lobbed it high into the air across the town square. As is typical in these situations, there had been little thought on his behalf on how this might inflame a situation. He didn't know if he intended to spark anything. He wasn't even sure if he simply wanted to be provocative. He certainly hadn't been aiming for anyone in particular. And so he hadn't intended for his missile to actually strike anyone at all. Yet it did.

Candy, meanwhile, was gently amusing herself on how terribly middle-class and grown up it felt to be drinking a blend of Sumatran coffee, fresh ground and steaming hot whilst simultaneously demonstrating against the rise of neo-Nazism in the provinces. It was hardly 1936 and the Battle of Cable Street she mused, how times had changed. By the time Candy came out of Starbucks however, she was shocked to be standing on the edge of a pitched battle, the consequences of someone, somewhere nearby, demonstrating a complete lack of thought.

Skinheads were charging the middle-aged Guardian readers and college lecturers, who in turn were running for their lives. Mask wearing anarchists were pulling their hoods up and tearing more blocks from the floor of the town square to hurl at the skinheads. Candy could see Mike, Amy and Titan stood at the safer, far end of the street where they had retreated to when the melee had kicked off but she couldn't get to them as they were the other side of what had become a battleground. She caught a glimpse of Debs, who was repeatedly striking a young man with what looked like a wooden pole, possibly being what was left of her placard after it was transformed into a weapon. The Police were struggling to contain the situation as there were clearly too few of them to cope with the sudden escalation of violence in the proceedings. They tried, in vain, to keep the fighting to a minimum whilst awaiting the arrival of reinforcements.

It was at that moment that Candy's head was suddenly and violently twisted around and she pirouetted on the spot briefly before seeing the ground moving towards her face in slow-motion. As she hit the ground, Candy caught sight of the two coffee cups bounce off the pavement, distributing a shower of dark liquid into the air and onto the street beside her as they did so. Again, Candy saw all of this vividly in super-slow-motion, like the detailed camera shots showing the droplets of sweat flying away from a boxer's face following the impact of his opponent's knock-out punch. She could see 'H' and 'Candy' scrawled in black ink on the white coffee cups as they bounced off the flagstones, lids lifted into the air by the force of being dropped.

Dazed, Candy tried to make sense of what was happening and, as the people around her started to come back into focus, she began to feel a hot, searing pain to the side of her head. Looking up from the cold pavement she could see the shape of a person, a man with a shaven head, wearing a tracksuit top and with large gold rings on his fingers, one in his eyebrow and another in his ear. He was standing over Candy and smiling broadly. One of his front teeth appeared to be made of gold too, Candy couldn't recall the last time she had seen someone with a gold tooth. It reminded her of growing up in the seventies; gold teeth, white dog shit and Texan chocolate bars...all lost to the world of the 21st century as H would undoubtedly say. She was rudely brought back from her confused nostalgic state when the man in the tracksuit top spoke to her;

"Perhaps this will serve as a reminder that

whenever you wear *that*..." he pointed to the *'Unite Against Fascism'* badge given to her by Debs and now on her lapel, "...you're fair game love, OK?" He sneered menacingly before he turned towards the square again.

The pounding coming from the side of her head was still disorientating and Candy found herself beginning to shake uncontrollably as she started going into shock. Unfortunately for Candy therefore, she didn't see the man's face as H wiped the golden-smile from it with a punch that landed square on his nose. She would later swear she saw both of his feet lift from the ground and then watched as he fell – again in super-slow motion - heavily to the ground in front of her holding his bloodied and shattered nose. As she lay there, she thought she heard the man start to plead for mercy and watched helplessly as H pulled him up by the front of his tracksuit top and land a second blow, this time to the man's blood-soaked chin. H let him fall to the ground once again. As she started to slip into unconsciousness, Candy would also swear she witnessed Debs arrive at the scene in time to land a heavy kick to the man's ribs; whilst saying something about the positive economic benefits of immigration and the sense of enrichment we all experience by living in a multicultural society of course.

There's a solitary man crying, 'Hold me',
It's only because he's lonely
And if the keeper of time runs slowly,
He won't be alive for long...

Chapter 12

"You here for the Mood Club love? Can you just tick your name off this list for me?" The reception worker again asked these questions too breezily for Mike's liking and in such quick succession that he had no time to answer either. She handed him a clipboard with the same questionnaire he had been given the week before.

"Answer these as best you can while you wait and give it to one of the staff when your session starts ok? And remember to give the pen back to me won't you?" She turned away before he had chance to reply and at that moment, Mike pondered whether *any* questions were *ever* answered in such a place.

He sat in an empty seat at the far side of the rather sterile waiting area and started to fill in the blank spaces and tick the boxes on his form. On a scale of 1-10, how did he rate his overall mood over the last week?

• How difficult had he found it to carry out ordinary household tasks? (7)

• Did he find it difficult or easy to socialise? (7)

• Had he found himself over-eating? (yes)

• Had he found himself not eating enough? (no)

• Was he using alcohol/recreational drugs to cope with his low mood? (yes)

119

- How were his sleep patterns? (9)
- How often had he felt the world would be a better place without him in it? (o)
- Had he attempted to do himself harm during the last seven days? (no)
- How frequently? (n/a)

He looked around the room; there were seven out of the original ten people who had attended the previous week and Mike wondered how many of *them* were contemplating suicide. As Mike was certain that suicide wasn't on the cards for him, he wondered if he actually was depressed at all. It seemed so normal in this place to ask if someone were either contemplating suicide or actually attempting it on a regular basis that he was beginning to feel a bit of a fraud even being there.

In the waiting area the group members were collectively avoiding eye contact with each other by taking their time completing their individual questionnaires. Mike hadn't really been looking forward to being patronised by *So-So-Sally-Anne-with-an-e* and her cronies once again and it looked as if a couple of individuals had gone further and voted with their feet this week. Mike looked around; Jess, Fiona and Mel were the three absentees as far as he could tell. Mike had always been good at remembering faces and names, a rare skill in teaching these days, and he reflected on their contribution the previous week. They had said nothing at all that he could remember. This, of course, was in contrast to the one or two responses or ideas that the others managed to register during the hour long session, a session that felt like an entire day. Bryan was there, looking at his watch and looking agitated, Carol managed a thin smile in Mike's direction and he nodded gently in response. It was the only form of communication between any of the people in the room.

When Na'er-lee eventually arrived to collect them at the appointed time, each of the group dutifully handed their pens back to the receptionist, who cheerfully said an enthusiastic "Thank you!" to each and every one of them in turn. They then followed Na'er-lee down the corridor to their meeting room. As they each sat down, Mike noticed 'Darren', a young man with a shaven head, a few piercings and tattoos, furtively looking Sally-Anne up and down and, when he saw that Mike had noticed what he was doing, raised an eyebrow as if to say "Nice". This week, Sally-Anne was wearing heels, a skin tight pair of leggings and a crop top which stopped above her waist...like a crop top tends to do. Sure, Mike had noticed that she was an attractive young woman but knew two important things;

(1) their 'relationship' was such that she was the professional and he was one of her clients so to look at her in the way Darren was felt wholly inappropriate and;

(2) she was in fact – like the majority of his female students – possibly only half his age so to look at her in the way Darren was felt, well, wholly inappropriate...once again.

Mike chose to ignore Darren and he sat down in the same seat as last week. He looked around, each of the group sat in the same seat as the previous week and so the three chairs left empty were those previously used by Jess, Fiona and Mel. Mike smiled to himself; it was comforting to know that it wasn't only his students who exhibited this behaviour. Even Maureen, who had been forced to speak first due to the location of

121

her seat, had sat in the same one this week. Once everyone was seated, Na'er-lee made an announcement to the group;

"Now, er, like while I've got your, kinda...um attention yeah? I just wanna let you all know, um, that like next week? Yeah? The room is...kinda, er double-booked? So we can't, er, like use it and stuff? So we're gonna miss next week and, um, like meet up the week after yeah? Everyone? Is that ok yeah?"

In response, the Gloom Club nodded, gloomily.

"So!" started Sally-Anne, somewhat predictably, "Now we've taken care of the housekeeping, so-to-speak, how are we all this evening?"

The group, also somewhat predictably, said nothing, choosing instead to look at the footwear they had chosen to wear this week. Unsurprisingly, Mike was wearing his old Dr Martens shoes. It was unsurprising due to the fact that Mike Powell owned just three pairs of shoes and one of these was, in actual fact, a pair of boots. Mike wore his old, cherry-red shoes during the spring and summer months. When the weather got wetter and colder he would switch to his black Dr Marten boots. His third pair of shoes weren't a pair of shoes either, they were a pair of trainers.

Mike remembered he had bought the day-glo trainers at the same time as he bought his gym membership about six years earlier. He had started a relationship with a fitness fanatic of a woman called Tracy who briefly taught Physical Education – or *Recreational Activities* as they were euphemistically called - at Highdowns. Tracy had spent nearly a full term trying to persuade

Highdowns' students that this time should be spent in physical activity rather than snogging in the common room which is how most of the college had used the time up until then. As a consequence, Mike had admired Tracy's focus and tenacity, plus she was clearly very *fit* and wore a lot of shorts and tennis skirts, so he asked her out. She swore that her next life-project was to make Mike fit and healthy. The trainers cost him over £70 and the year-long gym membership cost him nearly £200. The relationship lasted a little under a fortnight and, consequently, the trainers remained in their box unworn - except for trying them on in the shop – and the gym membership was never used. Mike received an annual reminder of this failed relationship from the gym when it came to renewing his membership and every year, Mike smiled as he put the letter in the recycling bin and sat back in his leather chair.

Following the meeting last week, Mike hadn't felt much at all, not better, not worse, just not much at all. He had spoken to Amy after the first meeting and criticised it roundly. He was critical of the practitioners, their amateurish efforts and methodologies. He was cynical of their motivation and dismissive of the low level content. Mike then found himself crying uncontrollably when he got home from the pub. Later, Amy had put this down to the session bringing Mike's challenges to the surface and into sharper focus for him. Mike wasn't sure if this was correct but he did concede that he had actually found himself feeling worse for a time. He concluded that he was probably being impatient and needed to give Mood Club more time. He also knew that, as the NHS was footing the bill – however much he felt they may be being overcharged – he had a duty to stick with it. He recalled Sally-Anne last week saying how people couldn't be replaced during the course. Mike had already noted the three absentees and hoped *their* consciences were troubling them.

Demonstrating her reluctance to cover old ground, Sally-Anne asked Na'er-lee and Gabs to recap what everyone had learned during the previous meeting and how everyone's week had turned out after their first experience of Mood Club. As per the previous week, Maureen was forced to start due to her proximity to the flipchart. She barely protested and simply mumbled something about it being good to know that other people felt the same way as her.

Mike had already thought that this had been his only positive lesson from his involvement in Mood Club. He reflected that Maureen's view, as it concurred with his own, was a valid observation and he hoped that her low self-esteem wasn't the result of bullying, or she might never recover if she continued to sit in the first seat. He just wished that he had been given the opportunity to speak first as he wouldn't now need to think of something different to tell the group before Na'er-lee and Gabs reached him.

This was *so* depressing. In fact, Mike had started referring to the Mood Club as the 'Gloom Club' when he spoke of it to his friends, well, to Amy and Sid anyway as he didn't speak of it to the others at all. He felt its only positive aspect was that it was just *so* crap, that it rendered the experience ironically quite funny. He chose not to share this with the group. Instead he meekly said something about the mutual support and reassurance he had been given by everyone the previous week had made him feel safe and able to share with them all. The group all looked at Mike displaying their most sympathetic, and their most supportive and most reassuring, facial expressions. Mike felt sick.

Bryan was next. He explained that it felt like a positive outcome that some group members had made the effort to arrive punctually for the first time this week and that as the group had also now passed the ten minute point, it was good to know they weren't going to be interrupted like they had the first week. His eyes darted sideways to the left towards Carol and then back to his shoes. Carol looked a little cheesed off at the comment and Mike caught her eye by smiling sympathetically. She narrowed her eyes back at him. Sensing the increased tension between Carol and Bryan, Gabs quickly moved the group on. Geoff was next. Gabs asked him what *he* got from the first group session. He visibly tossed the question around in his head for a few moments and, without a hint of irony in his voice, answered "Homework?"

After a few more, frankly less humorous answers, Sally-Anne handed over to Na'er-lee to lead on the findings of the group's week of research.

"Well, did everyone, er, like, *do* the homework?" She sounded like she was expecting an '*AS IF!*' answer but she continued, "Did anyone spot any, er, like, patterns or *wha'everr*?"

The Gloom Club steadfastly refused to answer.

"Did anyone spot anything like, er, your mood was better when, like, maybe, you were busy or somethin' like that?" ventured Na'er-lee, widening her eyes like a nursery school teacher talking to pre-school kids. Mike looked around the Gloom Club; no-one was sitting on the floor cross-legged. No-one had a scabby knee or a

125

runny nose that he could see. He looked back at Na'er-lee and realised that her gaze had fallen on him.

"Mike? You wanna, er, like say somethin' then?" she enquired.

Without hesitation and surprising himself on the swift nature of his response into the bargain, Mike answered,

"Yes!"

"What do you mean?" asked Na'er-lee, seemingly alarmed and taken aback momentarily by a positive response.

"I was just answering your question in the affirmative. What I mean is *yes*, my mood *was* better when I was busy doing something and was worse when I had time to think or when I was – *like* - doing nothing?" confirmed Mike, trying to out do Na'er-lee both in the patronising stakes AND in the *needlessly-sounding-like-a-question* stakes.

Na'er-lee smiled with her whole face, a wide-eyed, awestruck smile that pretty much lit up the room. She looked at each member of the Gloom Club in turn and then at Gabs and Sally-Anne-with-an-e. Her expression seemed to be saying "See...I can actually get this shit to pay off. My work here is, er, like done?" She then looked back at Mike, still radiating gratitude and admiration;

"Cheers for sharing that Mike, I mean, it must've been, like, er, proper challenging for you?" as usual she sounded like she was asking a question but this time Na'er-lee just nodded for what seemed an eternity and looked at everyone else in the group as if to express how courageous Mike had been.

Somewhat disappointed that prizes for stating the blindingly obvious weren't on offer, Mike sat back and listened to each of the practitioners explain that, being busy was the key to the group's recovery. In turn they described how taking part in an activity or just physically setting a goal and going all out to achieve it was the next step.

Gabs spent about five minutes reeling off a list of, what she called, 'pleasurable and routine activities' that Gloom Club members could consider doing to improve their frame of mind. All the time, Mike noticed that Darren was leering at Sally-Anne, clearly with his own private definition of 'pleasurable' in mind.

"For this week's homework we are all going to think of an activity we enjoy and we are going to set ourselves something called a SMART objective. Does anyone know what a SMART objective is?" Gabs asked, looking around the room whilst making quotation marks in the air with her fingers.

On hearing these words, Mike was transported back over twenty years of teaching practice and training sessions and his heart sank. Being asked to set a 'SMART' objective was tantamount to being told to start thinking 'out-of-the-box' in his mind and he felt like vomiting for the second time that evening. He also hated people making 'air-quotes'. Remarkably, it seemed that no-one in the room, other than Mike and Gabs, knew what a 'SMART' objective was; let alone how to set one. To rectify this, Gabs used the flipchart, and nearly ten minutes of Mike's life that he would never be compensated for, to explain the concept.

Rory, whom Mike thought was quiet yet seemed intelligent and appeared to be experiencing very similar symptoms to his own, was first to speak. Mike had slightly warmed

127

towards Rory, even though barely a word had passed between them, but he felt they may share common ground. They were of a similar age too so Mike was interested in hearing what Rory had to say.

Rory explained that he was going to go to the cinema with a friend of his who was also his house-mate. He decided this would be on Wednesday after work, and that he could overcome any resistance from his mate's girlfriend in stopping it happening. Gabs agreed this was a good objective as it involved two pleasurable activities, meeting a friend and watching a movie, so would go a long way towards taking Rory's mind off his low mood. She then asked which film Rory might see and he replied with a sentence that brought Mike sharply back into the room;

"Oh, probably the new *Hobbit* one."

Mike recoiled in horror and instantly switched from seeing Rory as something of a potential kindred spirit into seeing Rory as something of a prog-rock loving, fantasy film watching tosser. Mike had spent years with a number of Tolkien and King Crimson obsessives at college and university and now worked with a few at Highdowns. They tended to work in the humanities department, taught English and/or drama and had found a new lease of life since Peter Jackson started making big budget movies. They also found it socially acceptable for the first time since they left university all those years before to talk openly about playing Dungeons and Dragons, going to English Civil War re-enactments or being fond of the album *Tales from Topographic Oceans* by Yes. They were always more likely to become naturists or Morris

Dancers. Consequently, they were quite unlike Mike. He was never destined to listen to a Yes album, see a Hobbit movie or take his clothes off in public. Mike would never do any of these things, he wasn't a weirdo after all and he secretly wondered why occasionally it felt like Punk Rock had never happened.

The remaining group members came up with a variety of mundane tasks and activities that were, in turn, scrawled up on the flipchart to be checked back on the following week. Tasks such as 'join the library on Thursday afternoon' and 'go to the gym on Sunday' were written on the flipchart next to the name of the person who had set them. Someone else said they would 'go for a run on Saturday'. Mike's objective was that he would 'take his two dogs for a long walk in the park on Wednesday and Friday rather than just around the block'. This was interesting on two fronts. Firstly, Mike perceived a small degree of warmth directed towards him from the others, with Gabs and Sally-Anne even tilting their heads to one side in appreciation of *Mike the animal lover*. Secondly, it was interesting insofar as Mike had never owned a dog, let alone two.

Mike knew what he was going to do. He wasn't yet sure it was SMART and he certainly wasn't yet ready to share it with the rest of the group. But he knew for the first time in weeks what must come next and he knew it couldn't make his situation feel any worse that it already did.

+   +   +   +   +   +

Back in the White Hart, Amy laughed when Mike told her of his pet dogs and how they had

129

featured, quite unexpectedly, in his homework task. Mike then explained what he *really* had in mind to do this week, in order to improve things.

"Look, it's NOT just that it's not a SMART objective. It's just that it's not a *'smart'* thing to do either!" insisted Amy when Mike explained his plan. "You could make things much worse for you and I hate seeing you like this. You need to start healing yourself rather than picking at the wounds you've already suffered."

Mike nodded as he sat at the bar but said nothing. His mind was made up.

...I'm ashamed of the things I've been put through,
I'm ashamed of the person who I am,
But if you could just see the beauty,
These things I could never describe,
Pleasurable ways of distraction,
This is my wanting cry.

Chapter 13

Two days had passed since Mike had decided that he should find Maddie to get things ironed out with her. He knew he could do nothing about the past but felt he could influence how things went in the future. Perhaps he could persuade Maddie to drop all of this pretence over Liam's father being 'dead' if he could show that he had cared all along and had wanted to be a father to the boy. Perhaps it wasn't too late to be introduced to Liam....perhaps; *just perhaps* it could be made to work. But first he needed to find Maddie; he couldn't sit around in a bar in London hoping she might pop back in again.

Mike started to flick through the results on his iPad after typing the words 'private investigator' into Google. He was astonished to find a national website helpfully called 'Find-a-local-private-detective.com' which clearly specialised in just such matters. "Whatever next?" he mused, as he typed his postcode into the website's search facility. It came up with the name of an agency in town, an agency that Mike had never seen or heard of but that was based – if the address was correct – in the very town where he had lived his entire life. Mike nervously called the number and dutifully left a message with his name, address and telephone number on the answerphone as instructed by the crackly voice he heard before hearing the machine beep at him.

Just taking the first step on his quest made Mike feel as if he was on the road to recovery. He knew he couldn't explain this particular objective to the rest of the Gloom Group but he knew he would now start to address some of the things that had brought him down in the first place. He made himself a pot of tea and sat down in front of the television in the cool comfort of his leather recliner. Mike hadn't long been sipping his first cup of tea, nor had he been looking at the programme listings for very long when there was a knock on the front door.

"Blimey that was bloody quick!" said Mike aloud, slightly startled and jumping eagerly from his chair. He put his cup down, straightened his shirt and went to the front door. On opening it he found a middle-aged man wearing a buttoned-up raincoat and carrying an umbrella. The man had a pleasant but slightly nervous look on his face, and Mike immediately noticed that he smelled of alcohol. Mike reckoned that if he had been asked to guess what the detective would look like and be wearing when he arrived, Mike would have described him exactly as he was seeing, and smelling, him right there.

"Er, hi!" said the man, "You won't know who I am but..."

"It's fine, I know who you are!" said Mike warmly, "Come on in, it's cold out there isn't it and we don't want to discuss all of this on the doorstep now do we?" He ushered the man inside.

"That's very kind, thank you Mr. Powell," said the man visibly relaxing.

132

Mike continued with his welcoming approach, "Look, I've just made a pot of tea, would you like a cup? Or I could make a coffee if you'd prefer, sorry but I haven't got anything stronger I'm afraid." Mike led the man into the lounge and gestured towards the brown armchair leaving the recliner, as usual, for himself.

"Oh bless you, cheers," said the man, briefly taking a moment to look around the room. "A cup of tea will do fine thanks, this is *very* nice of you Mr. Powell. Black, no sugar thanks." He sat down and Mike smiled warmly as he muted the volume on the television and went to get a mug from the kitchen for his visitor.

"And please, call me Mike!" he called out as he opened the cupboard and took out a bone-china mug decorated with red roses from the top shelf.

"Oh, yes of course...Ok, Mike...good...er, thanks!" replied the man, "And please, call me Clive!"

Mike stopped in his tracks for a moment and his blood ran cold. Surely, this was just a coincidence...of course it was. The *'Clive'* Mike was thinking about didn't know Mike, or possibly even *know of* Mike, and certainly didn't know where he lived. But he wondered how the detective agency managed to get someone here so quickly. It had been less than forty-five minutes since he had called their number. Mike's mind raced. Maybe one of their Operatives – Mike swore they would be called 'Operatives' – must have been passing, or living locally or something. Maybe one of them had coincidentally been in the office when he left his message. Yes that was it. One of them had been there, debriefing some poor woman whose husband had been caught

133

cheating on her. He had been showing her the photos they had captured and comforting her when the answer-phone kicked in. He had heard Mike leave the message and naturally thought to himself that simply locating someone to reunite them with an old friend had to be nicer work than delivering bad news like this to a vulnerable woman. Of course it was just a coincidence that the operative just happened to be called Clive.

Barely believing it but still feeling somewhat relieved, Mike said nothing and walked back into the lounge. His visitor was sitting in the armchair, smiling. He had removed his raincoat and Mike's lower jaw dropped to the floor to see that, teamed with a shiny patterned scarf underneath it, Clive was wearing a tweed jacket.

+   +   +   +   +   +

An eternity passed before either man spoke. Eventually Clive decided he should break the silence;

"I suppose having barged in on you like this I should explain why I'm here" he said, rather matter-of-factly. "Shall I?" he picked up the teapot, hesitating to look at the balaclava cosy for a moment and looked at Mike with eyebrows raised as he put the rose covered mug on the coffee table between them.

"Shall you what? Explain why you're here? Or do you mean 'Shall I be Mum?" said Mike, rather sarcastically.

"Both I s'pose," said Clive as he poured tea into the mug and moved to top up his host's mug too. Mike, with simmering silent hostility, placed his outstretched hand over the top of his mug and glared at Clive. Clive dutifully put the pot down.

Barely able to contain the fury he felt inside at this intrusion, Mike sat back in his chair and waited for Clive to speak again.

"Crumbs, where do I start? Look, when Jacek came to me and told me someone was looking for Madeline and me, well I had to find out who it was didn't I? I thought it had to be something to do with my work, I hadn't realised who you were until I spoke to her about it. I didn't realise it was linked to the day we bumped into your friend...er...what was his name? The drunken guy...he came in Jacek's place a while back...was a bit, you know..."

"Sid...his name's Sid!" interrupted Mike impatiently.

"Of course, er...thanks," said Clive, pausing for a moment before continuing,

"Anyway, when Madeline came in later that evening I showed your details to her and she eventually told me the whole story. She had given me bits of information over the time we've known each other but had left a few blanks too. I guess she was ashamed or whatever and it seemed inappropriate for me to ask really. I never used to think she experienced things like regret or shame in the early days but now, well, she has changed, y'know? Anyway, I mean, if she wanted to tell me more she would've wouldn't she? I prefer to work on the present and the future rather than worry about the past which, let's face it, none of us can change. Judge not, lest we be judged eh? Especially when one considers that there's a child involved in this situation we have here, and his care and wellbeing has to be paramount, don't you think?"

"Frankly I think this is more between me and Maddie – do you mind if I call her Maddie? - than me and you Clive, know what I mean?" said Mike.

With every word from Clive's mouth, Mike could feel his blood pressure rising and his chest tightening. Mike so infrequently got to speak his mind but now that the floodgates had been opened there was nothing stopping the subsequent deluge. Before Clive could respond Mike continued, the anger he was experiencing being clearly expressed in his combative tone;

"So do you mind getting on with telling me why *you're* here Clive and why Maddie isn't? I would like to speak to *her* Clive. No offence right...but I don't really want to speak to some jumped up twat in a tweed jacket and silk scarf about much at all, least of all my son. Once I've spoken to her I will get on with my life, yeah? At the mo, Clive, you're kind of just holding me up. You might be able to help me Clive; you really might, by just letting me know where Maddie is. I could use that right now but otherwise I'm not sure there's much more you can do mate. However, if you think you can help you have one minute to impress me, so fill your boots!"

Clive appeared undeterred. He looked squarely at Mike and tried to explain his position,

"I appreciate that you have things to discuss and I feel your irritation Mike but listen, I need to speak to you about some pretty sensitive stuff and you need to stay as calm as you can. I know I'm a stranger to you but it's probably better coming from me than it is from her. I'll take no more of your time than I have to and I'll be happy to get going as soon as, ok? You can't say fairer than that can you?" Clive held out his hands in a non-threatening, *you-can't-say-fairer-than-that* kind of way and raised his eyebrows. He continued, this time smiling wryly;

"As an aside, ha-ha, it's actually *quite funny* really, she said to me that you were SO laid back and easy going that you'd probably not even show *minor* irritation about all this. She reckoned she ought to have come but when I insisted I would take care of it, in case things got a bit heated, you know? She said I would soon see what a good guy you were and how this would literally be something of a relief to you rather than all bad news. After all, I'm here to put it all right again aren't I? And to think, I even stopped for some *Dutch Courage* on my way here this evening!"

Mike wasn't someone who lost his temper easily. In fact he lost his temper so infrequently, and hadn't lost his temper for so long, that he didn't know when he last got so angry that he wasn't in control of himself. Years of frustration and hurt had been rising inside and Mike hadn't seen either coming. Years of saying 'yes' when all he wanted to do was scream 'NO!' had been silently taking its toll. Years of hearing nothing from Maddie about the son he had never been given the chance to get to know were invisibly being stored in his subconscious. It all suddenly poured forth. The next few moments were a bit of a blank but when Clive's face started to turn from bright red to purple and when his eyes started to bulge as if they were about to burst, Mike regained control of his senses. Although still feeling anger, Mike decided he should perhaps loosen his grip on Clive's scarf and let him get up from the carpeted floor where he had pinned him, seemingly without warning, a minute or so earlier. Clive slowly and unsteadily staggered to his feet and straightened his now disheveled clothes.

"You were strangling me Mike! You tried to

kill me!" gasped Clive, immediately confirming to Mike that he had absolutely no ability to 'appreciate or feel' the irritation Mike had been experiencing after all. Mike was still shaking and, out of the starting gate yet again, his thoughts began to race once more.

His thoughts rounding the first bend, it was clear to Mike that Clive was no more than an interfering do-gooder of a boyfriend who wanted to pontificate towards an ex-partner of his girlfriend in order to sort out her loose ends. In his mind's eye, he was opening up on the straight and it was apparent to Mike that Clive was someone who would rather deal with Maddie's loose ends than allow Maddie to take responsibility for the loose ends that were of her own making, thus absolving her of all responsibility. It was all too much for Mike who, at every hurdle, looked at Clive with ever increasing and trembling anger. He briefly considered doing Clive more harm; if only to rid his own mind of the awful horseracing metaphor he was flogging to death when his galloping thoughts were stopped dead in their tracks, just as they reached the finishing post in fact.

Clive had been struggling to loosen the scarf from around his throat, the scarf which moments earlier Mike had been using as a tourniquet to stem the flow of air to Clive's lungs, and when he finally freed it he dropped the scarf onto the back of the chair. In doing so, he revealed a neck which was red and purple in colour. Oh, and also revealing a neck that was wearing the dog-collar of a priest.

"Oh for fuck's sake, are you shitting me?" exclaimed Mike, "You're a fucking man of the cloth? CHRIST ALL-BLOODY-MIGHTY

MADDIE'S ONLY GONE AND GOT HERSELF TUCKED UP WITH A FUCKING PRIEST! HA HA! NO WONDER YOU WERE SOUNDING SO SELF-BLEEDIN RIGHTEOUS!"

Falling silent after his outburst, Mike flopped down in his chair and momentarily contemplated what the maximum sentence would be for murdering a priest, and would it have a special term like *Theolocide* or *Vicarocide* or something. He placed his face in his hands, seemingly defeated. Clive, still rubbing his neck, sat down too and, now that his bulging eyes had started to relax again, looked at Mike through newly narrowed ones. The pause didn't last long this time;

"You're not quite how you were described to me, that's for sure," said Clive, not wishing to make light of what had just happened but still sounding more ironic than literal.

"Well, of the million or more people she *could* have ended up with, or *should* have ended up with, you weren't on my list," replied Mike, trying to lighten the mood but sounding more like he was throwing another insult in Clive's direction.

"None taken," Clive replied dryly.

Clive went on to describe how Maddie, with a twelve year old Liam in tow, had turned up at a soup kitchen he had been running near Kings Cross station a couple of years back. The line she gave him at the time was that she had just arrived back from Spain where, it seemed, she had been living something of a nomadic life with a group of French and Spanish musicians. She was penniless and hungry and had nowhere for her and her son to stay. Fearing for her welfare and that of her son on the streets, Clive put her in touch with a women's refuge and they gave her an emergency bed for two nights. This bought Maddie some time whilst he found something more suitable, staying with a parishioner. He told of how she said they had escaped a life of drugs, alcohol and uncertainty abroad and had returned to the UK, even though they had no family here anymore. Maddie told of how Liam's father had died many years before but that she received a little something each month from some kind of trust fund he had set up before he passed away. Clive said that this was where he stopped enquiring and she stopped explaining as it seemed too hurtful and intrusive to ask for more detail from her.

Clive went on to describe how he had helped them find somewhere more permanent to live and how Maddie found Liam a school where he could thrive. The boy spoke only broken English when he arrived yet was fluent in Spanish and French. Two years on he was tri-lingual and turning out to be quite the scholar too. Clive glowed with affection and pride when he spoke of Maddie and Liam. It was clear to Mike that Clive had deep feelings for them both as he described how they had fallen for each other over a period of time. Maddie even did a bit of volunteering at his church, the one across the road from the bar they frequented, and it seemed they had a simple, yet fulfilling life. Silence engulfed the men again and they each sat in contemplation, processing all that had happened that evening.

"And she never spoke of me after that and why she cut me out of my son's life?" Mike eventually asked, hoping Clive could shed some light on why he had never really figured in their lives or been a part of Liam growing up. He felt that Clive had more to say but he was proving to be, uncharacteristically, not very forthcoming

140

right now.

"It's difficult Mike, you see, after all of what she'd been through, I didn't want to pry. I always thought that given time, you know, she would tell me more and eventually I would get a fuller picture. But she didn't give me much more until after we bumped into Sid that evening. It was me who persuaded her to do what Sid suggested and write to you about the money. You see, it didn't seem fair after all this time. Then, after you tried to find us, she gave me the rest. It appears that she felt it would all come out in the end so finally decided to come clean. I think your friend gave her a bit of a fright and she'd been in fear for a while, I reckon she knew that he knew and that you had come looking for us because he had told you everything, so she told *me* everything".

Mike couldn't keep up with Clive. He scratched his head blankly with his left hand and held his right up to stop Clive from speaking for a moment. His expression must have said it all as Clive suddenly stopped and said;

"You actually don't know any of this do you? Christ Almighty!" he looked upwards as if to briefly apologise for taking his boss' name in vain and looked back at Mike.

"I take it Sid told you that he met us? What am I asking? You must have known, even if he didn't tell you he saw us, it was in the letter wasn't it? But the letter, *that's* why you came looking for her? Bloody Hell, Sid can't have told you after all, he didn't want you to know did he? He was being protective of you. Or was he just thinking you would welcome the extra monthly money and drop the whole thing? And yet Madeline has been going out of her mind – and since she told me so have I by the way – that you were coming for your

141

money! All the time, you wanted a part in Liam's life, because you don't know *everything*!"

Mike's head was spinning but he stood up. He wasn't sure if the overwhelming confusion he was experiencing was due to the thought of Sid being protective of him, the still black-hole sized gap in his understanding of what Clive was saying or the frankly bewildering number of rhetorical questions he had just heard, more in fact than Gabs, Sally-Anne and Na'er-lee would ever manage in one evening let alone one statement. He shook his head as if to realign his brain cells and looked down at Clive.

"Er...Come again mate?" Mike said, in a more conciliatory tone this time. In turn, Clive shifted in his seat for a moment and sat upright. He was uncomfortable again and, this time, as nervous as the proverbial kitten. He mewed softly at Mike;

"You had better sit down and prepare yourself Mike, this won't be very easy for you but I think it might be the time for *someone* to level with you at last." Clive looked and sounded more like a priest than ever as he sat forwards. Mike slowly sunk back down and wondered what was coming next.

"Listen Mike, when your friend spoke to Madeline – Maddie – it was already clear to me that I hadn't heard everything about her situation before I met her, but it became increasingly clear during the conversation that he knew very little about it too. When he found out the truth he basically agreed with my suggestion that she should write to you and stop taking money under false pretences. You see Mike, and there's no easy way to tell you this, but you are *not* Liam's father. Liam's father is dead. He was an old school friend who tragically died in some random car accident a few months after Liam was born. She said she conceived with him on a one-night stand after they bumped into each other years after losing touch. She was on a girls' night out and he was on shore-leave, he was in the Royal Navy I believe. Anyway, she never told him as she didn't know where he was and she was already with a steady guy, you. Soon after he died she upped and left. I guess it was grief and guilt and quite a deep depression that did it".

Mike was numb, like someone had hit him on the side of a head with something heavy and blunt, but without him feeling the impact or any actual pain at all. His view was cloudy and Clive's words were becoming muffled and vague. He couldn't focus and he felt nauseous. When he regained some sense of what was unfolding in front of him, all Mike could see was a face, it was Rod's photograph, in a frame standing beside a naval officer's cap on top of a flag-covered coffin at a military funeral.

It had been a particularly traumatic time as Maddie and Liam's disappearance was just a few months after the group's school friend Rod Bailey had died. Rod had been part of their gang at school but they had lost contact with him since he joined the Royal Navy. They heard nothing from him for quite a number of years until news of his death broke. Rod had joined up at sixteen and was one of the youngest sailors to see active duty on a destroyer in the Falklands conflict, surviving the sinking of his ship, HMS Sheffield whilst there. He was tragically killed by a hit-and-run driver years later whilst celebrating his birthday on shore leave in Plymouth. Rod had no family to speak of but his old school friends felt a sense of sadness and loss. This was in spite of not having seen him at all in the intervening years. These days they rarely thought of him but when they did, it was always with some affection.

"Mike? Are you getting this? Are you ok? Mike?" Clive brought Mike back into the room.

"I'm *so sorry* Mike, so *very* sorry" Clive sounded very sorry indeed. "I was actually only visiting you this evening to give you this." He produced a crumpled envelope from the inside pocket of his tweed jacket, he smoothed it out and handed it to Mike. Silently, Mike opened it and inside found a cheque made out in his name and signed by The Reverend Clive Dillon. The cheque was for £30,000.

"Mike, I wanted her to stop taking money from you as I want to adopt Liam and be his legal father. I also, after hearing how she was still taking money from you rather than from some phony trust fund she'd told me about, wanted to repay from my own money, everything you have paid so far. I hope this will cover it, I don't pretend to know how much it is in actual fact but I can give you this. I inherited some money when my father passed away and always thought I could put it to good use one day. This, in my book, is *that* day at last. I bought a nice new car with some of it and Lord knows the church has enough money so I wasn't going to give it to them!"

Clive looked to the sky for forgiveness for the second time that evening. He also instinctively knew that he had been prattling on for some time, to fill an awkward silence that may have materialized if he hadn't, so seizing his moment he made to go. In his book it was time to leave Mike alone with his thoughts. With Mike still in a daze, they swapped telephone numbers.

"Look, I want this to be a new beginning for you Mike. Madeline says that, as Liam has never known you, or even known *of* you, that this will somehow go some way to putting things right. Having met you, I realise that her assessment is somewhat different from the reality but I would just say that time will help, Mike. You obviously have a good life and some friends who care deeply about you." He picked up his scarf and raincoat and started towards the front door. As he walked into the hallway, he paused and turned to Mike;

"One more thing Mike and *this* I know for certain. These things happen for a reason and they test us in all manner of ways yet there's one intangible truth you would do well to remember; God is on your side!" and with that, a smiling Clive opened the front door and closed it quietly behind him.

Mike, still looking at the cheque in his hands and not quite believing it all, walked back into his lounge. No sooner than he had sat back down in his recliner and...er, reclined to contemplate what had just occurred, there was a knock on the front door again. He thought for a moment he would ignore it but then, thinking it might be Clive returning, he chose instead to answer it after all. When he opened the door, he found a small man standing outside. He too was wearing a raincoat, was probably in his early sixties and he reeked of beer and tobacco. With a puzzled look on his face, and resisting the strange sense of déjà-vu in his head, Mike said "Can I help you?"

"Yeah mate, my name's Godfrey," said the man and he coughed loudly. Wiping his sweating forehead with a white handkerchief he continued; "The agency sent me you see? You need someone finding...yeah?"

"Oh, yes," said Mike before quickly stopping himself again. "Er...er, well, what I mean is *no* actually...b-but thanks," stammered Mike, scratching the side of his head for a moment before he went on. "Um...it's just that, well, er, it now seems I've got God on my side."

Godfrey said nothing as the door closed in his face. He simply rolled his eyes and muttered "Huh, story of my life," before he turned and quietly walked away.

Life's about as wonderful as a cold,
Life's about as wonderful as growing old,
Life's about as wonderful as a tramp lying dead
in the road...

Chapter 14

It was Monday evening again and Mike found himself in the drab surgery waiting area once more, completing the same questionnaire as he had twice before. This time he was there with just five other attendees. Darren wasn't there and Mike hoped that maybe he had found whatever it was he craved so had no further need for Gloom Club. He also wondered if Sally-Anne-with-an-e felt troubled about the success rate of her lecture and? about attendees seeing the whole course through. Maybe, just maybe, this was in fact a lower hemorrhage rate than previous Gloom Clubs.

Weirdly, Mike had been looking forward to this week. He hadn't developed a sense of enjoyment in being patronised. He wasn't sure if he could carry off the lie about achieving his SMART objective of walking his imaginary dogs (both of which now had names and were actual breeds of dog that Mike had heard of, just in case anyone asked about them). No, it was because this session had been previously billed as the one "...where we would discuss 'over-thinking' and examine ways we could try to reduce the frequency we are doing this".

Mike knew he over-thought and over-analysed. His mind would gallop away and he would be lost in a world where his questions remained unanswered. To learn how to stop doing this, ironically, was going to happen in a room where questions weren't so much left just unanswered but where they seemed to go to die. Yet Mike hoped this session held the key to his happiness and a way out of the depression he was still experiencing. He was still crying at the drop of a hat, he still wanted to be alone rather than in company and he still found himself watching all manner of crap on his television to escape the dread he felt. He had also found himself staring at the cheque from Clive and Maddie, which was now perched on his mantelpiece next to the weird mouse sculpture he bought on a dope-fuelled visit to Amsterdam twenty years before. Most of all, he had Liam on his mind. It always came back to Liam.

Mike's unconscious thinking was suddenly awakened by Sally-Anne's voice;

"So! Everyone, how did we get on with our homework then?" she asked patronizingly, just to stick with the traditions of Gloom Club.

Sticking with tradition too, the Gloom Club said nothing in response.

"Let's start with the list shall we?" she continued, turning the page on the flipchart to the previous week's list of objectives. She started with Maureen and went along the line, each Gloom Club member responding – once forced – with how well they did at work, the gym, the cinema etc. Sally-Anne eventually came to Mike,

"Did you get your poor dogs out for a proper run like you said you would this week Mike?" Sally-Anne was pouting and furrowing her brow in anticipation of Mike's cutesy answer. She looked like she was trying to bring up a little wind.

"Er, well yes actually!" said Mike, a little too enthusiastically even for his own liking. "Malcolm and Vivienne – he's an Irish Red Setter and she's a wire-haired Lurcher you see? Anyway, they spent a good bit of time off the lead and everything. Both days. They loved it and I managed to get some exercise out of it too, we were all winners really weren't we? When I think about it...." Mike suddenly stopped talking and looked around the room. He realised he was talking too much; embellishing too much; giving too much detail. The expressions on everyone's faces confirmed this. He looked back at Sally-Anne who looked like she had managed to bring up the wind she was trying for earlier and was now just waiting for Mike to stop talking.

"So, that's good then," Sally-Anne finally summed up. She glanced sideways at Mike and continued; "Today everyone, we are going to talk about '*Rumination*', do we all know what I mean by '*Rumination*'?" she wrote the word on a new page on the flipchart with a squeaky pen and turned back to face the Gloom Club, her Angry-Birds ink-black eyebrows seemingly raised more in hope than in expectation.

The Gloom Club unanimously refused to answer her and chose to look shoe-wards once again.

Sally-Anne started to explore what people might typically do when they ruminate. And the concept was thrown open to the group to discuss. The group, in its now usual manner, found it impossible to respond. After an interminable silence, Paul eventually asked, quite bravely in Mike's opinion;

"What exactly *is* rumination then Sally-Anne?" The Gloom Club looked at Paul with a measure of admiration and awe. Everyone seemed immediately more engaged, if not yet responsive.

"So, *rumination*, what can I say? Well it's the compulsive focusing we do on the causes and consequences of our low mood rather than on any possible solutions. I would describe it as when we think about something for a long period of time without thinking about anything else. When something takes over our conscious thought and we are unable to let it go, *almost* when we obsess over something, but not *actually* obsessing? That's quite different and another class for a different day altogether!" she looked knowingly at Gabs and Na'er-lee, who were smiling broadly at her about some CBT Practitioner in-joke she had just made but which the rest of the group didn't understand.

Mike felt like the last couple of weeks hadn't been wasted and, at last, the Gloom Club might be getting somewhere. He certainly felt like Sally-Anne had hit his own nail firmly on its head...after weeks of repeatedly hitting her thumb. He looked around the room; her description had clearly and unanimously chimed more with the members' own experiences too. The sense of relief in the room was palpable. Gabs stood up and Sally-Anne sat back down.

"Right, I'm going to read something to you all and I want you to all listen and then we will ask you for a few observations, ok?" Gabs looked at the group for a moment and then started to read a passage from the book she was holding.

It was quite a long piece so some of the group ended up shifting uncomfortably in their seats. Mike felt as if he had travelled back decades to when he was in 'Story Time' in school. The passage centered on a depressed person coming home from work. Mike thought this rather insensitive given that most of the people in the room weren't able to work due to the debilitating affects of their depression. The person was described as getting on with making dinner, whilst also thinking aloud and coming up with lots of "Why" statements to themselves such as,

- Why do I feel so down?

- Why did I let that happen?

- Why did I find it impossible to avoid...?

- Why did it have to happen to me?

If he'd have been in a group session in college, Mike would have butted in with a quip along the lines of "Why can't I stop asking myself these stupid questions to which I already know the bloody answers?" but he chose to remain silent. Gabs then asked a simple question;

"Well, what do you all think of the passage?" she asked earnestly. "Anything at all spring to mind?"

True to form, the Gloom Group maintained its silence. Gabs tried another approach;

"Well, do any of you identify with parts of the passage? I'm thinking of the sorts of words the person is asking themselves. Anything at all? Thoughts?"

The group all identified with the words, sentiment and emotions described in the passage, they were all suffering with depression and low mood after all, they just didn't much feel like responding positively, for exactly the same reasons. Gabs read the same passage a second time, but this time she replaced the "Why" statements with "How" statements. The reworked statement sounded more like a problem-solver's wet dream. The statements being about things the group could do in the future rather than statements that were relating to things in the past and therefore impossible to change. Again, Gabs asked for comments or observations from the group on how the passage had been changed and how this affected the passage over all. All of this was true, yet they continued to respond to Gabs with silence.

"Well, let's see" said Gabs after a pregnant pause, "Let's try to unpick this shall we?"

She went over the obvious points in the statements which had been made relating to the past, the "Why do I...?" as opposed to the statements in the second version which related to the present or future, the "How do/could I...?". The latter statements were described as opportunities to start 'problem solving' and therefore of finding a way of improving the group members' moods. This was based on the assumption that to identify a problem that can be solved rather than experiences from the past that cannot be changed, is a positive thing.

Gabs told the group that they would do more on problem solving in the coming weeks. Again, the mood of the group seemed lighter at this revelation. Still silent, but with an air of anticipation, the Gloom Club waited for more. Gabs explained that the first step for her to help the group identify times when they were ruminating;

"Well, can anyone tell me when they think they *may* have been ruminating?"

Of course, she was greeted with the customary silence. Mike was tempted to come back at this point with something along the lines of, "Well, I'm not sure about *me* as such but I have a *friend* who I think may be ruminating and I think I am usually...er, I mean, *HE* is usually doing it mainly at night when he's alone..." But the group was still not ready for his humour and he remained unready to share it so, as usual, he too said nothing.

In Mike's mind, Gloom Club was quickly becoming Rumination Club. Three things were now becoming clear to him; the first rule of Rumination Club was to admit that they had all joined Rumination Club. Mike reflected on the whole *"First-rule-of-Rumination-Club-is-you-don't-talk-about-Rumination-Club"* adage having been left redundant by virtue of it's members all being depressed and preferring not to engage with anyone, about anything, in any way. This of course rendered it a topic of conversation they would never share. The group had proven that it didn't want to outwardly engage with other members of the group or with the practitioners themselves, so were unlikely to chat about it when they got out. They had all, without mentioning it however, recognised that they all ruminated.

The second thing that struck him was that reducing their ruminating might be the key to resolving some of their issues and thereby find a way of improving their moods, individually or collectively.

This neatly led to the third thing. Mike was, importantly, feeling that he was starting to share a level of camaraderie with his fellow sufferers. Sure they were a group of strangers to him, they were all very different to him of course, but he felt they were in this together for the first time. He now believed that they had a common bond. They had been thrust together by the random referrals

153

of ten different GPs across the county in which they lived, and then plucked, again at random, from a waiting list. They knew each other only by the names hastily scribbled on the sticky labels they were wearing. They hadn't shared much more than a nod or a smile since they first met yet were now experiencing a collective consciousness, a shared sense of being in the same boat and all knowing together that the way out of this was now obvious to them. Failing that, it could be that Mike was simply ruminating.

+   +   +   +   +   +

Later in the White Hart, Mike was sitting at the bar with Amy and he was nursing the same pint he had ordered when they first arrived, three-quarters of an hour earlier. Although calmer than he was when Amy had picked him up outside the health centre, he was still pissed off.

"I'm not going back Amy; I bloody well refuse to sit through any of that shit again! Sod the cost to the NHS, sod the telling off I might get from Dr Baker, sod it all. I know what I need to do now and that's just sort my life out myself like I've always done in the past." said Mike. He took another minute sip of his pint of JLB and stared at the bar rather than his sister.

"And I'll be there for whatever you need, ok?" said Amy, in an attempt to placate Mike. "But why did it get SO bad in there? What happened?"

Mike took a deep breath and started to tell Amy all about it. His tone was, naturally, rather sarcastic;

"Well, Gabs explained that we could identify when rumination was taking place by employing what she called, 'a clever two minute rule' which amounted to basically working out if you have been thinking about an issue, challenge or problem exclusively for two minutes without attempting to problem solve it. If the answer to this question is 'Yes' - although this is not illuminating - we are apparently ruminating." He looked at Amy who was by now, sitting upright with her hackles raised so high Mike would swear he could see them just above her head.

"The stupid PATRONISING BITCH!" she exclaimed, quickly realising that her volume was a bit higher than required for Mike's proximity and she took a look around to see if anyone had overheard her. A nervous looking disheveled guy with a pronounced facial tic was stood at the bar near them, he looked away when Amy caught him staring - or trying to stare – at them. She looked back at her brother and spoke more quietly than before.

"Well, did you say *anything* to her? You must've told her she was treating you like kids," she continued, clearly not understanding the rules of Rumination Club at all.

"I didn't have the chance. A woman *did* ask the sixty-four-million-dollar-question, like 'What should we do if we realise we ARE ruminating?' and I thought to myself, 'at last...the bit of a defence strategy I have been waiting for patiently since I was first enrolled in the Mood Group/ Gloom Group/ Rumination Club all those weeks ago...the very reason I have stuck at attending through weeks one, two and now three...the moment of reflection and self discovery that would inevitably lead me to sanity and the ability to have an adult conversation without crying..." said Mike, sounding like an evangelist preacher. Amy sat silently and open-mouthed, waiting.

Mike continued;

"In my head I was asking 'What is the answer Oh wise one? PLEASE TELL US POOR IGNORANT AND DESPERATE SOULS HOW CAN WE STOP RUMINATING?'"

By now Mike was preaching to a transfixed Amy and, unknowingly, also to the five other customers who were still in the bar and hanging on Mike's every word.

"Do you want to know the answer Amy? DO YOU?" with eyes widening, Amy nodded and so did Tel who was standing close behind her, although in hindsight it might have been a coincidental twitch.

"Dearly beloved, the answer you have been searching for, apparently, is – and I quote the wise words of the best CBT practitioners the NHS can buy – 'When you use the two minute rule and realise that you ARE ruminating, *try* to stop thinking about that subject and try to think about something else instead!'"

Amy paused for a moment and then threw her head back and laughed, uncontrollably. Mike paused for a moment and then chose to join her.

Tel and the other customers of the bar went back to their conversations and secret dealings, none the wiser. Eventually, and through the tears, Mike spoke again;

"My initial thought at the point she came out with that gem was – and again I quote the words spinning uncontrollably around my head on hearing Gabs' wisdom – 'WELL THAT'S FUCKING AMAZING...YOU COMPLETE ARSE!' Do you know how many weeks I've been waiting and for that? Well, as I said, I may not go back for fear of beating the shit out of her and her CBT pals. All I can say is that *Rumination will be my ruination.*" Mike made out a shape with his hands like it was a sign on a wall or a well known advertising slogan or tag-line, "Maybe I should get it printed on a T-shirt. I'm beginning to think that their apparent incompetence is actually a very clever postmodern methodology to cure people of depression. I mean, its *so* crap that it's cheering me up, so it's probably FUCKING BRILLIANT!"

Still smiling, Amy dried her eyes. Before she could speak, however, Mike spoke again;

"Oh yeah, do you know what else was said? When we finished for the evening, Gabs told us we would have to miss two weeks due to the holiday break and we should come back on Monday 21st when the group would reconvene. She asked us to continue with our SMART objectives until we meet up again and we should all note down the times we noticed that we were ruminating. Then, and this is the *very best* bit of all, *So-So-Sally-Anne* stepped up to the microphone and closed the group by saying to us all that, without a hint of irony in her voice of course, that she hoped we all had a *VERY HAPPY* Easter!"

*I've been up for days and I feel like a laboratory
rat
Inside a maze and I reel in the monotony of
Screaming at the moon in the middle of the day
But as long as I can see it then I know I'll be ok...*

Chapter 15

Mike hadn't been to church for years. He hadn't celebrated Easter for years, except for maybe consuming more chocolate than he did any other weekend. Easter was ordinarily just a time when he would enjoy the longer break from work. This year it was different. In fact, this year *everything* was different. Mike hadn't been to work since before *Reading Week* more than half-a-term earlier and he didn't yet know when, or if, he would be going back. It was also different as he was sitting in the back row of a church that was miles away from where he lived. He was taking part in an Easter service, which was different too. The surroundings were unfamiliar to him, as were the people that surrounded him. The whole unfamiliar occasion was given an added air of mystery as, by his feet, Mike had brought along a large red-vinyl record case.

For the first time in a long time Mike's mind wasn't racing. He was finally focused on one thing and one thing only. He felt he wasn't ruminating; he was just looking to solve a problem. Mike looked around the church. He was searching for someone, maybe a small, slight woman, with dark hair and sparkling eyes who looked like an older version of Maddie, or who might also look a bit like a priest's wife. He wondered if he would see her, and if she might have a young teenager with her. He thought about what Liam might look like now, would it be like Maddie or would he look more like Rod did when they were kids. He scoured the congregation but the only person he recognised was the priest giving the sermon.

Clive (*I'm a Believer* – The Monkees) was pretty good at his job Mike found himself thinking. Not that he had recent experience of any other priests to compare Clive to of course, but Mike understood the message being conveyed and that it was being communicated intelligently rather than condescendingly like the sermons he could remember as a kid. Maybe it was because Mike was now much older, or educated that it seemed this way? Or maybe it was because he had met Clive and, although not liking him too much, Mike felt he was probably a good guy in general. Maybe he thought it was a good sermon as he had been feeling so vulnerable of late. That the message Clive was giving about the end of some things and the start of new things; new beginnings; of new life; of fresh starts and clean slates were more relevant to him now. Maybe, just *maybe*, this was all just because Mike's mind was racing again.

As the service ended and the righteous people of NW6 and the surrounding boroughs filed out of the church, Mike found himself glued to the pew on which he had seated himself an hour earlier. Was it really a whole hour since the service had started? His mind started to wander and he stopped seeing the details in the faces of the people who passed him. He couldn't really tell if they were young, old, male or female. They were just faceless and he started to question the merits of even visiting this place. As he did so, a voice

159

suddenly cut through the dull, lifeless shuffling sound of god-fearers heading off to their Sunday roast lunches;

"Mike? Mike is that *you*?" It was Clive.

"Er, yeah, looks like it!" said Mike sounding a little sarcastic without meaning to. "Have you got a mo?"

Mike stood up. Clive gestured for Mike to follow him through a wooden arched door behind him. Mike followed Clive and found he was in a small ante-room which was stacked high with dozens of plastic chairs, a couple of spare wooden pews and a huge bookcase against a wall which had all manner of hymn books and prayer books arranged in neat rows on its shelves.

"I can't stop long Mike, I'm supposed to be at the front door shaking hands with the great and the good of Camden and Brent!" said Clive cheerfully, yet nervously, whilst looking over Mike's shoulder towards the door. "The Curate is there but most of the congregation will expect to see me..." then adding, as if it was an after thought, "...Oh, and Madeline isn't here in case it's her you're looking for."

A small bell rang in Mike's head when he thought about Clive's postscript and he looked at the priest, who had briefly looked skywards before looking back at Mike, smiling again. Mike knew Clive was lying. Like he did when his students were lying about "dogs eating homework" or being late for lectures after "missing the bus", Mike instinctively knew this was when *he* was able to step in and take charge of the situation. Mike, at last, had something of the upper hand.

"No problem Clive, I'm happy to wait until you're done here, or done outside, or done wherever. I need to give you something for

160

Madeline but I need to explain something about it...if you don't mind of course." Mike held the record case up to Clive before turning and leaving the room with it. He went outside and sat on a small stone seat near the church gates and watched as Clive shook hands and swapped smiling platitudes with his flock.

Clive saw off the last of the church-goers and, as a light rain started to fall, he gestured to Mike. As Mike walked up the path towards the front door he heard someone following him. There was the 'tap-tap-tap' sound of heeled shoes and Mike glanced over his shoulder to see an older woman with horn-rimmed glasses and wearing a scarf on her head walking some way behind him. Mike continued until he reached Clive who quickly and nervously ushered him inside the church foyer and closed the big wooden door behind them. It slammed shut and Clive pulled the large black cast-iron bolt across to secure it.

"Ha! Got to call it a day at some point haven't you Mike? They'll keep me all day if I don't draw a line somewhere!" said Clive, nodding towards the outside and visibly sweating. "Now what were you saying earlier? I have a couple of minutes before I need to go out and do my Easter visits, the ill and infirm Mike, they need time with me too you know! You said you had something for Madeline didn't you? I'm happy to take it if you like. I told you she's not here didn't I? Yes, of course I did, she wanted to visit some friends for the weekend, I sent her off last night, Liam too!" he looked skywards yet again.

"Good job gambling is a sin Clive, you'd be a terrible poker player!" said Mike "Are you ok? You seemed to be relaxed enough during the service earlier. You were pretty good up there by the way,

161

yet you don't seem too comfortable now. It's almost like your mind is racing or something." Mike was enjoying watching Clive squirm a bit. Clive started coughing loudly and, just as Mike was going to pat him firmly on the back, there was a heavy bang on the door behind him. A voice with an unusual, possibly European accent from outside called out "Clive, Clive are you there?"

Mike looked at Clive, who had stopped coughing very suddenly and was standing stock still.

"CLIVE!" said the voice again and the person who owned the voice banged at the door once more.

"We're closed for the day now!" shouted Clive, "There will be another service tomorrow at eleven in the morning and all other daily services are displayed on the noticeboard by the gates," he turned to Mike, "We have a lot of migrants from Europe in this area. Like Jacek who owns the bar opposite. They seem to think the church should be open from dawn to dusk everyday like it is at home you know? I try to re-educate them in the way of the church presence here but they take a while to understand!" he shrugged his shoulders in a *what-is-a-priest-supposed-to-do* kind of way.

Mike said nothing, he turned to the door and slid back the heavy bolt and pulled the door open. It was the old woman who had been following Mike up the pathway earlier. Only she had taken the rain soaked scarf away from her dark hair and was wiping the raindrops from the lenses of her glasses. In doing so, it was clear that she wasn't old at all. Maddie looked up at Mike with a glint in her eyes, she was looking older and her accent had taken on something of a more European tone during the years she had spent abroad. She smiled

162

and calmly said;

"Hello, fancy bumping into you here."

Mike had played this moment out in his mind during countless sleepless nights over the years. He had rehearsed every line and insult he ever wanted to unleash in Maddie's direction. Recently he had been provided with even more unwanted material with which to inflict damage. This was on top of years of hurt, disappointment and resentment that he had been slowly growing inside him, all stored up for this very occasion. He knew he possibly would only ever get this one opportunity to really let her know what she had put him through and how he felt.

Mike did what he could to control his mind from racing away with everything that was buzzing around in it at top speed. He cleared his thoughts, took a deep breath and gently placed the red-vinyl record case on the stone floor in front of Maddie and said quietly,

"You should have this."

He turned towards the door, walked out of the church and headed for home.

I never thought that I would see the day,
I never thought that I would give you away
What if none of your dreams come true?
I can never run from you.
There's never been a 'How Do You Do?'...

Chapter 16

It was the fourth week of Rumination Club and Mike felt he had been listening to Elvis Costello, on repeat, all his life. The same old questionnaire was handed out to the five people who could be bothered to turn up after the extended Easter Break. Mike wasn't surprised that he still wasn't feeling like suicide but he was surprised to be hit immediately with the task of thinking up an objective for the following week the moment he had sat down in his seat. He was also surprised to see that Maureen was the absentee this week and also that Sally-Anne-with-an-e was starting with *him.*

"So everyone, how did we do with our objectives over Easter? Did we spend more time eating chocolate eggs rather than doing our homework?" she asked in her now customary tone. In response, the Rumination Club members stuck steadfastly to their plan of saying nothing. It had become something of a ritual interrogation; the practitioners would ask questions, usually in a patronising manner and the response would be akin to giving one's name, rank and serial number, only without giving the name, rank or serial number.

Seemingly in a break from the usual routine, and a break from the rules according to Bryan,

Sally-Anne looked along the even shorter line of ruminators and said,

"Gabby, would you be kind enough to pop out to collect any stragglers?"

"Gabs, Sally-Anne, I prefer Gabs!" said Gabs, curtly.

"Ok lovey, *sorry*. But could you? *Pleease*?"

Gabs rolled her eyes, she glanced at Na'er-lee who did likewise, and then left the room to gather the stragglers. It must have seemed to Sally-Anne that the group had shrunk beyond the normal levels and, as it clearly couldn't be relating to the content of her delivery, it must consequently mean that there were some latecomers this week.

Gabs returned a few moments later, alone.

The group started to share its successes and failures in achieving its objectives since the last meeting. Everyone got to hear how many walks Malcolm and Vivienne had been on over the previous week, despite the bad weather, and there was even the inclusion of a couple of Boxer dogs they had regularly been meeting up with in the park. Mike was getting quite pleased with his stories; the group seemed to be hanging on his every word. He wondered if any of them secretly hoped to bump into him one day, so they could meet these lucky pets for themselves.

One group member – *Mel* – announced to everyone that her objective in the coming week was going to be to spend more time with her young son, specifically on Tuesday, Thursday and Saturday mornings. Everyone seemed to think this sounded like a nice idea, assuming as they did that her son probably lived with an ex-partner or a carer whilst she was recovering from her bout of depression. Mel went on to explain that she has felt neglectful of her son as she has been very busy recently doing her exercise video - her SMART objective for the last two meetings - so hasn't spent much time with him recently. This is despite the fact that he *does* in fact live with her. Mike tried to rid himself of the image of this poor child sat in front of CBBC all alone whilst he could hear his mother panting and 'feeling the burn' in the next room. For a moment he considered calling social services...mental scars were inflicted by less than this Mike thought.

Carol took her turn. She talked about the constant rows she had with her teenage daughter and how she needed to repair their relationship.

"Look, I've always refused to allow her to watch crap TV, especially all the bloody reality shows and the populist stuff that we get shoveled down our throats on a Saturday evening, y'know? She, in turn, objects to this as she reckons it makes her stand out at school as being a bit *'weird'* as all the other kids are full of *'My Cat Can Dance'*, *'Pop Factor'* and *'Get My Big Celebrity Baker Brother Out of This'* whilst she doesn't know what the fuck's going on. They are all apparently talking about the latest plotlines that are being voted for by the general public and she feels like she's on the *outside* of it...I've told her she'll thank me when all her friends' brains have turned to effing mush and hers hasn't, but she won't have it." Carol looked tired and Mike felt for her. But she continued, unabated. She was pretty relentless:

"She wants to know stuff like; what designer the vacuous judges are *wearing* this week, or what *Ain't & Decline* – or whatever their flippin' names are – said to whoever...it's all *so* bloody pointless but she can't understand. It's simply a victory of style over substance; of marketing expertise over talent...it's all so cheap and fucking tawdry! I was exposed to all that stuff when I was a kid and ended up working for the N.H bloody S...I work long hours for low pay and no recognition. I don't want that for my fourteen year-old daughter." She pulled a face as if to vomit whilst looking around at the others. Although Mike would have admitted to being sympathetic, the others looked at her as if she was just plain weird. Carol, silent once again, wondered if maybe her daughter was right after all.

Finally, following other various tales of minor victories and a few confessions of individuals' shortcomings, it was time for Rumination Club to talk about problem solving and a way to identify when they could do this to improve their mood. Na'er-lee stood up and Sally-Anne sat down.

"Great!" said Na'er-lee, somewhat unconvincingly, "Let's...er, like throw a bit of, um, like theory at you?" and she removed the top from her green flipchart pen.

"Has anyone ever heard of, what in CBT terms we call, *Natural* Automatic Thoughts – or NAT's - as they're known? You can see why I get to, like, do *this* bit can't you?" and she wrote NATs in big letters on the flipchart, she replaced the cap on her pen and put it down.

If the group *did* see why this was they certainly weren't letting Na-'er-lee know.

"Well, these are the thoughts that, er, like jump into our minds constantly throughout the day? So maybe thoughts, like, about what we will have for dinner later? Or like, what's on the TV tonight? Or maybe, like, what's happenin' at work?" she looked at her colleagues, who looked back at her and smiled. "Well, they're called

167

NAT's!" her summing up was, as far as Mike was concerned, rather superfluous. Na'er-lee picked up the red flipchart pen and looked back at the group.

"Well next, I wanna, um, like, tell you when these NAT's become *Negative* Automatic Thoughts?" Without blinking or foreseeing the confusion she was about to create, she wrote NAT's in red on the flipchart and continued speaking;

"Now *these* NAT's are when we think negative things, er, like automatically? So like when we say stuff like *'that will never work'* or *'I always get this wrong'* and *'they don't like me, I'm a failure'*? Well I'm going to, like, train you to reduce the times that these NAT's spring into your heads? Ok? Would that be useful? Yeah?"

Bryan piped up with something of a brave question,

"So, if we have two types of NAT's and one of them is a good one, completely natural and all that and the other is more negative. Can't we call the good ones 'Good NAT's – or GNATs - instead? Just so we can tell the difference 'cos, I don't know about anyone else here but I'm in danger of getting a little confused I must say."

As a couple of the other ruminators nodded in agreement, Mike found his voice,

"If we write GNAT's on the board it's ok up to a point but it's still going to *sound* the same as NAT's as the G in GNAT is silent...and it's even more confusing when you consider that it's actually Nat that's writing it. Maybe we should just stick with red NATS and green NATS?" Mike was finding his feet as well as his voice. It was also an opportunity to be both funny and fuck with the heads of the other group members. Perhaps he *was* feeling a little better.

The group was confused. The practitioners were confused. So Na'er-lee tried to help;

"Ok, if you are a bit confused I'll give you an example yeah? Let's say Sally-Anne is like, walkin' down the road and she sees Gabs in the distance? She waves and calls out to Gabs and, like Gabs doesn't respond? Ok? Now, Sally-Anne might have a NAT that mayb.."

"Is that a Natural or Negative Automatic Thought? A GNAT or a NAT?" interrupted Geoff, looking like he seriously needed to know the answer rather than having spotted the opportunity to have fun at her expense. Mike looked at the other group members expecting a few of them to be smiling like he was, but he was pretty much alone in enjoying this exchange.

"We'll see won't we?" continued Na'er-lee, looking like she wished she had never started.

"Now Sally-Anne might be thinkin' a number of things, like, maybe Gabs didn't like her so was ignorin' her on purpose? Or that, like, she had maybe upset Gabs? At work? And Gabs was unhappy with her? So was choosin' not to answer..." Na'er-lee had an expression that was screaming at everyone "YOU SEE NOW?"

"Or maybe Sally-Anne had called out 'Hello Gabby!' instead of 'Hello Gabs!' *like*?" added Mike, clearly enjoying himself at last. He heard a distant bell toll and fully expected to see tumbleweed blow through the room as he was alone in the 'enjoying himself stakes'.

"Yeah thanks Mike," said a red-faced Na'er-lee. She turned to her colleagues to offer a silent apology for involving them in the mess she was creating before turning back to the group.

"Y'see, there is, like really only ONE negative

reason why Gabs would really ignore Sally-Anne in the street and that would be if she was upset with her, which, um, er, wouldn't like happen of course as they are, like, best buds an' that? Now it's, like, much more likely that there are simple, non-negative reasons for her ignorin' Sally-Anne such as, like, traffic noise? Or she was in a hurry? Or she had her iPod on or stuff like that, yeah?"

There was a ripple of acceptance from the group.

"Because everyone here has a low mood and that, it's like, more easy to focus on the one negative more, despite the fact that there are, like, loads more positive or natural reasons for things to happen, yeah? So we need to find a strategy for turnin' this around. I want you, when you have a dilemma like this, to write down the evidence FOR the thought being real and the evidence AGAINST it being real on a piece of paper, yeah?"

The group nodded collectively. Na'er-lee continued;

"You'll see that, like usually, the evidence *against* is plentiful? And the evidence *for* is scarce yeah? Stop when you've got a list with lots of naturally positive and reasonable things on it and maybe, like only, er one negative reason, um you might be able to achieve a more balanced view and improve your, er, state of mind? Or mood, Yeah?"

"Hang on a minute; can you explain something for me?" Carol asked, seeking a little clarity. Mike smiled as he felt she, at last, was asking the sixty-four-million-dollar question;

"What if I have TWENTY-FIVE reasons why it's *not* a bad thing and only ONE that says it is...but I *still* think it IS the bad thing because the reason for it being a bad thing is SO friggin' overwhelmingly accurate?" She looked at Mike briefly, then back at Na'er-lee and then straight at both Sally-Anne and Gabs. Carol went continued;

"I mean, if Sally-Anne *had* been calling Gabs '*Gabby*' all week, or for weeks maybe, despite her protestations and then called her Gabby in the street too; maybe Gabs would have ignored her due to her anger and frustration. So it wouldn't matter how long Sally-Anne's list of good reasons for Gabs ignoring her was, even if there *was* traffic noise, she was listening to her iPod, she had dust in her eye AND she was running late. It could *still* have been that Gabs chose to ignore Sally-Anne because of the ONE negative reason, which is that she had needlessly pissed her off yet again."

The room fell awkwardly silent for a moment. Sally-Anne was as red-faced as Na'er-lee. Gabs was sitting bolt upright with her hands clasped between her knees. Mike could just about make out that she was struggling to suppress a smile. Na'er-lee finally broke the silence;

"Well, er, that may be the case every now and then but as humans we often tend to believe the worst and yet things are rarely as bad as they, like, um...seem? So, um...so we should, like, practice this, kind of, re-balancin' of our thoughts and, like, things will probably improve? Yeah?"

At this point the group, without speaking a word or looking at each other, unanimously agreed that this was shit advice.

+   +   +   +   +   +

Back in the White Hart, Mike couldn't help wondering how many of the group would have the stamina and determination to return the

171

following week. As he explained to Amy the way the evening had ended, Mike wondered if he could even face going back himself.

"You do know that they can't *make* you go back...or *fine* you if you don't? They *can't* do a *damn* thing Mike, so please don't put yourself through it any more," said Amy, emphasising almost every other word.

Mike knew he didn't *have* to go. He equally knew that he still *would*.

Candy says I hate the quiet places, that cause the
smallest taste of what will be.
Candy says I hate the big decisions, that cause
endless revisions in my mind.
I'm gonna watch the blue birds fly over my
shoulder,
I'm gonna watch them pass me by.
Maybe when I'm older, What do you think I'd see,
If I could walk, away from me?

Chapter 17

"Ignore it, it's probably Amy calling again. She's called three times already today. I reckon she's just phoning to see how I am but I don't want to speak to anyone, do you mind H?" H put Candy's telephone down on the lamp table where he had found it ringing. He had missed two calls from Amy himself that lunchtime. It was unlike her to keep trying without leaving a message on his voicemail or send a text but H had more pressing things on his mind to care very much about Amy. He vowed to call her later.

Candy sat back on the sofa and picked up the bowl of grapes she had been doing her best to finish all morning. She put two in her mouth at once and pulled a bit of a face when opening her mouth caused her bruised cheek to stretch slightly.

"If you eat another grape I swear you'll start peeing wine!" said H, taking the fruit bowl away from Candy and smiling broadly, "and don't you want some lunch instead of all this fruit?"

Candy poked her tongue out at him and rolled her eyes, simulating boredom at receiving a lecture but appreciating the care and attention being lavished upon her. It had been nearly a week since the incident at the counter-demo and the bruising to her face was still, as she described it, a *'holy shade of purple'*.

Candy's parents were away for a fortnight, celebrating an extended Easter holiday with old friends in the West Country. To save them from worrying about their only daughter, Candy hadn't told them what had happened to her the previous weekend. When she'd been seen in the hospital she was told that she wasn't concussed and had been prescribed some strong painkillers to help her recovery. The doctor said she just needed some rest and recuperation. He also signed her off work for a week which Candy appreciated as she didn't want to sit in front of the bank's customers all week looking battered and bruised. H was concerned for her state of mind however, so had barely left Candy's side. He had even been sleeping on her parents' sofa at night so he could be at her beck and call.

"And why *do* we give ill people grapes? I can't say I've ever known what medicinal properties they have, other than their alcoholic by-products of course, but they seem to be a requirement for anyone who feels poorly. I can see that flowers can cheer a bird up..." he nodded at the blooms he had bought Candy from the *Shell* petrol station a couple of days earlier and were now drooping out of the vase he had stuck them in "...but grapes? *Really*? They don't have the same effect as chocolates or flowers do they?" H stuck another Thornton's *champagne chocolate truffle* in his mouth and screwed up the now empty crinkly plastic tray it had come from, tossing it into the waste paper basket next to Candy's father's writing desk. H believed that what he called *'posh chocolates'* – in his mind this was any box costing more that a fiver that included something called a 'truffle' rather than *Celebrations* or *Miniature Heroes* - were the *'right kind'* of chocolates for a woman. He just hadn't mentally developed this theory to include petrol station flowers as yet.

"And if you eat another one of those, two things will happen!" said Candy, "One; you'll need to work out twice as hard when you get back to the gym to rid yourself of the fat you are putting on by finishing my bloody chocolates and two; I'll punch you SO hard because you're not leaving any for me!" Candy launched a blow with her fist towards H's shoulder but swung through air as he dodged it, giving her a big chocolatey grin.

Candy looked at her face in a chrome hand-held mirror for the umpteenth time that morning. She winced as she turned her face from side to side; trying to see if the bruised left-hand-side was swollen by comparing it to her right cheek. She looked at H and tears welled up in her eyes, as they had every time she had inspected her injuries.

"I might be able to disguise the bruise with make-up but I can't do anything about the size of it, can I H? I look as if I'm in an abusive relationship or something, a poor defenceless woman. The reality is that I can't even find a man who wants me for who I am and *now* look at me! I'm fucking hideous!" The tears Candy had been storing up all morning burst forth and she sobbed uncontrollably.

Dealing with female emotion of any kind wasn't something that came naturally to H. Sure, he could cope with anger, usually he would simply meet it with a great deal of his own, but this situation was very different. This emotion was being shown by a woman who had suffered at the hands of a man who was just like H himself. She was the victim of violence from a coward of a man who would rather lash out physically than engage in debate. A man who had been cast aside by his family perhaps, or by an education system that wouldn't do more for him if he couldn't help it meet a target. He was spurned by a society that didn't care about him or how he might achieve his real potential.

What's more, dealing with this emotion was even more challenging for H when he considered that it was Candy, the woman he had always loved, who was experiencing such devastation. She was inconsolable. To have described H at that moment as being somewhat out of his comfort zone was an understatement of epic proportions. H knew that it was at times like this he could be relied upon for two absolute certainties; to *do* the wrong thing; and to *say* the wrong thing. He put his arms around her and held her close to him, tightly. It was at this moment H decided to change the habits of a lifetime. Speaking softly, H said the right thing for the first time ever;

"You're not hideous Candy, not at all. In fact I think you're the most beautiful woman in the entire world."

Estuary Girl, you're not the one,
You don't belong to the world that I'm from,
Your lazy words blow like confetti in the wind,
In the wind...

Chapter 18

"You'll find mugs in the cupboard above the coffee maker; and make me one too would you? I like the strong one, in the purple coloured silver pod...milk no sugar ta!"

Sid shouted to the girl in his kitchen, hoping she would master the intricacies of the chrome espresso machine without him having to get up and show her how. He needed a strong coffee after the night he'd had, having firstly played in the house band on the television Grand Final of *Pop Factor* the previous night and then having partied with the cast and crew until the early hours. It had been a late, heavy session and he was, at last, now surfacing back in his flat with...with, what *was* the name of the girl who had travelled through the small hours all the way back to *his* place? All Sid could recall was that her place was miles away in Essex or Kent or somewhere; that she hadn't needed asking twice; and that it had been a lot of fun once they got back to his. Sid switched his mobile phone on and it buzzed immediately;

Bzzz...Bzzz...Bzzz...Bzzz...Bzzz...

"Bloody Hell, someone wants me in a hurry!" he said, as the girl walked back into his room carrying two small white mugs.

"Whassat?" the girl replied.

Transfixed, Sid paused for a moment to take

in this sight. She was small, beautiful and *very* young. She was wearing an old *'Vive le Rock'* t-shirt of Sid's that he had given her last night when she told him she didn't want to sleep naked. Her short, spiky bleached-blonde hair contrasted perfectly with the jet black shirt, which was just long enough to cover her dignity but still give hints about her perfect physical form. He remembered choosing the t-shirt for this very reason. Sid couldn't help but still wonder, given what they had been up to for the couple of hours preceding the request for clothing, why she - or any woman for that matter - would want something to wear afterwards. He was always happy to comply. Sid loved seeing a girl he had brought home the night before wearing an item of his clothing the morning after. It seemed like a trophy, as if his conquest was made complete somehow and that the wearing of his clothes was like him leaving his mark on her. It also saved him from trying to carve a notch in his antique, brass-framed bed.

"Oh, er, nothing," replied Sid, his senses re-awaked.

"This is yours 'andsome!" the girl said, leaning across the bed to hand Sid the mug and kissing him gently on the cheek. In doing so, she exposed just enough of her cleavage for Sid to think about grabbing her and starting all over again. He resisted the urge, choosing to sip his coffee.

"Thanks er...thanks babe!" Sid said, "What time do you make it?"

"Dunno!" she said, sounding too carefree and un-rushed for Sid's liking. He liked to get rid of girls as early as he could the morning after and he already knew it was fast approaching one in the

178

afternoon. She looked nice – she looked great actually – but Sid knew there must be something up if Amy had called him five times already and he didn't want to call her whilst the girl was still there and do the whole *"No, Amy is not my girlfriend, she's just my mate's sister and a childhood friend and we're looking after her brother who's feeling a bit down..."* routine with, despite all they did last night, a relative stranger. And frustratingly, he still couldn't remember her name.

"Where's me phone?" she finally asked, "I should look to see what's been said about last night I s'pose, don't ya reckon?" she looked at Sid with a beguiling smile. He smiled back and took another sip of his coffee. The girl pulled at the edge of the duvet and peered underneath; then she looked under the pillow and then under a glittery white shift-dress left abandoned on the floor. She scratched her head and in doing so, lifted the t-shirt up enough to expose part of her pert, naked backside. Sid was again beginning to think that he should simply switch his phone off and enjoy the start of a new day when she suddenly spotted her shiny mobile telephone cradled in a white stiletto-spike-heeled shoe by the bedroom chair.

"A-ha..." she said, "...'ere it is!"

She sat back on the bed and switched it on. It buzzed ferociously, much more so than Sid's had a few moments before. He momentarily wondered why. How many friends did this girl have? However Sid knew he just needed to get the message through to her that it was time for her to leave rather than choose to inspect all of her messages and then, naturally, decide to stay with him a bit longer.

Bzzz...Bzzz...Bzzz...Bzzz...Bzzz...Bzzz...
Bzzz...Bzzz...Bzzz...Bzzz...Bzzz...Bzzz...
Bzzz...Bzzz...Bzzz...Bzzz...Bzzz...Bzzz...
Bzzz...Bzzz...Bzzz...Bzzz...Bzzz...Bzzz...
Bzzz...Bzzz...Bzzz...Bzzz...Bzzz...Bzzz...
Bzzz...Bzzz...Bzzz...Bzzz...Bzzz...Bzzz...
Bzzz...Bzzz...Bzzz...Bzzz...Bzzz...Bzzz...

"Look, um...er, er...*love*, before you start looking at your messages and updating your status an' that..." Sid started to speak but stopped again when the girl put her hand up to stop him.

"Oh ok, right, 'ang on a mo...*Babe*? *LOVE*? Please don't tell me...don't say you can't..." the girl's voice trailed off as the reality of the situation began to dawn on her. She shook her head a couple of times and drew a large breath,

"YOU DON'T REMEMBER MY FUCKIN' NAME DO YA?" she shrieked before, almost to herself, she went on;

"Huh! That's fuckin' priceless that is! He's different to the young boys on set I says, seems like an alright kinda bloke he does, someone who's been around a bit and knows a bit about life an' *the business* an' all that."

Sid gulped, sensing she was on the verge of exploding with indignation once more.

"Look, it's not like that..." he interrupted, trying to explain himself, "...It's just, well, we all had a *lot* to drink and that...didn't we? I mean, bloody hell we were wasted when we got here, *then* we had a couple of spliffs as I recall...so don't get pissed off that I can't...er, I mean...I..."

Sid was floundering. He was usually pretty good at this bit and couldn't understand why this morning he should be struggling. Sure, the girl was stunning...and she looked *very* familiar now that he had time to drink some coffee and think about it a little longer. But he just felt Amy *needed* him urgently and he couldn't get her out of his mind. The girl looked at her mobile phone and then held her hand up to stop Sid talking for the second time. He didn't much care for that kind of treatment normally, but this wasn't turning into a normal day. Sid took advantage of the chance for a breather and then, with the silence still hanging in the air, she coldly said;

"Can you put the telly on please? The news maybe?"

Puzzled, but glad for the opportunity to pause the proceedings a little longer *and* get the girl to put her hand down again, Sid picked up the remote control and turned to the BBC News channel on the 52-inch flatscreen television on his bedroom wall. The room remained silent for a few minutes, save for the muffled sound of the newsreader that the girl had turned down to number three on the volume setting. Sid and the girl sat, quietly sipping their coffee until the story the girl had been waiting for came up.

"There!" she said before repeating herself more loudly and pointing animatedly at the television, "THERE!"

She turned the volume up for the lunchtime report that had just started. The one o'clock headlines started rolling and Sid watched in horror as the reason for her rapidly deteriorating mood became clear. It was all slowly coming back to him now.

"Can ya see why I'm pissed off now?" the girl asked before continuing without pausing for breath or a response;

"The judges said I won 'cos eleven-and-a-fuckin'-half million people picked up their 'phones and voted for *me* last night to win the Grand Final, FOR ME! I'll be on every front page this morning and I will be number one in the charts next Sunday with a cover of a poxy REM song I don't even like. And it seems that everybody in the entire country now knows my fuckin' name...MY name is, you might say, on everyone's lips this morning. Across the entire United fuckin' Kingdom today, people are talkin' about my performance last night...everyone that is except for the useless pig-headed bloke I chose to SHAG AFTERWARDS!"

No fun, my babe, no fun.
No fun, my babe, no fun.
No fun to hang around, feeling that same old
way,
No fun to hang around freaked out for another
day.

Chapter 19

As Mike was handed the same questionnaire to complete as the previous four meetings and as he was again asked to return the receptionist's pen, he paused to wonder if anything was ever done with the information contained in his tick box responses. He ticked the box to say he wasn't remotely thinking of killing himself. He wondered if he would be presented with some kind of graph after successful completion of the six-week course showing the gradual improvement in his mood. If it was impressive enough he could stick up on his fridge at home or better still, on the wall behind him at work. It might look like one of those sales charts that used to be on the wall behind the boss in seventies sit-coms or in newspaper cartoons in the same period. Maybe he would see Doctor Baker at some time in the future and she would refer to it as if it were his latest school report.

"Thanks love!" said the receptionist cheerfully when Mike handed her biro back before following Gabs down the corridor to their meeting room. There was no Geoff by the looks of it so the Rumination Club membership now numbered just four. Once everyone had been seated, Sally-Anne-with-an-e started the session in her inimitable style:

"So, everyone ok this week?"

The group, as usual, refused to answer. Sally-Anne, as usual, did not see this as a negative and continued;

"So, this evening we'll hear about your attempts at maintaining your positive moods and we'll look a bit more at problem solving, ok? Yes?" Before the group could throw a little more silence in Sally-Anne's general direction, she turned to Gabs;

"So Gabby, would you please be a *complete love* and pop out to see if there are any stragglers this week before we get going? Would you? Thanks!"

Gabs glared at Sally-Anne, went red in the face and then silently left the room, gently closing the door behind her. Mike wondered if maybe it was being called 'Gabby' again despite her continual protestations; or maybe it was a dawning realisation that the time she spent in Rumination Club was pointless and that her talents lie elsewhere; or maybe Gabs genuinely spent the next hour looking for stragglers; maybe it was a combination of all of these factors. All Mike knew was that he, and the group, would probably never see Gabs again.

The remaining Group members took turns at relating their success in achieving such testing objectives as joining the library and borrowing a book; going to the gym more than once (*twice* in fact); and even babysitting. When Mike's turn came, he shared another weekly installment in the lives of his fictional dogs. The group *'Ooh-ed'* and *'Aah-ed'* when Mike explained how Malcolm had to go to the vet that week after swallowing a large safety pin and how Vivienne had pined for him all day. He told of his joy when the vet gave him the news that the pin had safely passed through his naughty dog and how he and Vivienne had gone to the vet to collect the little rascal later that evening. Mike told everyone how he had bought them matching studded dog-collars to celebrate Malcolm getting the all clear. Ironically, Mike was never happier than he was when talking about his dogs.

Sally-Anne then split the group into two smaller groups and asked Na'er-lee to join one whilst she took charge of the second. Mike thought it curious that Sally-Anne might call these 'groups' rather than 'pairs' given the rapidly diminishing numbers involved in Rumination Club. He chose, however, to remain silent.

"So, I want each group to write down things that we like about ourselves; qualities we like to be known for; achievements we have made; positive things around us etc. Once we have all done this, we can talk about them, ok?" suggested Sally-Anne, as usual rather more in hope than expectation.

Na'er-lee joined Mike and Bryan and tried to expand upon the idea behind the exercise as Bryan was struggling to understand its purpose;

"Well, its like, er, people sometimes like remember their failures? Yeah? And don't always, um, er, like recall when positive stuff is achieved an' that? Maybe you have strengths and, um positive qualities? Yeah? We should, like, spend more time focusin' on the good stuff that we do when we are, like, down in the dumps an' that?"

Bryan frowned but said nothing. Na'er-lee continued;

"Well, look. What if like your best friend, or a relative, or someone at work, like, sort of, asked what they thought of you? Yeah? Like, your good

185

points an' that?"

"I don't have many friends as such, I've been described as not really being much of a 'people-person' at work..." said Bryan suddenly "...but I am *always* punctual...and I am honest and I'm polite and well-mannered!" Bryan sat back in his seat and looked at Mike, somewhat triumphantly having thought of three qualities in quick succession. Na'er-lee smiled at Bryan and then looked at Mike to make his contribution;

"Do you know what Bryan?" responded Mike dryly, "I reckon you ARE a people person. Look at the way you thought of everyone's learning when you came up with the *ten-minute rule* on week one. You knew we would struggle to learn all of this *really complicated* stuff if we kept getting interrupted and, having good manners yourself, you also reminded us all that being punctual is a polite thing to do when other people are relying on you to do so."

Bryan looked pleased to hear that he had been such a positive influence on the group, so much so that he was respected by members of it too. Na'er-lee simply looked impressed with the depth of Mike's emotional intelligence. The level of Mike's sarcasm and impatience grew, yet still went unrecognised by his audience;

"Me? I think I'm probably out of my depth in the company I'm keeping here. But I'd stick my neck out to say that, apart from being an animal lover of course, I also find it easy to empathise with people, I'm patient and I think I have a good sense of humour, although I know some of my friends think I am too sarcastic."

The rest of the session was spent speaking, or in the clients' cases listening to, the practitioners speaking about problem solving and how to do it.

Sally-Anne had a step-by-step guide of how to problem solve and wanted to share it with the Rumination Club. As far as Mike could see, things were about to get so much tougher for all of them.

"So, this step-by-step approach to overcoming your problem of ruminating will change you from thinking 'Why have I got a problem?' to 'How shall I solve my problem?' See? The following six steps are how you can take control of your thoughts and act in a way whereby you can manage your challenges and deal with things that affect you in a positive way, ok?"

Sally-Anne seemed pretty sure of herself. Mike just couldn't help but think that an entire SIX steps might be a bit of an arduous task simply to work out if he should wear his blue jeans or his black ones; or if he should order a pizza or a Chinese to be delivered. But he regained some of his patience and decided to listen to her wisdom. Meanwhile Sally-Anne took the group's silence as permission to continue;

"So, Step One – work out exactly what the problem *actually* is, yes? We can't do anything about it until we can define it now can we? And remember, you must be SMART, ok?"

Mike rolled his eyes, realising that the levels of condescension were inevitably going to rise. Sally-Anne went on;

"Step Two – Think of solutions, ANY solutions are ok at this point so don't discriminate, yes? I want you to brainstorm people!"

Brainstorming had Mel in a bit of a quandary it seemed. She furrowed her brow as if she was worried that she'd never get through her whole exercise video and look after her son as well as brainstorm, there simply weren't enough hours in

187

the day. She raised her hand but Sally-Anne just dismissed it;

"I'll take questions at the end, this is very important! Step Three – Choose an option, the one you think is the best for you and think about the possible consequences. You could do a cost/benefit analysis to identify the Pro's and Con's if you like? One for the long-term and one for the short-term? Yes?"

She was clearly reading this from a manual called either; *Wind-Ups-For-Dummies* or; *How-to-Piss-People-Off-In-Six-Easy-Steps*. She turned the page and went for the next step;

"Step Four – make an action plan to put your chosen solution into, well, into action!" Sally-Anne grabbed the small piece of air in front of her and clenched it tight in her fist in front of the group. Mel gasped, Bryan frowned and Carol looked at Mike and then back at Sally-Anne with a *'What the fuck?'* look on her face. Sally-Anne was clearly on a roll;

"Step Five, everyone, is simply DO IT!" she shouted, with a manic smile and wide eyes, staring at the ruminators. Mel looked like she might explode with the excitement, Bryan looked just about as puzzled as he had at the start of the process and Carol just quietly slid her left arm into the sleeve of her jacket, closely followed by the right arm. Mike was transfixed. As an example of people-watching, this had to be the best he'd witnessed in years. Sally-Anne, seemingly recovering from the climax of step number five spoke again, somewhat breathlessly this time;

"So. Now, step Six is important ok? Step Six is when we all have to look at what happened, it's a review yes? Did it work? Or shall we return to an earlier step and try again with a different option?"

She looked around the room and as she did so, Carol stood up. Picking up her handbag she turned to Sally-Anne and spoke,

"So, if I were YOU, *L-o-v-e-y*, I'd return to Step One. Once there, if I was you of course, I'd work out my problem - which is clearly that I am not cut out for this work - and then I would simply FUCK-OFF!" Carol turned to the group and wished everyone the best of luck before smiling at Mike and walking out of the room.

Sally-Anne, much to her credit, didn't bat an eyelid. Mike wondered if she had experience of this kind of behaviour from previous groups. She turned to the three remaining ruminators and simply said, with gold medal winning levels of condescension this time;

"So, we all need to recognise when we are suffering a setback ok? I don't think Carol, *bless her*, was able to do this so I'm going to help you to spot things early to avoid becoming trapped in unnecessary vicious circles. Are you all familiar with traffic lights?"

She looked around the room, seemingly expecting one of the group to raise their hands. However, as there weren't any alien life-forms present, Sally-Anne felt able to continue without having to explain the concept of traffic lights in further detail;

"When we are *'in the green'* we don't need to worry do we? We can handle things ok can't we? It feels like we are in control doesn't it? All systems are go, yes? If, however, we find ourselves *'in the amber'*, how does that feel? Are we in danger of spiraling towards anxiety or are more unhelpful thought patterns creeping in? This could be a cue to change things slightly to get back to being *'in the green'* again yes?" She peered

189

at each group member individually as if to tune in to their thoughts. If she had succeeded she would have seen Mike weighing up whether he should be following Carol out of the door. He wondered if she was sitting in a bar with Gabs somewhere close by, drinking copious amounts of alcohol. The only thing he was certain of was that he knew he was being severely tested this particular evening.

"The amber is a cue to start coping. It doesn't mean you are certain to go into the red, OK? Just that it is a danger," she continued. Mike was almost certain that he was about to enter the red, just as Carol had done moments earlier. Mike was glad that Carol had chosen to leave rather than continue to sit in silence through this. He thought that if she had stayed, this would be the point at which she would have beaten Sally-Anne to death with her rolled up hand-out. Mike wondered, briefly, if she might commit suicide as a result of this, or at least contemplate moving from a zero to a one when she next completed the questionnaire. He also admired that she had the pride to not put up with the patronising any longer. He also recognised that his pride was a long way from fully returning.

"When we get to being 'in the red', and this is where Carol should have taken a step back everyone, we, er...well we should take a step back," Sally-Anne continued, a little uncertainly. "We can't just stop yet we also need to resist the temptation to do anything hasty, which could make things worse. We must remember the tools we have at our disposal and use them to plan again, yes? When we've done this we need to congratulate ourselves for managing a sticky situation, we really MUST do this, ok?"

+   +   +   +   +   +

As they sat on their usual *Rumination-Club-Debriefing-Barstools* in the White Hart, Amy listened with her mouth open and a fixed stare. She had been as impressed with Carol's outburst as her brother had been but as Mike continued with the tale of how the evening had unfolded, Amy struggled to remain calm;

"For homework this week we've all been encouraged to write down – using the amazing invention of the *traffic light system* she revealed to us of course – all of the occasions during the next week when we are feeling good, or 'green'..." Mike made an inverted commas shape in the air with the first-two fingers of each hand and grimaced as this was one of his least favourite things to do. He continued;

"...when we are feeling bad or 'red'..." more fingers;

"...or when we are feeling indifferent or 'amber'...!" Mike finished with another set of finger inverted commas and added a finger exclamation mark for good measure.

Amy smiled slightly but said nothing. She knew instinctively when Mike could be pushed to the limits of his patience and this evening was closing in on that moment. She instinctively knew that if she displayed anger, he might burst a blood vessel. Mike went on;

"Apparently, this is in order that we can start to get a feel for the times when we are more likely to feel down *before* we actually do. I'm already acutely aware of when these times are. And I certainly DO NOT require a traffic light system to identify that I feel *'in the red'* whenever I think of the Liam situation!" he made a final set of finger inverted-commas and in doing so, accidently knocked his glass over on the bar. There was very little beer remaining in it and the small amount that had once been the dregs of his ale slid silently along the varnished wooden bar and slowly dripped away over the edge and onto the floor.

"Look..." said Amy, quietly picking up a JLB Premium Ale bar-towel as she spoke and commenced mopping up the spillage, "...at least she didn't ask you all to give her *a-hundred-and-ten-per-cent*. You know how much you hate that!" and she smiled dryly.

Mike looked at his sister and frowned slightly;

"Why do you say *that*?" asked Mike, adding a sarcastic and over-sized question-mark shape with his fingers at the end of the question.

They both laughed and Mike started to feel better.

As he walked through his front door later that night, Mike wondered how many members of Rumination Club would actually bother to turn up with their homework done the following week. He certainly didn't feel much like going and for a moment contemplated adding the very thought of attending Rumination Club just one more time as being the first item on the list of things he felt *'in-the-red'* about.

He also simultaneously felt relief that Sally-Anne-with-an-e hadn't asked the group to give her *a-hundred-and-ten-per-cent* as he knew he would have been arrested for inflicting some terrible pain upon her person with half a dozen flipchart pens.

What I did that evening,
What she said that evening,
Fulfilling my hope,
Headlong I go for glory.

Chapter 20

As Mike stumbled down the stairs in his confused, half-asleep state, he yelled at the person knocking repeatedly at his door;

"OK! OK! I'M COMING...OK?" and then mumbling under his breath continued,

"...for fuck's sake, I'm jus..." and he hurriedly pulled an old *London Calling* t-shirt over his head. He swung the door open and as he did he stopped dead in his tracks. It was Clive.

"Fucking Hell Clive!" Mike didn't sound particularly pleased to see him, "What do you want...and what the fuck are you doing here at *this* time of the morning?"

"Yeah, er...sorry Mike..." said Clive, nervously toying with the edge of the still-furled umbrella in his hands, "...but may I come in? Madeline asked me to come and see you and as..."

Mike clearly wasn't massively impressed with Clive's opening gambit either so continued in his admonishment;

"For Christ's sake, she doesn't contact me for fucking years and now I can't shake her off. What is it now? Is she not entirely sure she hasn't fucked my life up enough eh? Does she want to give me another kicking to make sure? Be nice if she could at least do it herself rather than send a messenger from God, or do it at a reasonable time of the fucking day...or is sleep deprivation part of

193

her grand plan? Eh?"

Although he knew it was nearly eleven-thirty, Clive said nothing; he just looked sheepishly at Mike and waited for him to stop ranting. Mike slowly calmed down and gestured to Clive to follow him into the lounge. Clive stepped inside, closed the door behind him and, after wiping his feet on the union flag doormat, he followed Mike. As he walked into the house Clive could see that Mike was still not taking a great deal of care of himself or his surroundings. The lounge was littered with detritus from numerous takeaway meals, a dozen or so beer bottles and discarded clothes lay on every surface. Mike stood in the middle of the room, oblivious to the mess and scratched his backside through the tatty jogging bottoms he was wearing. He clearly hadn't shaved for days.

"Look Mike, it's not good news I'm afraid. I think you'd better sit down," said Clive in a low and slightly grave tone.

"Is it ever when it's to do with Maddie – sorry *Madeline* - is it *ever* Clive?" replied Mike flippantly. But suddenly understanding the look of anxiety on Clive's face, Mike stopped talking and slowly sat down in the leather recliner. He gestured silently to Clive to take a seat also. But rather ominously, Clive remained standing.

"There's no easy way to say this Mike but there's been an accident and, well it's Liam, he's in hospital. He was hit by a car around the corner from the church and he's been hurt pretty badly I'm afraid." Clive paused for Mike to take the information in before continuing;

"It was an accident you see? He just ran out in front of it and, well...you hear of these things all the time don't you? You...you just don't expect it to be someone you know. Look, I know this is all a bit much, seeing as you've only just heard the news that Liam...well, that he isn't....you know..." Clive nodded at Mike and raised his eyebrows but tailed off; afraid that pointing out the obvious at such a time was unnecessarily cruel given the circumstances.

Mike sat, numb, slowly digesting the news. He eventually broke the silence;

"I don't understand Clive. Why have you come *here* and why are you telling *me* about this? Why now? Why, when it's abundantly clear that I have nothing to do with the situation and that I'm not wanted as *part* of the situation, as a part of Liam's life? I've never been a part of his life, I get that now. You told me why I was always excluded from his life, so now I understand Liam is nothing to do with me. You delivered the news yourself, remember? Now though, now you decide, or Madeline decides I suppose, to tell me about *this*. Forgive me but I don't get it. It's a shame that he's been hurt and I truly hope he makes a full and speedy recovery, just like I do whenever I hear of this kind of accident, but he's a stranger to me, isn't he? And so forgive me for not getting the point but...." Mike stopped talking. As his quivering voice ran out of words to say, he simply started sobbing.

Clive pulled a handkerchief from the top pocket of his tweed jacket and handed it to Mike, who promptly blew his nose in it and handed it straight back. Not batting an eyelid Clive spoke quietly;

"It seemed like a good idea, the right thing to do. Mike, it's clear to me that you still care deeply about Liam and that the recent news hasn't changed a thing. It's also clear to Madeline now,

195

that's why I'm here. After you left that red case with us on Easter Sunday she spent a bit of time looking through it. She didn't show me at first, I thought maybe it was stuff that mattered to the two of you, from a long time ago. I thought maybe it was photos and stuff like that from when you were together. But then she showed me how you had written to Liam as he grew up. I saw how you had given him details about you and your life. News updates of key moments, like when you changed jobs and at which school or college you were working at and how your career was progressing. She showed me the birthday cards and Christmas cards you wrote but couldn't send too. I saw the photos you put in so that he might recognise you if he ever looked for you one day and the photos of your sister and of your friends."

There was no response from Mike and Clive was left to wonder if visiting was such a good idea after all. He picked up his umbrella and turned to go. Before he did he added;

"Look, Madeline never realised how much you had cared about Liam or what she had done to you. She knew you had tried to find her at first but that you had stopped soon afterwards so she assumed you were over it. She knows differently now. Very different in fact. But knowing how you felt meant that she also knew you would want to know about Liam and the accident. She's not proud of what she did Mike but she maintains she would have done anything for her son. Look, just call me if you want an update or if you want to know more, ok? I'd better get back and see how they're both holding up. Call me though, right?"

As Clive opened the front door, Mike put his hand on his shoulder, startling the priest who up to then hadn't realised Mike was following close behind him.

"Christ Almighty!" he exclaimed, hurriedly looking skywards for forgiveness as always before adding, "Don't do that!"

Mike had dried his eyes and was looking shabbily forlorn in his scruffy attire and unkempt hair.

"About Liam, is he going to be ok Clive?" he asked softly before hearing himself go further than that. "I mean, I'd like to know if there's anything I can do."

Clive paused for a moment, which gave Mike enough time to process what he had just said to the priest. Was he really offering help to a man-of-the-cloth, an ex-girlfriend who had treated him so abysmally and someone else's child, a child he didn't even know? Could it be that in his depressed state he had weakened to the point where he wasn't thinking straight at all? Would Maddie take advantage of the situation as always? She could exploit his kindness and generosity and leave him in a difficult and sad position at some point in the future yet again. Mike soon realised he was simply ruminating as usual. His rambling thoughts were interrupted by Clive;

"I know this is a bit presumptuous Mike, a bit random I guess, but..." Clive paused briefly and then asked, "...what blood type are you?"

"Eh? Oh...it's...er...O. It's O negative actually" said Mike. He had recovered from the unexpected question and his earlier emotional outpouring sufficiently to unscramble his brain to start talking once again. Clive looked at Mike through narrowing eyes and then said;

"Look I hear it all the time in my work and I know that, when people hear about someone else's misfortune or loss they usually say '...*and if there's anything I can do...'* but did *you* mean it when you said it?"

He looked at Mike for a response but Mike just looked blankly, straight back at him.

"I mean..." continued Clive, "...when you see someone you haven't seen for ages you usually say *'...hi and how are you...'* but you're not expecting them to *actually* tell you how they are, are you? Otherwise we priests would never get anywhere as we'd always be listening to people talking about their illnesses, family troubles and..."

Clive was floundering and beginning to feel he would never make any sense ever again but Mike knew exactly what he meant. It was an old talking point that he and Sid would debate into the small hours. Interrupting Clive, Mike suddenly said,

"I know what you mean Clive and yes, I meant what I said. If there's anything I can do, I would like to help if I can."

"It's just that Liam has nearly used up the supply of his blood type at the Queen Mary," said Clive. "He is O negative too. O type blood isn't an uncommon blood type really – although O negative is slightly more so - but it's also pretty special because you can give it to any..."

"...to any person who needs it and has any *other* blood type." chimed in Mike, finishing Clive's sentence for him. Before he could ask how he knew so much, Mike said, "Like I said, I have O negative myself Clive".

"Well stocks are really low at the moment Mike, Queen Mary's Blood Bank team is appealing for O type donors. Madeline and I can't give him our blood as neither of us are suitable. I know it's quite a way but would you be agreeable to give some? Liam may need more surgery when

198

he's stable and..." Clive knew he was possibly overstepping the mark and awaited the full force of Mike's temper to be unleashed. Without hesitation, however, Mike simply agreed to help;

"'Course I will. And Amy, er, that's my sister, is also O negative so I'll call her. She's pretty squeamish but she'll give anything for a cuppa and a sugary biscuit, trust me!" With a renewed sense of purpose Mike went back into the lounge and rummaged around for his mobile phone "I'll call her!" he yelled to Clive, who was still stood by the front door.

"Thanks Mike, I don't know what to say other than thanks a million! I'd better get going but let me know when you're coming...a text will do if you like...and I'll let the hospital know ok?" Clive put his umbrella under his arm and closed the door behind him as he left.

As Mike called Amy he was grateful that he had decided not to start taking the anti-depressants prescribed to him by Dr. Baker as it may have been the difference between being able or unable to help Liam.

+   +   +   +   +   +

It was just over an hour later when Amy arrived, with Debs in tow, at Mike's. By this time he had showered, shaved and found some clean clothes to put on. As he opened the door he was greeted by his sister;

"Hey big brother, how's it going?" and she breezed past him into the hallway. Debs followed silently behind, rubbing Mike's left arm and tilting her head to the side slightly as she passed him, in an unintentionally patronising manner. Amy walked into the lounge and pulled a face at the state of the place. Trying not to let her disdain show in her voice she continued cheerfully;

"Debs has O type blood too, how *great* is that, so I twisted her arm to come along, I tried getting hold of the others but for some reason no one seems to be answering their phones today. I spoke to Titan, they don't know what blood type they are but they said they will check it out for future reference. You know what they're like though, they'll probably ask that any blood they give be sent out to the victims of mining disasters in Chile or Himalayan goat-herder victims of avalanches or some such thing. Hopefully the others will call me back though, you never know how many more of us O types there are!"

"Actually we're only about seven percent of the population I think you'll find," interjected Debs, "Well, O *negative* is anyway. Not sure how many have O positive blood but O negative people can only receive O negative blood so its academic really," she sounded so matter-of-fact but somehow Mike already knew it was unlikely that there would be more than three of them visiting the hospital today.

As they climbed into Mike's car his mobile rang.

"Ooh I love this tune!" said Debs, "It reminds me of school discos and Saturday morning TV...*then I saw her face, and I'm a Believer, not a trace, of doubt in my mi...*"

Debs gleefully sang along for a few bars until Mike switched the phone off, simultaneously interrupting Debs' karaoke rendition of the Monkees' hit whilst also forcing Clive into leaving him a voicemail message.

Although Clive may earlier have been able to put his mind at ease, Mike wasn't in the mood for talking, preferring to discover for himself what news there was when he arrived at Queen Mary's later. As Debs went to protest, Amy stepped in to divert her attention from Mike's apparent rudeness;

"How about we listen to the radio for a bit eh?" Amy suggested diplomatically and, before anyone could answer, she switched the radio on and sat back, fastening her seatbelt. Taking Amy's cue, Debs did the same. Mike looked across at his sister, then glanced in the rear-view mirror at Debs and started the engine of his Ford Fiesta. The three travellers remained silent for a while as they drove away from Mike's house and headed for the motorway towards London. Amy concentrated on playing with her phone, Mike appeared to be concentrating on the road and Debs found herself looking around the interior of Mike's car. It smelled fresh and clean and the rear seats looked like they had never been used before. Unlike other cars Debs had sat in recently, there was no litter, dirt or any belongings to be seen. It was cleaner than Mike's home for sure and probably cleaner than Debs' flat too. So clean that Debs could no longer ignore it and decided to break the awkward silence;

"Is this a new car Mike? I mean its immaculate back here. Has anyone *ever* used these seats before me?"

Mike looked up and glanced back at her. He didn't really want to start a conversation. He was still worried about Liam and was wondering how he might be faring. The radio had distracted him for a while but now Debs had burst that bubble and wanted to engage in a conversation about nothing of consequence. He was, of course, still feeling a little agitated. Sensing his irritation, Amy

201

interrupted for the second time since the start of the journey;

"Debs, who else can I call about giving blood? I've tried the usual crowd but is there anyone you can send messages to? It'd be really helpful. Maybe everyone you call before a demo or whatever? I'm going to try the guys at the gallery and I'll put in a call to Nigel at the White Hart. If he's ok with it we can put some posters up. Even if they're not O negative, it'd be worthwhile to get a few more people as donors anyway, wouldn't it?"

"I tell you what!" said Debs suddenly, "We should start a campaign at Uni. There's thousands of students so we might be able to generate enough interest to get the National Blood Service to do a regular day in one of the sports halls or the Union or something. It's such a great cause and all, I'm sure there'd be interest. Shame they don't pay though, students will do anything for a quid. Now, if we were talking about sperm donors it would be a different thing. The place is choc-full of wankers!" she laughed dirtily. Amy did too, she looked at her brother, he was smiling for the first time since she arrived and Amy felt safe to tease him for the first time in what felt like ages.

"I reckon Mike could donate sperm successfully, don't you Debs? He's not doing anything else with it at the moment is he? Except wasting it I s'pose!" The girls laughed again. "I reckon he'd make a fortune. It's not as if he's seeing anyone at the moment – or *ever* actually – and it's not as if he's doing much else with his life" Amy and Debs continued laughing, more loudly than ever.

Mike looked at Amy and pulled a face. It had once been a regular routine of hers, talking about his misfortunes with a friend such as Debs in front of him as if he weren't there. Over the years he'd become accustomed to Amy making fun of his sad life and realised it hadn't happened for a while. He was trying to fathom why this was. Had he really been so low that she didn't feel able to do it? Did she think he was *so* fragile that he couldn't take it? *Was* he actually so fragile that he couldn't take it? Or maybe he just had been so pre-occupied with everything he hadn't noticed?

For the first time he could remember, Mike used the Rumination Club *two-minute-rule* to avoid a longer examination of his inner thoughts. He threw Amy one of his *pissed-off-big-brother-dealing-with-a-piss-taking-little-sister* looks and, rather sarcastically, said;

"I love it when you're this funny Amy! You should been on the stage, you really should...with a razor sharp wit like yours!"

Without faltering and whilst Debs was still chuckling behind her, Amy came back;

"And if he carries on buying cars like this he'll never have women lining up to date him either will he? Look at it, a Ford Fiesta, bloody hell, talk about *dull*! Can you hear him now, on a blind date or something like that, when you or I have lined him up with a friend? He'd be sitting there, moaning about the waitress being called '*Star*' and how crap the tea is and that they haven't made it the right way..." she paused to look at Mike accusingly and then continued "and then he offers the girl a lift home. She asks [in a high-pitched voice] *'Ooh yeah, that would be nice, what car do you drive?* and in reply he'd say, [rather grandly] *'Well, I have a Ford Fiesta Zetec, the 2012 model actually'* and she'd make her excuses and quietly call a cab!"

Amy and Debs laughed hysterically and Mike

couldn't help but laugh too. Despite everything that was going on in his life and the reasons for their mercy dash today, he found Amy funny. He put up a weak defence, more to encourage her to continue the mockery than bring it to an end, Amy loved it when Mike was self-deprecating;

"Look there's nothing wrong with this car. It was *Supermini of The Year* when it came out; it's agile yet frugal; its back seats fold down to make it even more spacious and it is designed, in and out, to appeal to young and old alike!"

The girls laughed hysterically again. When she eventually controlled her laughter, nearly a full minute later, Amy turned to Debs in the back;

"Do you know what Sid always said about Mike's cars Deb? Do you?" she turned to Mike but continued talking to Debs, who was sitting forward to hear Amy whilst also wiping a tear from her eye. Mike was already pulling another face; he knew what was coming;

"Well, Sid always asks Mike why he insists on buying Vicar's wives' cars!" said Amy before doubling up, tears streaming down her reddened cheeks. Debs screamed in delight and fell back laughing once again too. Mike was smiling and his cares, albeit temporarily, had been left behind.

He hadn't heard this particular story for quite a while but Mike recalled how Sid used to mock him when they were younger. Mike and Sid had passed their driving tests within weeks of each other when they were both seventeen. Mike had been saving for a car for months and was determined to get one as soon as he could whereas Sid was happy riding his Suzuki motorcycle. In fact Sid never did buy a car when he lived at home. Soon after Anita passed away he chose to pack everything he owned into a rucksack and move to London, guitar in hand, to seek his fortune. Mike's savings didn't really amount to much so his parents eventually took out a loan to buy their son's first car. Mike made the payments on his parents' loan out of the wages he earned working in the local greengrocers on Saturdays and Sundays.

The first time Sid came back from London to visit Mike he was driving a 1975 two-litre Ford Capri. It was the much sought after 'John Player Special' version, painted glossy black with gold detailing, just like the Formula One car driven by their boyhood heroes. Sid swore that the car was his. Mike suspected that his busking and pub gigs would barely have covered the petrol so secretly believed that Sid had either borrowed it or stolen it to impress everybody at home and give the impression he was doing well. Nonetheless, it had been only six months since Sid had left and already he was driving what the boys would once have described as a *'film star car'*. Back in the real world, Mike's parents' money had bought him a 1976 Mini in *'Harvest Gold'*, a description which Sid called a euphemism for *baby-sick-yellow*.

Sid would come home to visit whenever Mike came home from University and he would always be driving - or riding - something flash and fast. He would turn up on a Norton Commando 850 one visit and then arrive driving a three-litre Granada coupe the next. There would be a superfast Dolomite Sprint followed the next visit by him driving an old Pontiac Firebird with a massive phoenix decal on the bonnet. One summer he even turned up riding a huge trike, made from a VW chassis and powered by a Mini Cooper engine. This was when they were in their very early twenties and Mike had recently

205

replaced his trusty Mini with a Mk1 Ford Fiesta in electric blue. He had bought it out of his last student grant cheque, using the Mini as a part-exchange. It was the end of the summer and Amy was at home when Sid arrived. At that time in her late teens, Amy used to impress her Art School friends with tales about Sid, unbeknown to him of course. She would regale stories of how this *rebel-without-a-cause* friend of her older brother would visit from time to time, describing the adventures he was having in London recording and playing with various, almost famous, bands.

That particular weekend Mike had been thrilled to see Sid pull up and, despite seeing the huge trike he had arrived riding, Mike quickly took his friend to see his new purchase. Although it was about eight years old, the Fiesta was in immaculate condition. It had a new stereo and, being a hatchback, was far roomier than Mike's old Mini too. He pointed out to Sid that it meant that when he came home from University for good later that year, he could bring back everything he owned.

"But mate, I don't get why you would buy *this*," Sid exclaimed pointedly. He was looking the car up and down whilst smoothing back his hair which had been blown all over the place as he hadn't been wearing a crash helmet on the trike.

"It's been really well looked after mate, it's got loads of extras and it's low mileage too. Only one careful lady owner!" said Mike triumphantly whilst dusting a speck of dust from the top of the green tinted windscreen.

"I can see that Mike, wow look Amy, a wing mirror on *both* sides, whatever will they think of next?" Sid's mocking tone didn't enthrall Mike, but Amy was sniggering so Sid continued;

"Luxury grey velour upholstery, imitation leather gear-knob cover, a two-and-a-half-watt tape player and, wait a moment, is that a genuine glove box and cardboard parcel shelf Mike? You won't know yourself now. The old Mini has been well and truly put in the shade by this awesome machine hasn't it?" Sid mimicked Mike's voice "...*and only one careful lady owner!* Bloody Hell Mike, was she married to a Vicar or something? 'Cos that's the only person I can see driving something like this!" Sid threw his head back and laughed loudly. So did Amy.

Back in his updated 2012 Fiesta, Mike was growing tired of Amy having all the fun at his expense;

"Do you really need to torture me like this all the time? It was SUCH a long time ago and you only thought it was funny then because Sid turned up on the flippin' trike looking cool, do you remember that?" Mike asked Amy as she slowly stopped laughing. Amy noticed he was smiling broadly and looking more like his usual self than he had for weeks. Mike went on, "And I seem to recall you weren't *SO* cool yourself though, remember? You screamed like a Banshee when he took you out on it, you were even crying when you got back to the house! Remember that Amy?"

Mike was right, Amy recalled with horror how Sid had driven the trike at such speeds that she had literally feared for her life. She cried for most of the ride but Sid didn't realise as they were travelling so fast he couldn't hear her sobbing behind him. Amy couldn't let him know she was scared by tapping him on the back as she was too busy gripping hold of the bars either side of her seat.

"Oh yeah, so I did!" said Amy, looking into

the middle distance. "I never went on another ride with Sid did I? To this day I've not been on another motorbike and I rarely even get in a car with him, he can be a bloody maniac!"

Amy looked back at her mobile phone, Neither Sid, Candy or H had called her back as yet. She wondered where they might all be and what they were doing.

"Why are they all ignoring my calls? Shall I try them again?" she mused aloud. Then Mike spoke;

"Look don't worry about them, we'll be there in a mo. I just want to thank you both before we arrive for coming along today. I know it's weird and all, especially given how this has all turned out, but it really means a lot to me and maybe it will make a difference to Liam too."

Amy saw that there were tears welling up in his eyes and Debs leant forward and gently rubbed his arm as she had when she first arrived at his house earlier that morning. This time, however, Mike noticed that it felt more supportive than patronising and he smiled despite the way he was feeling. As he drove into Queen Mary's Hospital car park and started looking for a parking space, he hoped it was time things started to get a little better.

So cut the rose in full bloom.
'Til, the fearless come and the act is done
A love like blood....

Chapter 21

"Ok then smarty-pants how exactly do you use this thing?" asked Tania, holding up the instructions to the light once again and squinting at the tiny writing as hard as she could. She took her designer glasses off – the lenses were plain glass after all - and looked yet again but still she couldn't make out the detail.

"Give it here love, it can't be that hard surely?" said Tim holding out his hand. Tania looked crestfallen and passed the small booklet to Tim. She put her glasses back on, went over to the kettle and said;

"Well if you can work it out you're a better person that I. Do you want a cuppa?" she asked, turning on the radio and holding up a packet of Green Tea and shaking it in Tim's direction.

"Ooh yes but...actually...can I just have a normal cup of PG sweetie? I feel the need for something a bit stronger than *that* today" and he nodded towards the *Fairtrade* tea packet Tania was holding, somewhat dismissively.

"Course you can" she replied and she put a tea bag in each of he two small white cups she had placed on the worktop. Before she could pour water from the kettle onto them, however, Tim spoke again;

"Sweetie? Would you mind? Could I have a normal mug today too please? You know I just love the *Habitat* bone china cups but they're pretty small and we don't have anyone coming 'round do we?"

"Yeah, no worries my lovely! And do *you* mind if we listen to Radio 2 this afternoon instead of the iPod? I'm not really in the mood for free jazz today. I think I'd rather have some music you can hum along to and some chatter," said Tania cheerfully and she reached into the far back reaches of the cupboard. After a few moments and some chinking and tinkling of china she emerged with a *Cadbury's Crunchie* mug from last year's Easter egg and a *PG Tips* mug adorned with a cuddly monkey, a free gift they received after purchasing numerous boxes of said tea. She dropped a pyramid-shaped tea bag in each and poured in some boiled water whilst humming along to a nameless boy-band tune on the radio.

Meanwhile, Tim was reading the small booklet and simultaneously examining the step-by-step photographs that accompanied it. His tongue had been sticking out of the corner of his mouth for a minute or so whilst Tania made the tea but then suddenly he spoke;

"Look this is it. You put a drop of water on *there* to moisten it and then you prick your finger with this little thing and get some blood on....*this* little stick here!" Tim waved a small needle and a white plastic strip at Tania, who was watching intently but also looking a little queasy by this stage. Tim continued undaunted "...then you put a blob of the red stuff onto this card and wait. Once the pattern emerges you compare it against *this*..." he held up another card "...and the one it looks most like is *your* blood type and Bob's your metaphorical uncle! See? That's quite simple really isn't it?"

Tania smiled lovingly at Tim and handed him

a steaming cup of tea;

"You *are* clever aren't you? I don't know what I'd do without you Tim," Tania cooed before adding, "I just know our blood will be compatible anyway and I know that, if ever you needed it, I would be there for you." She smiled knowingly and nodded at the blood testing kit, "Not sure I like the idea of a *small* prick though!" As they laughed, the video-com buzzed. Peering at the small black and white monitor by their door, Tim could see it was Candy and H standing outside the locked wrought iron gates that prevented members of the public accessing the block of apartments in which Titan lived. Tim buzzed them in and Tania switched the radio off. By the time Candy and H had reached Titan's front door, Eric Dolpy could be heard coming from the iPod and Titan were sipping hastily-brewed green tea from stylishly-small china cups.

"Ooh, that looks a *lot* better Candy!" said Tania, looking at the side of Candy's face whilst kissing her on both cheeks. "You can hardly see a thing. You can hardly see a thing now eh Tim?" she looked at Tim for confirmation. Tim peered at the side of Candy's face and agreed;

"Yeah, wow! That's improved hasn't it?" Answered Tim enthusiastically and he held out his hand to greet H. H left him hanging there for an awkward moment or two and then shook Tim's hand, squeezing hard. Tim winced before also kissing Candy on both cheeks and gesturing for them both to sit down. Candy didn't look convinced of their judgment on the state of her bruising but she smiled weakly and sat on the small sofa. H sat down next to her, wriggling like a dog settling into a new basket as he did so. Tania pulled a brightly coloured leather bean-bag into the middle of the room and sat down too. Rubbing his still-numb right hand to get his blood flowing again, Tim moved to refill the kettle and having done so, switched it on. He flexed his hand a couple more times and pulled a face before turning to his friends;

"Right then, shall I grind some fresh coffee? We've got some frankly amazing Guatemalan Bella Carmona or a really full-bodied Arabian Mocha-Java if you're interested in a darker, more chocolatey undertone?"

Tim's request was greeted with a frisson of excitement from Tania and yet with a degree of bemusement from Candy and H. Tim stood there, silently awaiting a response, his question seemingly hovering in mid air. He knew there was no tumbleweed in the flat and no church in this part of town but in his head he would swear he heard a distant bell toll. After what felt – in Tim's mind - like three or four days had passed, Tania stood up and broke the silence.

"Hey, maybe you'd all prefer some tea?" she asked, moving to the kitchen area of the open-plan living space and opening the larder. Then, more to herself than her friends she started to go through the list of speciality teas and infusions there were to choose from;

"Now, I think we have *Oolong* which is a black tea from China, we have green tea of course, made from Chinese *camellia*..." She turned to the guests, involving them in her thought process once again by explaining, "...it's a healthier tea which has less tannin..." and before anyone could say anything she continued in her tea explorations, "...Then there's *Matcha*, a Japanese powdered green tea. We've got a red herbal tea called *Rooibos* – my *absolute* favourite – and we

212

have a really nice Waitrose organic *Camomile!*"
Tania turned back to face everyone with a big
smile on her face, only to be greeted by more
silence. It was Tim's turn to deal with the
awkwardness and this time he intervened more
quickly than Tania had earlier,

"Wow, I didn't realise we had *so* many to
choose from sweetie! We *are* spoilt for choice
aren't we? I think I'll have another green tea, it's
so refreshing! What about you two?" he asked,
turning to Candy and H.

"Hasn't *Tinia* got anything less pretentious?"
asked H impatiently.

"Pretentious? *Moi?*" asked Tim without the
slightest hint of irony.

"Oh, don't be so impolite H," said Candy,
slightly embarrassed by H's obvious irritation.
She turned to Tania and asked, "Er, have you got
anything like an English breakfast tea Tania? Or
something like that?"

Tania peered back into the cupboard and
pulled out a box of *PG Tips* teabags. She held
them aloft to her friends and asked,

"Like this?"

"Ooh, lovely!" said a relieved Candy, "White
no sugar for us both please".

Tania proceeded to make two more cups of
tea and Tim sat down on a footstool he pulled
from behind the sofa where Candy and H were
seated. He looked at them for a moment and then
asked;

"Did Amy get hold of you too then? I take it
you spoke to her and that's why you're here? It's
terrible news isn't it? Blimey, given everything
that's gone on and that recently...well, I mean,
poor Mike eh? Bloody Hell! I just wish there was
more we could do to help. When we heard abou..."

"Whoa hold on! What are you talking about Tim? H interrupted Tim's flow, holding his hand up. "What's happened now? Is Mike ok?"

Tim explained about Liam's accident and how Mike and Amy were travelling up to somewhere in London to give blood. He went on to explain how Amy had spent time calling everyone to see if they were compatible donors as hospital stocks were pretty non-existent. Tania handed a mug of tea each to Candy and H and sat down on her bean bag again. H explained to Titan that both he and Candy had missed a number of calls earlier that day from Amy and had tried calling her back a few times without success.

"Yeah we thought she was being pretty insistent, considering it's a Sunday afternoon and all that. Anyway, we tried to call her again just before we got to *Titan Towers*..." he said, looking around him as he did so "...but it's going straight to voicemail now, so I guess they must have arrived at the hospital. You two not going then? No *Top-Class-Titan-Blood* to spare?"

"We're not sure if we're a match or not yet. It's a long way to go just to be told *'no thanks'* by the hospital staff. But we've bought some blood test kits to see if we're a match or not. You could always do the same I guess. Of course it's unlikely we'll be compatible, but we ought to find out what we are, even if we can't help Liam out it would be helpful to know, given our plans to travel," said Tim.

"I give blood already," said H, "I'm type AB though and *Madam* here is A neg," he continued, turning to Candy and addressing her directly "I checked when we were in the hospital last Saturday, so neither of us are any good for the boy by the looks of it."

"Ok, yeah, of course," said Tania. "Anyway, if we *do* get to go on a long-haul destination next year it would be safest to know our blood types before we go, eh sweetie?" she said, looking at Tim, "Just in case of emergencies of course. We're looking at going on a trekking holiday to Vietnam and Cambodia next spring by the way," she added.

"Well look, you could give blood anyway even if you're not a match for the kid. Hospitals are always after more," said H, then mischievously added, "...them Vietnamese will give you whatever blood they have in the fridge if anything happens to you out there by the way, IF they've got a fridge in their hospital or wherever you end up that is. They'll feed you meat from a dog and give you whatever blood they can find. Let's hope you don't get sick eh? It comes to something when you realise you are better off in a mainland European hospital these days doesn't it? With the butchers they have for doctors in Spain and Turkey too! I went to the far-East once, back packing I was. Loads of adventures I could tell you about. Bloody Hell, the birds and the booze, it'd blow your minds....but the doctors and that? Christ, no thanks very much, it'd just give you both the shits I tell you."

Titan simultaneously pulled the same horrified face. Candy nudged H in the ribs and threw him a glance. Expertly changing the subject she pointed to a framed and mounted photograph on the far wall;

"I like that picture Tania, is it new?" she asked, feigning interest.

"Oh yes, we picked it up in a gallery in Soho the last time we were in London. It's a limited edition photographic print of Sting playing the

215

lute whilst Trudie Styler does some form of tantric yoga in the background. We found it spoke to us both on a deep level so we bought it and had it framed. Tim says he liked it because of the way the...now let me remember what it was he said...the *iconicity of the negative space visually and conceptually activates the distinct versus the in-distinct.* Isn't that right love?" she looked at Tim for qualification of his analysis. Before he could answer her, she continued,

"I like it because I'm just a huge fan of Sting's work..." Tania broke off before quietly adding under her breath, and in Candy's direction,

"...and I think he looks pretty *hot* too, don't you Candy?"

Candy was forthright when it came to such subjects. So she gave her answer in the only way she knew how;

"Nah, to be honest I've always thought he was a bit of a pretentious twat actually Tania. Look, he was originally a Geordie teacher; then he was speaking with a *Cool-Urban-Chic London* accent as soon as *The Police* made it big; and when it became groovy to come from working-class areas in the nineties, he goes all North-Eastern on us again, like he'd never been away from the place at all. Talk about a phoney!"

She pulled a face but was on something of a roll, so continued;

"You can certainly see why Copeland and Summers prefer to stay away from him, even if they're not financially better off without him. And I ask you, all that time he spent personally going around sticking the bark back on the trees in the Amazonian rainforest and the crap about *five-hour-long-tantric-sex-sessions* and yoga and that stuff...well..."

Candy paused for a moment wondering whether to continue and then chose to say something else that was on her mind;

"...look, shall we say it's just that I prefer my men a little more un-reconstructed these days?"

And with that, Candy squeezed H's arm. H visibly appeared to grow about three feet taller and put his arm around Candy's shoulder, he was grinning broadly. There was a moment of silence whilst Titan absorbed the meaning of what they had just witnessed and what had been said.

"Bloody Hell! When did *this* happen then?" asked Tania when the penny finally dropped.

"Oh, you know...its been on the cards for ages, it's just taken me a while to beat her self-respect down to the point where she's so emotionally vulnerable and low that she can't defend herself against my irresistible charms any longer!" said H nonchalantly but looking like his smile might one day have to be surgically removed. "And now that she's decided she can't live without me..."

Tim interrupted H;

"We can call you *Handy* can't we? *H-A-N-D-Y* see? H and Candy equals *Handy!* That's pretty *handy* isn't it?" he exclaimed, gleefully clapping his hands together like a five-year-old on Christmas morning. H glared across at Tim but Candy saw what was coming and headed him off;

"Look it's very early days yet Tim. You are the first to hear about it and you two are the *only* couple around here who are anywhere close to the style of Tom Cruise and Katie Holmes..."

"...and with the brains and charisma of Peter Andre and Katie Price!" quickly added H, grinning sarcastically.

"Look, we'll just be 'boyfriend and girlfriend' for the time being and see where we go from there won't we?" Candy looked at H to put him straight again, he was still obviously pleased with his 'Peter and Katie' comment but now was swelling with increased pleasure at the whole 'boyfriend and girlfriend' description used in Candy's précis of the situation. It was very soon admittedly, but nothing could be too soon when it came to Candy in H's eyes. Guessing how he was thinking, Candy smiled at H...and H saw the room light up.

As they later went to leave and as H helped Candy on with her jacket he turned to face Tim and paused. With a quizzical look on his face he nodded towards the iPod dock and asked a question of his host;

"I don't suppose this is old Eric Dolpy playing is it Tim? If I'm not mistaken it's his 'Out to Lunch' album isn't it. You know it never ceases to amaze me how everyone sees this as the *be-all-and-end-all* of improv jazz."

Tim froze.

With the straightest of faces, H continued,

"Yeah, I quite like the abstract tonal qualities but I prefer his earlier stuff like 'Iron Man' or 'Conversations'. But over all that be-bop based stuff I just love Ornette Coleman; you must like him, yes?"

Tim failed to thaw out, much as H had expected in truth. By this time Candy and Tania were also struck dumb but were hanging on H's every word, mouths open. He went on once more,

"Yeah, when you think that Coleman's 1960 album 'Free Jazz' coined the name for the genre, you have to sit up and take notice don't you? To think he was there at the beginning and yet *still* winning awards like the *Pulitzer* in 2007 for later works like 'Sound Grammar' you have to hand it to him. Remind me next time I'm coming around and I'll bring you some stuff you can borrow?" And with that, H carefully escorted a silent Candy out through the door and closed it behind them, leaving an open-mouthed Titan inside.

"What the hell was all *that* about?" Candy finally managed to ask, still puzzled about what she had just witnessed.

"Oh I'm just playing with him. I saw an Eric Dolpy CD on the side last time I came 'round here. Look, Tim gets on my tits right? So I'm just showing him up a bit to prove anyone can read *WikiFreeJazz* and be a page ahead of the rest!" H laughed, sounding not dissimilar to Vincent Price in an old *Dracula* movie and continued;

"Look, I know they've been together since they were kids and they've had this bloody portmanteau-style 'celebrity' name long before *Brangelina* or *Kimye* but they are NO different from the rest of us. Neither of them have had a relationship with anyone other than each other and they are so perfectly matched in levels of pretentiousness that are unlikely to ever do so!"

Candy was still smiling broadly, she knew H was right. She rubbed his arm and, in an understanding tone joined in with H's rant,

"They ARE pretentious aren't they? All that tea and coffee stuff, what a laugh! I bet they drink PG Tips and Nescafe all the time we're not around. They travel miles to shop at farmers' markets, independent butchers, fishmongers, bakers and fruit and vegetable shops to show off but I bet they use Lidl as much as they use Waitrose. I saw a copy of the *Guardian* on the coffee table but I reckon there were copies of *Take A Break* and *OK Magazine* in the up-cycled raffia paper rack!" Candy snorted when saying 'up-cycled' as this was a term used frequently by

Titan. In response, H laughed heartily.

"And what about all that carry on about going to Vietnam and Cambodia! How ridiculous is that?" asked Candy rhetorically, "They've never been anywhere other than Turkey, Tenerife and Torre-bloody-molinos!"

H laughed at Candy's observation and added;

"And if they ever get married I hope they take on a double-barreled surname, with Tim's surname being Small and Tania's being Cox I cant wait to hear them introducing themselves!"

H laughed yet again, Candy grabbed hold of his waist tightly and started to laugh along with him. She pulled at H's jacket lapel and, through her giggles she said;

"I can't talk; with a name like mine I reckon I should've been a Country and Western singer! I suppose we're off out now to see if we can buy some ancient jazz CDs, Ornette *someone* was it? We'd better bloody-well have some before we get invited back here then hadn't we?"

"Too right!" said H and he stepped into the lift and pressed the ground floor button. As they descended to the lobby he turned to Candy.

"Look, I know it's early days and all that but I'm no good at dancing around elephants you know? So what are we to do about *You-know-who*?"

Candy looked at him, she knew he was talking about Sid but didn't really want to have *that* conversation. She looked away and softly said;

"It's in the past now ok? Never again. You'll just have to trust me on that."

H took Candy by the arm, swung her around and planted a deep and passionate kiss on her lips.

Out of body and out of mind,
Kiss the demons out of my dreams,
I get the funny feeling it's alright...

Chapter 22

"Look just drink the water there and I'll get someone to bring you a nice cup of tea in a mo. Don't try to stand up yet...but it might help to stabilise your blood pressure if you dangle your feet off the side of the bed. Remember, this is your first time so if you feel at all faint, just lie back down and stay there as long as you want, ok Amy?"

The nurse added a few scribbled notes to the clipboard she was holding, smiled briefly at Amy and was gone. Amy could hear the gentle squeak of the nurse's rubber slip-on shoes growing increasingly faint as she walked down the corridor and away. Amy had always loved how nurses could be so assertive yet inoffensive when they spoke to patients. They spoke directly about difficult subjects and yet did so without any bullshit. They certainly didn't take any nonsense and Amy admired this skill. She had toyed with the idea of training to be a nurse when she was younger and choosing her path through life. However, as she often felt queasy in a butcher's shop, Amy decided that a busy A&E Department or, worse still an operating theatre, was probably no place for her. Through her momentary distraction, Amy suddenly heard a familiar voice, talking somewhere;

"Is that you Mike?" she called out to the wider-world outside the pale blue curtain that shrouded hers.

"Amy? Are you all done then?" came the reply, still familiar but still from a place unknown to her. "Where are you?" the mind-reading voice had beaten her to the question on her lips and Amy found herself replying;

"I'm here Mike!" at once giving him a clear response and yet no real answer at all.

"Yeah, ok...but *where* exactly!" Mike's voice verged on laughter.

"Sorry...er, well I'm behind a light-blue curtain. I'd come and look for you but the nurse told me not to get up yet. You know how light-headed I get someti..." and with that, the curtain behind her parted slightly and her brother was stood by her bed, chuckling. Behind him Amy could hear gentle laughter coming from a variety of other directions. Mike was giving her one of his looks.

"Amy, we're *all* behind light-blue curtains!" he laughed as he pulled the curtain back a little further, at once enabling Amy to see the length of the room. It was more like an old fashioned hospital ward. All Amy could see was light-blue curtain material. A few had been pulled back slightly and in between these she could see people lying on beds, drinking plastic cups of tea and looking in her direction, all of them smiling. Any looked back at Mike, slightly red-faced;

"Yeah, well, ok" she said, "And how was I supposed to know? I could've been anywhere" she looked back at her feet, dangling over the side of the bed, she was swinging them back and forth like a sulky eight-year-old.

"Are you going to try to stand up then?" asked Mike unsympathetically "And you'd better pick your bottom lip up before you do, or you'll trip over it!" He laughed a little but his mirth was cut short by the sight of his little sister who, immediately as she stood, fell backwards again, knees buckling beneath her.

"WOAH there!" he said as he grabbed her under each arm, stopping her from falling to the cold white-tiled floor. Mike gently raised her enough to sit her back onto the bed and released his grip. He lifted her feet up to the level of the bed and Amy slowly pulled herself back into the foetal position. Mike covered her with the soft blue knitted blanket and called out to Debs who was further down the ward;

"Are you ok to grab another cuppa Deb? One for me too while you're at it please. I think we might wait a little longer before trying to get this little one home! It'll give me time to see how Liam is doing anyway."

Debs' head appeared from behind a curtain a few beds down.

"Yeah no worries, I'll see what I can find. If I can, I'll get some good old NHS digestives too!" she replied cheerfully and disappeared in a cloud of light-blue.

+   +   +   +   +   +

"There were only three of us in the end, only three who could donate *his* blood type you see?" Mike sounded apologetic as he explained to Maddie and Clive why he hadn't turned up with an army of friends, family, work colleagues and students from Highdowns to rescue Liam in his hour of need.

"Mike, what you, Amy and your friend have done is wonderful really," said Clive, and he tried to reassure Mike by resting his hand on top of

Mike's own. Mike hurriedly pulled his hand from under Clive's and looked at Maddie.

"How is he Maddie? Is he doing ok? What are the doctors saying? And what happened exactly? Was it an accident? I mean, I know he's a kid but surely to God he can cross the road without..." Mike trailed off, realising two things; one, he wasn't giving Maddie an earthly chance to answer his barrage of questions and two; she would struggle anyway, given that she had started to cry.

Clive went to speak but Maddie took hold of his hand to stop him before he could intervene again. She seemed to understand that Mike needed to hear it from *her* this time. She gathered herself and Mike, patiently waiting, somehow knew it wasn't going to be easy for either of them. Maddie blew her nose and dried her eyes. She looked at Mike;

"I've right royally fucked this up haven't I? I mean, God I've fucked it up good and proper for sure," she said. She glanced sideways at Clive for a moment but he was too busy looking to the sky to get absolution for Maddie's profanity. She looked back at Mike and continued;

"He's pretty poorly Mike. There have been some internal injuries and bleeding, they've removed one of his kidneys and his spleen too. They might operate again later; they think he might lose the other kidney. And it's entirely my fault, my poor baby is in there with pipes and tubes and wires and everything sticking out of him and it's MY FAULT!" she broke down in tears once again and Clive put his arms around her. He smoothed her hair back and tried to comfort her as best he could, but Maddie was inconsolable.

"Look it's no-one's fault as such is it?" offered Mike, "I mean, these things happen all the time don't they? A kid steps off the kerb without looking, they lose concentration or they've got their headphones on and are in a world of their own, or a driver comes around a corner too quickly....was the driver going too fast Maddie? Was that it?" Mike looked like he was getting angry but suddenly his mood changed. It was dawning on him that there might be worse still to come.

"Hang on, if he's lost a kidney and his spleen already, three blood donors won't be anywhere near enough will it? If they operate again he'll need lots more. Loads more in fact. What are we going to do? I'm happy to give more but I don't suppose they'll take more from me yet will they?"

"It's ok Mike," said Clive calmly. "The hospital put a call out to other local donors and they've had a pretty good turn out I believe. Everyone in that ward where you lot gave blood are giving blood for Liam – or any other emergency case today I guess – it was a really good response. The hospital was pleased anyway."

Mike felt reassured but as he sat back down on his chair, Maddie spoke again,

"It's my fault though Mike, as usual I made a mess of things. Like I always do I suppose."

"What do you mean Maddie?" Mike asked, somewhat tentatively, "Why is this your fault? Do you mean Liam didn't just lose concentration like other kids do? Are you saying it wasn't an accident?"

"Look, we don't need to get into all that now do we?" asked Clive, "I mean, this is no time for the blame game. I think we need to keep a united and supportive front for Liam at the moment and see what we can do to help get him through all of this. There'll be plenty of time for post-mortems later...er, well, I didn't mean...er, an unfortunate choice of words, I'm sorry...it's just that what I mean is that we can all help Liam NOW and then we can see what happens once he's up and about again, ok? You know what kids are like, they'll have you out of your mind with worry one minute and then before you know it they're out and about, in the park playing football and staying out late. I'm sure he'll be fine Madeline ok? And you'll all get over this I'm sure."

"Well thank goodness he's got you and God on his side eh Clive?" said Mike, sarcastically. He was growing impatient and becoming unafraid to show it. Clive frowned at Mike but did what his god always suggested at such times and turned the other cheek whilst Mike continued,

"Look, I'm sure things will pan out ok and all that but can one of you *please* just tell me what happened?" He looked more insistent and Maddie knew it was time to be honest with him for the first time in living memory. Clive sat back down and with resignation, folded his arms. Maddie adjusted her hair slightly and dried her eyes once again. She looked at Mike and started to tell him, voice trembling, about what had happened.

"Listen, when I said it was *my* fault Mike, it *was* my fault. Liam and I had been having an argument and he ran off. I tried to stop him but he was so upset it was impossible to catch him." Mike went to interrupt but Maddie continued before he could squeeze a word out. He went cold when he heard her words;

"He found your case Mike. He found the red case you left with me when you came to the church at Easter with all of that stuff in it. I had misjudged the situation so badly, I didn't realise how you had felt. I saw that you had been hurt by it all so much more than I thought you would've been. I wanted to get rid of the case but somehow I couldn't. I wanted to tell him about it but somehow I couldn't do that either. By the time I realised he was going through my stuff he had read the cards and letters. I tried my best to explain it all to him but we had a blazing row as you can imagine. He said all sorts of horrible things, given what I had told him all his life and that's when it happened."

Mike was numb, his mind, usually so prone to racing, seemingly wasn't functioning at all. He could only feel the pressure rising behind his eyes and could only hear the sound of his heart beating, not fast, just beating loudly. Was this what a stroke felt like? Had he just had some sort of seizure? He couldn't move his head; he couldn't speak; his arms and legs appeared to be made of lead; he wasn't even sure for a few moments if he could see or hear any longer. Then it dawned on him that he was starting to ruminate so, realising that normal service was at last resuming, Mike felt able to explode;

"For fuck's sake, I hope you aren't even *contemplating* saying that some of this is somehow something to do with me, that this is *my* fault for showing up after all these years! You were right earlier Maddie, you were right when you said this was *your* fault! This IS your fault; you ARE to blame; your actions have caused all of THIS!" he stood up and looked around the waiting room in which they were sat and mentally pointed to each of the invisible problems in his head. The problems that had undermined so many aspects of his life since she took Liam away; the missed opportunities; the failed job applications; the failed relationships; his inability

227

to listen to anything other than punk rock songs that were decades old; his shitty taste in cars. Basically for everything that had ever gone wrong in his adult life, Mike wanted to blame Maddie. He looked back at her; Maddie was stock-still and staring at Mike with a look of horror on her face. Clive sat quivering, struck dumb by the force of Mike's anger. Mike wasn't even nearly finished,

"Oh but you can be relied upon to do *one* thing right can't you?" he snorted. "You can be sure that you hurt *everyone* else and still escape without a scratch can't you? It couldn't be you stepping out in front of a car – or better still a fucking bus – could it Maddie? Oh no, you have to drive an innocent kid to doing it rather than you. Well do you know what? I hope he makes a full recovery and lives a fucking long and healthy life. Do you know why? Well I'll tell you. Two reasons why Liam should have a long and healthy life are, one; he deserves to as he hasn't done anything wrong but be born into this world to the wrong parents and two; he can be a constant reminder of what a fucking twat you can be. He can make sure you are reminded of your actions so that your guilt lasts until the DAY YOU DIE."

Mike turned to Clive; he tilted his head slightly and spoke, this time a little more softly,

"And *you* Clive, what are *you* going to do? Your god has spoken I guess, but he's exacted his retribution on the wrong person surely. How will you explain that to Liam when he comes around, IF he comes around of course, and what about to the rest of your flock eh? Surely they'll see you as a bit of a failure if you can't even keep your own young *charge* safe? If I was you Clive I'd get the hell away from this woman now. You've seen what a destructive influence she is and what she's capable of man, so get out while you still can."

"Look Mike, whatever you think of all of this, you have to understand that I really care about Liam. I care deeply about both Madeline and Liam in fact." A tear fell from Clive's eye as he spoke. "I'm determined to be a good father to him and everything that being a father means. I know I'm probably not *cool* enough for his tastes, but then again I doubt very many fathers are cool enough for their kids, whoever they are."

"Your point being, Clive?" Mike's irritation had not subsided and he was half-preparing to blow again.

"Mike, it was always going to be tough to take on someone else's kid, of course it was. His father is dead and there is no extended family that we know of right?" he looked at Maddie for confirmation and then back at Mike again. "But suddenly in his world Mike, Liam saw there might be more. There may not have been a father out there but there had been someone who had helped support him through tough times; someone who had quietly wanted more than a long distant relationship with him; who wanted to share things with him; be a role model and all that. Look, what I'm trying to say, badly I know, is that the reason he ran away from Madeline after the row is that he was going to look for you. He took the most recent photograph of you and was hell-bent on finding you. Liam was in a really confused state of mind and can't have been looking where he was going. The driver had no chance of avoiding him....."

Mike didn't hear the rest of Clive's sermon. He slowly sat down on the red plastic chair and started to cry. Mike had long believed that he had been Maddie's only victim but now he could see that he wasn't alone. He needed to remember that the tissue of lies was, however, the *only* thing he shared with Liam. The poor kid in the High Dependency Unit was suffering too. There was no denying that Liam had been poorly treated, not that Maddie had intended it this way, and by running away maybe he was just demonstrating that he had inherited Maddie's impulsive and emotionally charged streak. Clive and Maddie silently watched as Mike wept. Mike was desolate. If he could have erased the previous few weeks and return to before he knew Liam was Rod's son, the news that Liam had tried to contact him would have been the best news ever. Now though, it made things even more heartbreaking. He also knew that Liam was just a kid and was more important in all of this than he was himself, however desperate he might have felt. It would be more difficult for a child to overcome such things than it would be for an intelligent, rational adult. As he sat with his head in his hands, Mike suddenly heard a familiar voice behind him;

"Ah, here you are you miserable old bastard. Looks like you wanna get outta here, am I right?"

Sid was stood in the doorway to the room, resplendent in ripped jeans, biker jacket and black motorcycle boots. He had an unlit cigarette hanging from the corner of his mouth and he was smiling. Mike looked up and took in the sight;

"You thinking about turning your hand to catalogue modeling then?" Mike asked, wiping the tears from his eyes and raising a smile once again. It was so good to see him. He turned to Maddie and Clive and said;

"I've said all I want to say to you two ok? I want you to keep me updated on Liam's progress but I can't get involved in this any further. Please don't let Liam contact me, I think it's for the best, for *all* of us." Maddie and Clive nodded in quiet unison. Mike slapped Sid on the shoulder and pushed past him into the corridor. Debs and Amy were there too, Amy had a little more colour in her cheeks than she did the last time Mike saw her, she also had about five biscuits in one hand and a plastic cup of tea in the other.

"What a fucking day eh?" Mike said to all of the assembled. "If I live to be a hundred, I'll never have another day like this!" Turning to Sid he went on; "And you...what are doing here? And how did you find us?" Sid was still smiling;

"Look, I spoke to H and Candy and they told me what happened so I came. But there's no time for all *that*, do you wanna get outta here or shall I just fuck off without you?" Sid held his hand up before Mike could speak and continued; "And before you give me your answer I should tell you I've got a brand spanking Triumph Bonneville T100 outside in black if you wanna ride?"

He looked at Debs and Amy and added, "My *little bonus* from the nice TV people for helping someone win *Pop Factor* last night you understand?" before looking back at Mike; "So think carefully before you answer my question...do you wanna get outta here?"

Amy spoke before her brother could gather his thoughts. She was clearly thrilled with what she was hearing.

"Ooh, don't say who won Sid, I've recorded it but haven't watched it yet!" she exclaimed and she clapped her hands together like a performing seal as if to emphasise her excitement.

Mike pulled a face at his sister and pulled his car keys from his pocket. He jingled them in front of Sid's face;

231

"Sorry mate, I'd love to but I've got the car".

Sid snatched the keys from Mike's hand and threw them to Debs who caught them expertly. He looked back at Mike and, with a knowing grin, said;

"Look mate, it's a *girl's* car ok? So just let a girl drive it home!"

I used to make phantoms I could later chase
Images of all that could be desired.
Then I got tired of counting all these blessings,
And then I just got tired...

Chapter 23

As he looked around the magnolia coloured space in which he found himself, Mike still couldn't believe he was standing in the waiting room at the Health Centre once again. It was the final week of Rumination Club and, after enduring the previous meeting the week before, he had been determined to simply provide feedback without putting himself through the ordeal of attending. He completed the same questionnaire as always, but this week bravely resisted the urge to tick the 'Yes' box on whether he had considered ending his own life during the last seven days and the 'o' box on the number of times he had attempted this. He resisted these temptations as he knew that the two occasions he would have remotely contemplated suicide were just *after* the previous meeting and whilst he was on the way to the Health Centre *this* week.

There were only three attendees in the waiting room, including Mike. Bryan and Mel had made it and Mike realised there was no Carol following her outburst the previous week. Also, rather unsurprisingly, there were only two practitioners present. Mike was correct in his assertion to himself last week that they would probably not see her again and assumed that Gabs was possibly still looking for stragglers.

Sally-Anne with-an-e commenced

233

proceedings in her inimitable style by informing the group that it was going to be a shorter session than usual. Mike recounted to everyone how his beloved dogs were enjoying the regular exercise they had been getting since he had been attending the group and the group looked pleased that they had somehow contributed to the greater welfare of such wonderful pets. Mike promised that he would build upon this new exercise regime. Once everyone had briefly shared their successes and failures and proclaimed their plans for the following week, Sally-Anne addressed the group.

"So, as I've said, we will only take about half an hour of your time this week everyone. I'm sure you all have things to do and what we intend for this evening is for you to reflect on your learning from the last few weeks, ok? So, tell me, did you all get to grips with the traffic light system we talked about?"

As was customary the group refused to answer, although Mike let out a little sigh at this miracle of planning on the practitioners' behalf. He had agreed to meet Amy in the White Hart at the usual time and was now contemplating sitting alone at the bar for half an hour waiting for her to arrive. Sally-Anne broke the silence by addressing Mike directly;

"So, Mike? Did you manage to look at the times when you are '*in the red*', or feeling *a 'little amber'*, or maybe when you are '*well into the green*'? Mike?" Sally-Anne made finger-inverted-commas so frequently within the one sentence that it was all Mike could do to control the urge he felt to snap off each of her digits in turn. He answered Sally-Anne angrily in his head;

"Well, Sally-Anne-*with-a-fucking-e*, apart from feeling '*in the red*' whenever someone does *'this'*..." he paused and made a matching pair of inverted commas with his fingers, "I do know when I am in the *red*. I also know when I am *in the green*, when I am feeling a *little bit amber*, which of course is basically when I'm neither *red* nor *green*. I am also acutely aware of when I am being a bit of a *cowardly yellow* and also when I'm *brassed-off* or even when I'm *singing-the-fucking-blues* ok?"

Although what he actually heard himself saying was;

"Er, yeah, um...thanks."

Sally-Anne didn't press Mike further, preferring to turn to Bryan and Mel and ask them the same question. Like Mike, Mel said she had done her homework. Bryan, however, looked a little sheepish and seemingly by way of an admission said,

"Well, no, not really. I had a bit of trouble with the idea and wondered if you might go over it again for us?" He paused and looked at Mike and Mel before continuing, uncharacteristically, "...That is, if the others don't mind?"

Realising that the shorter session was about to get a whole lot longer and also recognising that Bryan had suddenly become aware of others' needs and wishes, Mike smiled and nodded accordingly, as did Mel.

Demonstrating her aversion to recapping, Sally-Anne turned to Na'er-lee and smiled weakly. Na'er-lee stood up and addressed the group;

"Do y'know what? I think we can, er, like, maybe go over this again yeah? An' when we're all, like, ok with it an' stuff, maybe we can finish up for the time being, yeah?"

When Rumination Club eventually finished and, instead of a shorter session a whole hour had

235

passed, everyone said their goodbyes and went their separate ways. Mike wondered if he would ever see any of the group or the practitioners ever again. This was despite being told of a '12 Week Review Meeting' by Na'er-lee. At the end of the meeting she had explained what group members should expect;

"You'll all, like, be invited to come to, er, a sort of meeting? It's called a twelve week review which, er, is sort of a follow up session an' that? It's, like, gonna be held in about a month from now though? OK?" Being faced with a short row of confused countenances she went on to clarify;

"It's, like, just that we used to, like, um, call it a 'Twelve Week Review'? As we held it twelve weeks after the sessions, like, ended? Yeah? But we changed it like 'cos we found that, er, no one would attend an' stuff? We reckoned it was, like, waaay too long after these, er, sessions had ended an' that, so we moved it to a month afterwards? It's just that, like, er that we just haven't changed the handouts?...Or the title...Yeah?"

+   +   +   +   +   +

Later that evening in the White Hart Mike recounted to a bemused Amy how Rumination Club had eventually ended.

"We were promised a letter inviting us to the *twelve-week-review-in-a-month-from-now*   in due course but I have a sneaking suspicion I'll either get the letter a week *after* the meeting has taken place or I won't get any invitation at all."

Amy smiled but there was clearly something troubling her. As Mike stared into the abyss that was his empty pint glass, she prodded him gently and spoke;

"Weren't you asked to give your feedback on how it all went? I mean, they can't just continue force feeding this horseshit to people and patronising them to death and expect no feedback, surely to god?"

"Oh yeah" said Mike, "I got to give my feedback alright, we all did! As there were only three of us, we all got to give feedback individually in front of the rest of the group so you can imagine, given how reluctant to speak we still are, how that went. I mean, how inappropriate was THAT? To ask us for feedback in front of the others? Can you? Basically I just offered some brief and positive platitudes along the lines of; *It was engaging* – although it wasn't; *It had been fun* – although it hadn't; *That it was positive that we had felt included* – although we didn't; *That it wasn't at all patronising* – even though it was; *That it had been useful* – but of course it really hadn't; we even agreed that we *no longer felt alone* – even if we felt we did!"

Amy smiled and put her hand on Mike's shoulder. He sighed and she looked at her brother and sighed too;

"So you didn't tell them anything negative at all? Surely you could have used your tired old cliché about how *'there's no such thing as failure, only feedback'* so no-one got upset or hurt by it? They'll never know how crap they are unless they get that from people like you Mike. Let's face it, none of the other numbskulls sitting there are going to tell them what's what and they obviously don't take the dwindling numbers into consideration of how well – or otherwise – they are doing!"

Mike sat silently for a few moments thinking about Amy's question, which was left unanswered. He heard her ask someone behind the bar for two more drinks and he thought long and hard to locate a negative or two he could have mentioned. He took the beer that Amy held out to him and said;

"It was pretty much how it always is Amy so I don't know what I could've fed back to them as a negative. It was *just* as I had been expecting I s'pose, my expectation levels were just *so* low..." and he paused for a moment before adding, "...although as it was the last week, it would've been nice if I'd have been able to talk some more about the dogs just one more time I guess".

It's not a case of telling the truth, some lines just
fit the situation,
Call me a liar - you would anyway.
It's not a case of aiming to please; you know
you're always crying.
It's just your part, in the play for today.

Chapter 24

"Well it *was* the very end of a *very* long week of rehearsing, recording, re-rehearsing and re-recording mate. I'd used all sorts at first to keep me awake; then more to send me off to sleep; and then more still to get me awake again. Just to keep to the schedule like. It was fucking punishing man!"

"Is he still whingeing about the other day and his un-erring ability to piss women off?" Amy asked Mike as she re-joined her brother and Sid at the small round table in the corner of the pub. She looked at Sid, who in turn was looking into an empty whisky tumbler in his left hand. Sliding a house-double of some unknown whisky across the table towards him she turned her attentions to Mike again, saying;

"Well he's only got himself to blame. I mean he ought to know how to treat a woman by now didn't he? He's a middle-aged lothario who's never held down a relationship with a member of the opposite sex and then he whines and moans when a woman he's shagged dumps him when she realises that he can't even be bothered to remember her name!"

"Look I'm still *here* OK? I can hear you, and she didn't '*dump me*' alright?" said Sid whilst

239

making speech marks with his fingers, "We weren't in any kind of relationship or anything. We met, we enjoyed each others' company and the rest....well, y'know, the rest just happened as it often does. It was never destined to be anything other than what it was. As for being *dumped* as you put it, sure she yelled a bit and then asked me to call her a taxi – *which I did* – and then she left. That's how I happen to like it. Simple as that!" Sid sipped at the whisky then held it up to the light and looked at it with narrowing eyes. He smelled it and frowned.

"As far as I am concerned Sid, you deserve everything you get," said Mike who, if he was being honest would have admitted that he felt more antipathy towards Sid in that moment for his visible punctuation marks than for the way he treated his women.

"But it wasn't *just* a woman; it was *Linzi-Jeen Newton* for goodness' sake! Not only is she *H-O-T* but she's number one in the charts right now!" exclaimed Amy. "...AND by the way she's only about half your age Sid, you're old enough to be her father, you know that, right? Bloody hell you really blew it this time." Amy sat back and picked up her drink, having well and truly rested her case. Sid looked across at Amy and then at Mike, he smiled and with a glint in his eye said;

"Look, it wasn't me that *blew* anything ok? It was *her* in fact!" he beamed as he delivered the line and Amy went pale for a moment, she gulped. She certainly didn't need this level of detail. But seizing the opportunity Sid continued unabashed;

"And I'm pretty glad she's NOT my daughter either...I mean, I wouldn't want any kid of mine doing the sort of stuff she was eagerly getting up to *that* night, *hur-hur*!" he picked up his glass, raised it in a mock toast towards Amy and drained it in one gulp. Sid frowned again as the taste of the cheap whisky fumes hit his throat before he and Mike burst into laughter; Amy pulled a face of disgust. Yet again, Sid continued;

"At any rate, she'll be number one for a couple of weeks sure, and then it'll be number seven next time around and number thirty-two the next. Then next year she'll be on Celebrity Big Brother or in the jungle. The year after she'll struggle to get a bit-part in Christmas Panto in Southend-on-Sea. Before you know it she'll be back flipping burgers in Chelmsford McDonalds and customers will be staring at her name badge and wondering what kind of mindless fucking Essex Country and Western fan spells their kid's name like *that!* She *was* hot alright, but I'll tell you something else, she..."

"Hi everyone!" called out Debs, walking up behind Sid and interrupting him in mid flow. She was with Titan. Tim went to the bar and engaged the man behind it in conversation about wine whilst Tania and Debs sat down with the friends.

"How's Liam Mike? Any news?" she asked, touching him on the arm gently as she did so. Mike furrowed his brow slightly and moved to speak. Debs, Amy, Tania and even Sid leant in towards him. Mike swallowed hard, sipped his beer and swallowed again. He looked around the table and spoke quietly;

"Yeah, I got a text from Clive this morning. Liam's still holding his own and responding ok to treatment. He's stable now but they still think he might lose the second kidney as it's not functioning at all well. They're looking at his tissue type to see what kind of match they may need from a suitable donor as a fall back. Kids

241

quite often have to wait a long time for a decent match as the number of people who die carrying a donor card is far lower than the number of people waiting for an organ...although Clive seems to think children get some priority over older people or something. At any rate, he's going to be pretty poorly for a while I guess."

"Bloody hell," said Debs, "They must all be going through it at the moment. Imagine that, you're basically waiting for someone to die tragically so that your own child can survive and have a normal life again. What are the chances of a living donor Mike?"

"To get a decent match his only realistic chance of a quick transplant would be from a close family member so that's pretty much out of the question" Mike was clearly feeling gloomy again. "If he had a healthy sibling, you know a sister or a brother maybe, they *could* have been a good match, but he hasn't. Maddie has done so many drugs over the years she's not really well enough and his dad is deceased and had no living family as far as everyone knows. Clive reckons that good matches can be found so, as there's no likely hope of a living donor anytime soon he's waiting for a decent match from a dead stranger."

The friends fell silent. They were quietly absorbing Mike's words. Their solemn mood was suddenly broken by Tim, who arrived at the table carrying a tray. On it were a small brown beer bottle, an empty half-pint glass with a stem, a glass of what appeared to be red wine and a tall glass of orange juice. He was obviously unhappy about something;

"I don't know *why* we come in this place I really don't!" he said, putting the tray down on the table and tutting loudly. He looked at the faces around the table and, still standing on an invisible soap-box, continued; "It's not as if we haven't got a decent wine bar or two in town now. And what about the little independent micro-brewery in Hope Street? The Warren Arms? We should be in there drinking their craft beers instead of the slop you've got there Mike." And he nodded at Mike's JLB glass, which was half empty, rather than half full as usual.

Tim sat down heavily and handed the orange juice to Debs, the red wine to Tania and placed the brown bottle of beer on a wet beer mat in front of him and the empty stemmed-glass next to it. Tania took Tim's hand but before she could speak, he shook his hand free and continued with his complaint, wagging his finger as he did so;

"All I asked for was a decent red, *'Maybe a Rioja?'* I said." Tim turned to Sid, "You know... a 2009 would be nice or perhaps even a 2005? I mean, 2009 was a good year but really it's best drunk early of course. The 2005 on the other hand, is just *extraordinary*. So, what does the barman say in reply? I'll tell you shall I? He says *'We've only got this Merlot'*, that's what he says, and it's in a box...A BOX for crying out loud! And then, just when you think it can't get worse...it gets *worse*! They still don't do freshly squeezed orange juice in here, no matter how often I request it and then I ask for a craft beer and I get a bottle of *this*!" Tim held up a small brown bottle of beer with a bright green label, "He said it's an IPA from an independent brewery but I just know it came from the same cash-and-carry where he bought the god-awful bottles of UHT orange. I didn't even know anyone still made UHT orange for goodness' sake!" Tim sat back, seemingly exhausted. Tania took hold of his hand once again

243

and gently spoke,

"Mike was just telling us about Liam and how he's getting on sweetie. He's still quite poorly you know."

"Oh yes, er...of course, s-sorry to hear that mate..." stammered Tim, looking at Mike a little guiltily before picking up his beer and pouring it into his glass, "...is there anything we can do?"

Mike treated the question as if it were rhetorical and switched the conversation to another subject.

"Well, look, that's enough of all that for now, I was going to ask if anyone has seen H and Candy at all? I haven't seen them in a while and just wondered if there was any truth in the rumours I've been hearing!"

It seemed that no one had seen them since they visited Titan and spilled the beans about being an item. It was exciting news, given that Candy was always being pursued by H whilst she busied herself pursuing Sid, the leather-clad elephant in the room who nobody was mentioning this evening. Sid explained that he had in fact seen them the day after the 'Pop Factor' final and they had informed him of the accident and that Mike had gone to the hospital to give blood. He had been looking for Mike and Amy as he had missed some calls that same day so was riding around looking for them on his new motorcycle.

+   +   +   +   +   +

"There's not really anything else to tell ok?" Sid was drunk by the time he, Mike and Amy walked along the road to Mike's house after the pub closed. Sid started to let on more than he had intended about bumping into H and Candy.

244

"I was on my way to Titan's, I'd already been to Candy's but there was no one in, and just as I parked the bike in the road by the Off Licence I saw Candy standing on the corner. I went over and started to talk to her. She was her usual self, all coy and that, she said she liked the bike and then H suddenly comes out of the Offy with a couple of bottles of plonk. She, just as suddenly as he appears, stops talking to me and starts to look all shifty. She decides to leave the talking to him obviously and *he* gets a bit funny with me; looks like I maybe can't speak to her any more or something because he's with her now. I'm surprised that he didn't give me a slap for good measure to be honest; you know what he's like. Anyhow, she stayed pretty silent throughout the whole *warning-shots-across-the-bows* thing, so I guess I know where I stand eh? She *did* tell me about Liam's accident though. Turns out Titan had told them all about it a few minutes before I showed up. As soon as I heard that, I was on my way." Sid made a gesture like an airplane taking off into the distance before adding, as an aside;

"Do you know what he said to me before I left though? Christ! That bloody H told me I would never be trustworthy. He said I would be like a teetotal landlord or a thin chef...beyond trust! Do you get that? Do you? Cos I sure as hell don't!"

Mike and Amy glanced at each other. They may have been drinking but they still instinctively knew exactly what H meant by his statement and consequently they knew Sid would always be under H's scrutiny. Secretly, Sid knew this too, but he refused to admit it to Mike and Amy.

Mike took his keys from his jacket pocket and opened his front door. As he stepped back to allow Amy to walk inside, Sid pushed past them both and wandered straight into the lounge. Mike and Amy took off their coats in silence.

"I tell you what *guysss*..." continued a now slurring Sid as Mike and Amy joined him in the lounge, "...H had better add a *sssilent woman* to his lissst of people not to trust, if he knows what's good for him...getting with *her* that ish!" He slipped his leather jacket off and let it fall to the floor. Sid held his left hand up like a notepad and, taking an imaginary pencil from behind his right ear, Sid made as if to write on the invisible page;

"Right, the *lissst* goes as follows; (1) *Sober-Ssteve-of-the-Ssurrey Arms*; (2) *Gordon-Fucking-Iron-Man-Fucking-Ramsey* and (3) *Coy-Candy-The-Ever-S-s-so-Fucking-SILENT!*"

Shouting his last word and, finishing his imaginary list with a flourish and an overly-dramatic yet still invisible full-stop, Sid slumped into the reclining armchair.

"You two should stay," said Mike, smiling broadly. He looked at Amy and said, "The spare room has clean bedding, Sid can kip on the sofa. Now, I'll stick the kettle on, tea and biscuits all 'round, yes?"

"Ooh that'd be good. Mmm! A nice cup of tea," nodded a smiling Amy. They both looked at Sid for an answer, he was fast asleep.

And I've lived, that kind of day,
When none of your sorrows will go away,
It goes down and down and hits the floor
Down and down and down some more -
depression.

Chapter 25

"So, Mr. Powell, from what you're feeding back to me the CBT wasn't really much of a success or much of a help. Am I correct in my assessment?"

Dr Andrea Baker was sounding like Sally-Anne-*with-an-e* all of a sudden, starting sentences with '*So*' and ending them with a tone Mike perceived as condescending. Mike had been called into the surgery to see her as his latest sick-note was due to expire and he had requested an extension. He didn't really have time for it, today of all days as he had places to go and things to do. Well, ONE place to be and ONE thing to do actually. But Dr Baker wanted to hear more about how he was feeling before issuing the new note, which was odd as Mike had come to believe that GPs distributed sick notes like people distributed confetti at a wedding. It had always been his experience that colleagues at Highdowns and previous institutions where he had worked, appeared to have been signed off for seemingly very little. His experience with Dr Baker however, was starting to appear different.

"Look doctor, I'm not saying that it was a waste of time and money you understand, just that I still feel very low. I have no motivation to do anything; I'm close to either tears or bouts of anger at the drop of a hat; I tend to stay indoors rather than go out anywhere unless I'm dragged out by friends; I can't sleep some nights and then others I just can't get out of bed. I seldom cook for myself and my house is a mess most of the time. And all the time I can feel this tightness in my chest, this weight on me that I can't shift. It feels a bit like someone's died. I'm not suicidal; I just can't see any purpose in my life. Do you know what? I even feel guilty that I feel this way and that I must be bringing everyone around me down too, so I tend to stay away from others when I'm able to. I ask myself, *'What have I got to be depressed about?'* and I can't find an answer. I've got so much to be happy about in my life, it makes no sense to me that everything looks so damned bleak" and as if on cue, Mike started to cry.

"Here you are," said Dr Baker, holding a box of tissues in Mike's general direction, "I didn't mean to add to your burden, it's not that I'm critical of your attitude or anything. From the sounds of it you did rather well to actually turn up every week. I know most people would have dropped out along the way. It's rather that I've heard this kind of thing before about the Mood Club and I'm beginning to think we need to do a full review on its effectiveness and maybe an impact assessment." She looked back at her desk and scribbled a few words on a small-white form on a pad in front of her and tore the top page off. Handing it to Mike she said,

"Try not to worry about how you feel ok? I know the CBT may have been a bit below your capabilities but look at it this way. They talked sense, however patronising it might have been at times I grant you, but they did. All that stuff about spotting what triggers your low mood and what enhances your mood; the problem solving techniques and the need for motivation and planning. I appreciate it's maybe a bit of a bore when talking about SMART objectives and having to think consciously about doing it all but, once we get used to doing it, we find it becomes an unconscious process once again. Sometimes the motivation to do something happens after we actually start doing it, do you know what I mean? Sometimes we have to force ourselves into starting something we'd really rather not do and then, almost miraculously if it's me doing the gardening for example, we find that we have achieved something positive and the feeling is pretty good!"

She was still smiling at Mike as he looked at the sick-note in his hand and started to process what Dr Baker was saying. He knew it all made sense somehow. He knew that some of the things he had done recently regarding the Liam situation were things he hadn't felt like doing; had even feared doing; but he *had* felt better once he had done them...hadn't he? The sick-note was for another month and Mike felt a sense of relief when he saw that he could stay away from the pressures of work for a little longer.

"Thanks Doctor," said Mike, with a sense of relief quite obvious in his voice. "And sorry if I went off a bit there, I think I was misunderstanding what you were saying about the Rumina...er, I mean about the Mood Club. Another of my symptoms at the moment is to jump to conclusions I s'pose. I'll bear in mind what you've said and see where it gets me, ok?"

Dr Baker tapped a few words out onto her computer. She looked at the screen, read the sentence back to herself, seemingly to confirm its accuracy, and then looked back at Mike.

"As it happens, I've just seen an email about the CBT sessions in my inbox, do you mind if I have a look? It might be relevant to what we have been talking about," she opened the email and read it silently before Mike had time to consider her question, let alone answer her. When she finished reading, Dr Baker turned to Mike with a wry smile;

"Well there you go, as if to prove everything you've been saying!" she said. "I have been emailed by someone from *Talk it Over* who is informing me that the twelve-week review, planned for *next month* for some bizarre reason, won't now be taking place. Apparently the room is already double-booked and there were only three people left at the end of the course, so a practitioner is going to telephone each one for an individual follow up. Sounds like it's going to end in the same inauspicious way in which it started!" she clapped her hands together and laughed.

Mike looked at her with an *I-told-you-so* look on his face and smiled, feeling slightly vindicated. He said nothing.

"And one more thing before you go Mr. Powell," continued Dr Baker, "If I may be so bold as to suggest this. Please stop asking yourself questions like *'Why me'*? and *'What have I got to be depressed about?'* Ok?"

Mike looked puzzled, particularly as Dr Baker, like so many others he had encountered in recent days, chose to make the dreaded mistake of emphasising the inverted commas she saw in her head with her fingers. She avoided his disdain by continuing with some simple common sense advice;

"It's just that you might as well ask what someone has to be *'diabetic about'* or what someone has to be *'asthmatic about'*...it really makes no sense at all to ask that question; because it makes no sense *as* a question; so it serves no positive purpose at all. Do you see?"

I saw the shape of things to come,
The future in your eyes.
The love you always meant to give,
The bodyguard of lies.

Chapter 26

As the teapot suddenly appeared in front of him, its masked eyes menacingly staring him out, Sid was jolted from his slumber. His eyes were still half stuck together and his head was full of cotton wool and jack-hammers. He groaned inaudibly and was about to voice his complaint when he heard a familiar voice;

"That was quite a night!" said Amy, rather too breezily for Sid's liking; "I've made tea!"

"Is there any coffee?" mumbled Sid whilst unscrambling his senses. He gasped for air and grasped for his cigarettes.

"Yeah...and *good morning* to you too! I'll go see what I can find," replied Amy, turning on her heels and disappearing as quickly as she had appeared.

Sid sat up, he gripped the arm of the chair to steady himself and, squinting in the daylight Amy had allowed to flood the room, he fumbled in his pocket for his Zippo. He drew a cigarette from the crumpled packet he found in his shirt pocket, straightened it out as best he could and lit it. He took a deep and long drag on the cigarette, inhaled the smoke and started to exhale. As he did so, Amy walked back into the room and Sid suddenly started to cough, uncontrollably. It was an extraordinarily loud hacking cough that set off the jack-hammers in Sid's head once again. It also made Amy pull a face. She walked past Sid and quietly opened the window to let some fresh air into the room and let some of Sid's smoke out. She turned to him, held out a small-white cup and saucer and simply said,

"Coffee. Black."

Sid held out his hand, Amy noticed that it was shaking slightly but she said nothing. She handed him the cup and saucer and poured a few drops of milk into a cup for herself. Amy picked up the teapot and as she started to pour herself a cup of tea she looked at Sid again as he sipped his coffee. Blinking hard, he looked up at Amy through his puffy bloodshot eyes.

"What *was* I drinking last night Amy? More to the point, what was I *thinking* to be knocking it back like that on a school night? Now that *Pop Factor* is out of the way I've got some stuff I need to do at TinCan. I'm about three or four jingles short of what's needed to cover the bills this month y'know? All thanks to the long run Linzi-Jeen had in the show. One thing I know is that her triumph – and *the Triumph* I ended up with – won't carry on paying the bills afterwards. Oh and where's Mike by the way? You not rudely roused *him* yet then?"

"Blimey, you're not very rock-n-roll *today* are you Sid? Not so much '*rebel-without-a-cause*' as '*rebel-without-a-clue*' I reckon!" Amy laughed, "What were you doing drinking '*on a school night*'? Are you *serious*? No one talks like that anymore, well, no-one under sixty anyway!" She sipped her tea and continued unabated, "Mike, you'll be surprised to learn, has already risen, washed and gone. He had to see his doctor first thing to get his sick note extended and he got a text from Clive overnight so I think he's going to take off to London for the day when he gets away from the surgery. I hope it's not more bad news. Anyway, he did ask me to see you managed to get up and out ok without setting light to yourself or the house before he left!" She laughed again.

Sid didn't appreciate Amy's mocking tone and silently sipped his coffee. Amy poured a few more drops of milk into her tea to adjust the taste and stirred it again. She turned to Sid and, plucking the cigarette from his fingers and crushing it out into the ashtray next to him, spoke softly;

"Look Sid, I know you might not recall much of what you said last night, y'know, about Candy and all that, but I just want you to know that I'm always around if you need someone to talk to ok? I can always put time aside for a chat y'know, like I do for Mike? I just want you to know, that's all."

Sid snorted. He put the coffee down and, fumbling in his mangled cigarette pack for another smoke, he stood up. Finding what he was looking for, Sid started his second cigarette repair of the morning before placing the filter tip in his mouth. He lit the still-badly-bent cigarette and took a puff.

"Cheers Amy, I'll bear that in mind," he said, rather sarcastically and then added as he exhaled; "It's just that I'm not in Mike's league with all this...this *stuff* ok? It doesn't figure as much for me." He scanned the room for his motorcycle helmet whilst putting on his leather jacket. He ruffled his black hair, bent down to pick up the helmet which was beside the armchair where he had spent the night and he stood up straight again to face Amy.

"Look, I remember everything I said last night but cannot think of a single thing I might *need* someone to confide in about any of it. Candy was

254

nothing to me. None of the women I sleep with actually *mean* anything to me. It doesn't make any difference whether it's a Candy, a Linzi-Jeen Newton or anyone really. I truly hope Candy and H are happy together for the rest of their natural lives, I really do. She deserves to be happy for once, she's been unhappy for so bloody long. H, well he deserves some credit for his persistence too doesn't he? That man should be rewarded for knowing what his dream is, for actively seeking it out and pursuing it relentlessly, even if it means us lot having a crafty laugh at him behind his back from time to time. Hopefully she'll be worth the wait to him. And it'll certainly save the rest of the female population of this bloody town from his ridiculous advances; from being propositioned by him every friggin' weekend won't it? And Linzi-Jeen? Let's just say she'll do ok and hopefully she'll get five-stars on her McDonalds name badge even if she doesn't get a five-star review for her album." Sid untangled the strap on his open-faced motorcycle helmet before continuing;

"I'm not just saying that to save my fragile ego or my pride or anything like that so please don't start playing the *pop-psychologist* with me ok? I don't get close to women; I've never really got close to women, probably since my mum and Anita died. I didn't really know my mum that well and of course I was devastated when Anita died. To see her deteriorate from a *tough-as-old-boots* Irish matriarch into a shell of a woman in a few months was fucking horrible, I was heartbroken I guess, but it's not affected who I am or how I live since. I know this much. I've analysed it time and time again you see? I recognise it, understand it - and maybe its significance too - yet I don't *care* enough to do anything about it. I like my life, er,

255

correction, I *LOVE* MY LIFE ok? It's something of an adventure and one thing's for certain, there's plenty more women out there who'll happily join me for the next installment I can assure you."

He picked up the cup of coffee and finished it quickly. It had gone a little cold but Sid knew the little extra shot of caffeine, along with the wind he was about to feel on his face as he rode to Surrey, would wake him up fully so he could face the day ahead. He'd eat later of course, someone would send out for a takeaway, or get some pizzas delivered, or Nancy would take everyone's orders and go into town on a '*grub-run*' as they called it in the studio. Sid zipped up his jacket, tightened the cuffs and pulled up the collar. As he went to pull the crash helmet on, Amy spoke.

"I understand all that Sid and look; we pay judges to sit in judgment and you know I'm no *Daily Mail* reader so I'm certainly not judging you or your chosen lifestyle. And I'm not trying to interfere or anything, I promise you. I just want you to know that if you ever want someone to spend more than a few moments in your life; I'm here and always will be. Now, before I get all sentimental you just go careful on that bike. I've seen you on one of those things before and you're a flaming menace to yourself!" With that, Amy kissed him on the cheek.

Sid, feeling a tinge of regret at speaking so harshly to Amy, put his arms around her and hugged her tightly for a moment. Whilst he did so, something he wished he'd had the courage to do many years before fleetingly crossed his mind. He loosened his grip on her slightly and looked deep into Amy's eyes; he held her like that for a few more seconds and moved his face closer to hers then, resisting the temptation to do anything more, he kissed her gently on the forehead.

"I think I'd better split before..." Sid trailed off and, before Amy could fully come to her senses and realise what had just *not* happened, the front door slammed shut. Sid was gone.

What's gonna happen when the sky turns black?
What will you do when the sea comes back?
What if there's no way of moving back?

Chapter 27

Listening to the opening lines of the song, swirling around in his head again and again was frustrating beyond belief for Mike.

This is, the Happy House,
We're happy here, in the Happy House,
Oh it's such fun, fun, fun, whoah...

He had heard them almost continually since leaving the doctors' surgery and along the journey to the Queen Mary Hospital. He was now completely on edge. Why did he buy a car without a hands-free facility? Why did he buy a bloody Vicar's wife's car for Christ's sake? Why was Sid always right about such things? Why oh why had he chosen *that* song as a ringtone for the hospital switchboard number? Mike had thought it would be ironic but *now*? Now, he could just scream.

This is, the Happy House,
We're happy here, in the Happy House,
Oh it's such fun, fun, fun...

If Sid's mobile rang when he was driving, he would just answer of course, Sid being Sid that is. Mike of course was made of different stuff. He had pulled over once only for the phone to stop playing the tune. Mike would then try Clive's number but there would be no call connection. Clive was obviously in a place in the hospital where calls from a mobile phone could not be made and so had his mobile switched off. Was this why he was calling Mike from the hospital switchboard and not his own phone? Why wasn't he leaving a voicemail message with more information? Damn it!

This is, the Happy House,
We're happy here, in the Happy House,
Oh it's such fun, fun, fun...

If ever there was a time when Mike wanted to hear a sappy tune from The Monkees over one of Siouxie and the Banshees' finest it was now. Mike drove faster and faster, he re-read the text message from Clive over and over in his head.

Mike, there's been a development
in Liam's condition. Can you give
me a call when you have a moment
please? Just for an update - that
is if you want an update of course
– Many thanks, Clive.

God it was so like Clive to punctuate a text perfectly; with commas, apostrophes and not using the letter 'u' for the word 'you', he even used a pair of hyphens – *FUCKING HYPHENS IN A TEXT MESSAGE!* Mike was aghast at the fact that Clive even signed the text with his name. Mike had been ringing Clive's number since he woke that morning and periodically since. However, he had only managed to reach the mobile network's robotic, automated voice, which repeatedly told him it was impossible to connect him and that he should try again later. It was the same pattern all the way to Queen Mary's. Mike would call, the robot would answer. Siouxie would call, Mike would be driving and unable to pick up. Clive would again leave no message on the voicemail. Was it good news or bad? Had there been a deterioration or an improvement?

This is, the Happy House,

259

We're happy here, in the Happy House,
Oh it's such fun, fun, fun...

As Mike drove in through Queen Mary's gateway he snarled at the 5 miles-per-hour maximum speed limit sign that greeted him – no, which taunted him – as he left the main road and drove onto hospital grounds. Mike quickly found a parking space and switched off his engine. He left his car and walked past the ticket machine, neglecting to buy himself a permit to park. He marched into the newest wing of Queen Mary's which housed the Intensive Care Unit where Liam was being cared for. As he turned the corner next to the Family Room where he had last seen Maddie and Clive, he saw the reception area and there was Clive, with a white desk-telephone in his hand, punching numbers into the keyboard. As Mike made to call out to him his mobile rang again.

This is, the Happ...

Mike quickly silenced Siouxie's lamenting, sarcastic refrain and put his mobile back in his pocket. As Mike reached the reception area, Clive turned and saw him and handed the white telephone back to the receptionist. He turned to Mike, smiling, and spoke;

"Crumbs mate, I've been trying to get hold of you all morning, where have you been?" he sounded urgent and slightly desperate in his tone. It was, however, all Mike could do to resist the urge not to head butt Clive in the middle of the face.

"I know that Clive, for fuck's sake! I've been at the doctors *and* I've been driving. I've also been trying to get hold of *you* but you left no accessible number for me to call back on, your mobile is switched off and you flatly refuse to leave any information on my voicemail so my blood pressure is through the fucking roof. I've been at my wits' end since I got your message, not that you said much at all of course, so here I am Clive. Now, what's the bloody score? What's happened? How's Liam?"

"It's not great Mike, looks like he's going to need a kidney after all. He's been pretty poorly overnight. He's conscious and heavily medicated. Madeline is with him, and it seems the only way they can improve his prospects now is to get him a donor, fast. It won't be easy though. As you know he has no blood relatives so the hospital is going through the records to look for any good blood and tissue matches. The chances are pretty low at the moment as there are a couple of people ahead of him in the local area awaiting transplants but, if a good match turns up, he has his youth as an advantage over the others who are both a good bit older." Clive shrugged his shoulders in a rather despondent 'so who knows' manner and fell silent.

Mike felt for Clive at this moment. It was still obvious that he really loved Liam and he had clearly been running on empty for some time. He looked pale, pathetic and drained of energy. Mike felt inclined to put a comforting hand on Clive's shoulder but resisted this urge just as equally as he had resisted the urge to do Clive physical harm a few moments earlier. Mike was still deep in thought as Clive asked the inevitable question; the question Mike had been both secretly yearning for and dreading since this whole sorry episode had begun; the question that, if answered, would mean there was no turning back, not ever.

"Do you want to come and see him Mike? I know he would like to meet you."

The question hung in the air between the two men for what seemed an eternity. Mike was convinced that if he didn't answer, Clive would withdraw the suggestion as an aberration, a simple mistake, an error of judgment on his behalf. Mike listened to the silence and Clive quietly refused to take back the offer. Mike could hear his heart beating, loud and fast. He was sure Clive could hear it too, yet still Clive waited politely for Mike's reply. Mike heard himself break the silence, falteringly at first, as he agreed to spend a few moments with a boy he had not seen since he was an infant and never had the chance to get to know. And yet it was also a child with whom he still also felt a long-held and close connection; a child who had affected Mike's entire life in ways only he knew or could even begin to understand and a child who had suffered greatly through no fault of his own.

"Blimey...er...are you sure? I mean, yeah...um...why not? He does know *everything* now though Clive doesn't he? It's just that I wouldn't want him getting confused or upset or...whatever, you know?"

Clive nodded and smiled. He beckoned Mike to follow him and walked away down the corridor towards the end where there was a closed white door with a small window. Along the walls of the corridor there were drawings, collages and paintings, donated to the hospital by a local college. There were also photographs of Queen Mary's Trustees, the great and the good of the local community. Yet Mike saw none of this. Mike could only see the door, like a small pinprick of light in a long black tunnel, drawn out before him. His mouth was dry, his mind racing and he felt his legs getting weaker. For a fleeting moment he thought he may not make it to the end of his journey and then, as Clive pushed the door open, Mike suddenly found himself in a bright, white room.

In the room sat Maddie, looking pale and tired and sitting beside a bed. The other side of the bed was a large white machine on a trolley and Mike could also see a drip on a tall shiny metal stand. In the bed was a small child with tubes going into his nose and the drip running through a long tube into his arm. He had a white bandage around his head. Mike was temporarily transfixed by how *white* everything was. The bedding, the walls, the curtains, even the floor. Everything was white. Mike's gaze was eventually drawn back to the boy, to Liam. Mike saw that he too was white. His face was the colour of the bandages and the bedding, there was no pink in his cheeks or lips. As Mike stared, Liam opened his eyes. He didn't look so much like a small child any longer. He looked older than his years in fact. In contrast to the lack of colour everywhere else, Liam's eyes were dark; dark and sparkling like Maddie's.

"Hullo," whispered Liam.

"Er...yeah, hi!" replied Mike, his attempt at sounding 'breezy' sounded more like a simple man trying to establish contact with an alien life form he had bumped into whilst walking in the forest. As he struggled to come up with something better, Liam spoke again;

"Cool t-shirt."

Mike looked down at the t-shirt he had put on that morning. It was partially hidden under an unbuttoned green ex-Army issue shirt that he was wearing, a look he had been perfecting seemingly since he was a teenager, and the part that was showing was adorned with a picture of a man in silhouette against a brightly coloured star design, with the words '*August 1952 – December 2002*'.

"Aren't you getting a bit old for all that stuff these days Mike? You used to wear stuff like that in your twenties and thirties. I can't imagine the lecturers at work being impressed; it's not much of an example to the *students* either is it?" Maddie was her usual, charmingly sarcastic self but Mike refused to bite. Maybe she was just trying to lighten the mood, Mike wasn't sure. She was smiling broadly but when they were younger she had been prone to sneer at him occasionally, particularly in regard to the music he liked and the clothes he wore so he knew there was an edge to what she was saying. Once upon a time he would have bitten back, today it didn't matter at in the slightest.

"He's probably wearing it ironically Madeline, aren't you Mike? Lots of people wear band t-shirts ironically these days I hear. Isn't that so?" Clive looked at Mike for affirmation; he was smiling and raising his eyebrows in anticipation of Mike's response.

None came. Instead, and choosing to ignore everyone in the room except for the patient, Mike pulled a chair over to the side of Liam's bed and spoke softly to him;

"Thanks mate, it's a guy called Joe Strummer. He was a musician and was someone I looked up to when I was younger. Still do actually, ever since I was about your age I guess. He died when he was still quite young and I liked him and so his death made me sad. I met him a couple of times too y'know. Me and a friend bunked off school, and bunked the train too, to see his band The Clash in Brighton once when we were kids. We

264

got there early and got to go backstage when they were doing a sound check. They let us hang out for a bit and just chatted to us like we were grown ups, we loved it! We told them that we were in a band too and Joe said he would dedicate their song *'Garageland'* to us later that evening. He must've had a lot on his mind or something 'cos they played the song that night but dedicated it to *everyone* who played in bands rather than just us but we didn't really care too much. I bumped into him at the bar at another gig much later. He was with some friends so I didn't get chance to speak to him again other than say 'hello' and shake his hand." Mike was smiling, re-living these significant moments in his mind's eye and hoping it would impress Liam. Coming back down to earth, he continued;

"Anyway, he did a lot of good things when he was alive and lots of people carry on doing good things in his name to commemorate his life to this day. That's pretty cool isn't it? I bought the t-shirt because the proceeds go to good causes that were dear to Joe. Simple as that." Mike didn't even throw a glance at the others; this wasn't a point scoring exercise; he just looked at Liam and smiled, warmly. Mike was surprised at what Liam said next though, surprised and impressed in equal measure;

"I'm not a kid you know; so don't speak to me like I'm a stupid kid. I know who he was, that's why I said it was a cool t-shirt. I like him and some of his music too."

"Really? Well that's pretty cool too," said Mike, nodding his head in agreement with Liam's apparent good taste in music and ignoring the fact he had managed to irritate him so quickly after their first meeting. "Seems like we *both* appreciate the finer things in life then young man. But how on earth did you latch onto Joe Strummer? It's not as if your mum was ever a fan and I can't see Clive – no offence Clive – being into the *'Only band that mattered'*!" Mike laughed and Liam chuckled, albeit it briefly before the chuckle turned into a cough.

The obvious weakness of the boy in the bed brought everyone back to normality quickly. Maddie gently stroked Liam's arm and he fell silent again, catching his breath once more. Mike spoke again. He was intrigued by this kid; this kid who wanted him to be part of his life despite everything that had happened; this kid that *should* have been *his* kid. Mike found it mind-blowing;

"So, Liam, tell me how *you* came to discover The Clash then? They were a massive band for me and my mates when I was growing up. We used to go and see them play live back then but that was *hundreds* of years ago now! How come you're not into Green Day or Blink 182 or any of that kind of stuff?"

"Actually, I do like Green Day, they're cool I guess and I know they were influenced by The Clash and all that old-school punk stuff. But it was his band The Mescaleros that I liked first. I started looking at the earlier stuff he played later on, the early punk stuff with The Clash and the stuff when he was in that band called The 101ers. It's all pretty good, but I *really* like The Mescaleros, they were a bit wild. I prefer the stuff by The Clash that was sung by the other one, Mick Jones if I'm honest," said Liam, much to Mike's astonishment. It was clearly a subject close to Liam's heart as he went on, with Mike sat silently listening in amazement;

"Me and mum were living in Spain just before we came back here. We were staying in a place called Realejo in Granada with some musicians that mum was friends with. They took us to this ceremony where the locals had named a square after this English man called Joe Strummer. He was a bit of a hero there so they named a square after him. I thought it was pretty cool but also quite funny that it was an Englishman they were honouring and not someone from Spain. But the people there were dead serious about it all. Anyway, one of the musicians we were with liked Joe Strummer's band, The Mescaleros, that's why they took us to see the naming ceremony. Later on he played me some Mescaleros' songs and I really liked them too. They were different from all the Spanish pop stuff we used to hear everywhere and from the traditional Spanish music these people we were living with played. Then like I say, cos I like music and I like history, I looked up who he was on the internet and found The Clash an' that. And I liked them too. Though I thought their drummer and Mick were cooler than Joe."

Mike felt an inexplicable sense of pride, maybe also a small sense of vindication in front of Maddie, but mainly just a good old, huge sense of pride. Liam liked music *and* history. Bloody hell, he even had an opinion on the dynamics within the *Only-band-that-mattered*. If only Sid could've been there to witness it. Mike wanted to say something along the lines of *"That's my boy!"* but, given the circumstances, that clearly wasn't going to happen. Liam was smiling but looking tired so Mike sensed this was his cue to leave the family together.

"Look, if it's ok with you, I'll get off for a bit now and let you get some rest ok?" he looked at

Liam who nodded at him. Mike turned to Maddie and Clive, they looked exhausted too and Mike felt warmly towards them for the first time in a long time.

"Will you come back?" asked Liam quietly. Mike spun around; Liam's question had taken him rather by surprise.

"Oh...er, well if you would like me to? Of course, I'll pop back in the next couple of days, er..." Mike turned to look at Maddie and Clive, "...if your mum is happy about me coming back that is?"

Maddie smiled back and moved slightly, which gave Clive a gentle nudge, thereby preventing him from nodding off on her shoulder.

"Yes it's ok. We'd *all* be glad if you came to visit again wouldn't we?" she said. Clive nodded in sleepy agreement and smiled too. Mike held his hand up in a *'see-you-later-then'* kind of way and left the room, gently closing the door behind him.

Mike hadn't felt this happy for a long time and, as he walked away from the door to Liam's room on the cushions of air under his feet, he started to notice the pictures that adorned the walls of the corridor. As he paused to better examine a pop-art style collage that reminded him of something Sir Peter Blake might once have produced, he heard a familiar voice.

"Ha! Small bleedin' world!" said the smiling nurse stood behind him, seemingly out of nowhere. She was dressed in a deep red surgical-style uniform of baggy trousers and baggy tunic, topped off with a baggy red hat. Mike turned towards her and paused, awakened from his daydream by this pillar-box of a woman but still not quite finding himself able to identify her.

"Er, yeah...Hi!" he replied, disguising his

uncertainty as best he could. "How are you?"

She pulled the red hat off and ran her fingers through the shock of red spiky hair that lay beneath it, her badly-bitten red nails revealed too. Mike saw that she was very pretty, and *very* familiar. She rolled her eyes theatrically at him and spoke again;

"What? How am I since my bloody meltdown in that friggin' meeting you mean? What an effing embarrassment that was eh? I really showed myself up there didn't I? Mind you, I could easily have decked that patronising *Sally-Anne* I tell you, Christ she was a piece of work. Sorry, 'scuse my language! It's Mike, right?"

"Er, yeah of course, that's right, it's Mike," he replied, relieved that he now recalled where he had met the nurse before, "And it's Carol, yeah?" he enquired, sounding a bit too much like Mood Club Na'er-lee for his own comfort. Thankfully, Carol appeared to miss the similarity. He held out his hand to shake and Carol shook it, enthusiastically, for about ten seconds or so. Mike later mused to himself that ten seconds is a very short period of time in most situations but when someone is gripping your hand and wildly shaking it up and down, it's actually about eight seconds too long. After letting go of Mike's slightly exhausted hand, Carol continued;

"It's funny isn't it? I swear my language – no pun intended – is getting worse so it must be my bloody state of mind. Obviously I just feel the need to release the bleedin' pressure and swearing seems to do it for me...that is if I haven't got some dip-shit like Sally-Anne in my firing line!" Carol laughed. It was a belly laugh that made Mike smile broadly whilst also drawing a few puzzled stares from the reception staff at the end of the corridor. This amused Mike still further. Regaining her seemingly fragile composure once more, Carol went on. She was clearly enjoying herself more today than she did when she was in CBT;

"What are you doing here then Mike? I work here, but *you*? You must be visiting. You might be a bit bleedin' mental like me..." she tapped the side of her head with her index finger "...but you seem physically healthy so you're not getting treatment here and you don't work here, so who you seeing?" She was assuming a bit too much for Mike's liking and was so politically incorrect Mike's internal '*PC gauge*' went off the scale momentarily, but she was a breath of fresh air too.

"Oh, it's a bit complicated actually but you're right, I just came to see someone. Do you work in this department then?" he nodded to his left, towards the door at the end of the corridor, "It must be pretty tough". Carol leapt in, somewhat characteristically as it would eventually turn out, with both feet. Gesturing towards the door to Liam's room she said;

"It can be, take that young lad in there for instance. He's a lovely kid but he's had a bit of a rough ride and he's quite poorly. He's got a bit of a bloody weird family by the looks of it as well the poor little bugger. I mean, that lot are maybe Jeremy Kyle fodder, you know? In there it kind of looks to me like the makings of a *Tarts and Vicars Party*..." she trailed off, before quickly and apologetically adding "...sorry, are *you* family? You're part of his family aren't you? I have this tendency to run off at the mouth you see...people are always saying my mouth only stops moving when I pause to change feet. I know I should filter what I say before I say it, but I get so carried away. Why can't I keep my bloody mouth shu..."

Mike laughed. It was a *Carol-like* belly laugh that instantly arrested her self-loathing rant and put her back at her ease. It also drew more disdainful looks from the reception staff. Mike hadn't laughed so hard in a long time and when he finally managed to quell the laughter and regain his composure, he looked at Carol,

"You'd better stop for a mo, I might strain something....you *are* funny. Do you know what? You'll never know how close you were with the *'not family'* statement and your description of Liam's family was accurate too, believe you me! Anyway, I seem to remember that you don't have a TV in your house so what do *you* know about Jeremy Kyle?" he said, wiping a tear from his left eye before he heard himself go on to say;

"Listen, do you want to meet up for a coffee or something? I don't live around here but I get the feeling I'll be coming back to see Liam for a bit, just to dilute the damage being inflicted on him by his weird family, so maybe we could, you know, chat more? Do you know what? I'm not even sure what the protocol is for when you meet another member of the Mood Club out in public...maybe we should have ignored each other, I don't know. Anyway, it'd be nice to meet up if you're free...and want to...er, I mean..."

Mike had never really been very good at the whole *asking-a-woman-out-on-a-date* thing; that was more Sid's territory. This time, however, Carol wasn't looking at her watch, her phone or mumbling excuses about hair washing. She hadn't once told Mike that she had decided to give up on relationships or share some randomly made decision to join a convent. As he ran out of steam

271

– and words – Mike saw that Carol was still smiling, in fact she was beaming.

"That'd be nice, give me your number," said Carol, "Then I'll text you my shifts and you can let me know what suits your working or visiting patterns, ok?" She fumbled in the pocket in her baggy red trousers and handed a mobile phone to him. Mike took it from her and keyed his number in and then pressed the green key. His phone vibrated softly in his pocket and he pressed the red button on Carol's mobile to end the call before his voicemail kicked in.

"There!" said Mike, "Now I have your number too...er, that is, I have your mobile number too, not your actual *number two*!" he sniggered and handed Carol's mobile back to her. She grimaced at him and glanced at her phone briefly, before slipping it silently back into her pocket. Realising he probably sounded more like a stupidly immature fourteen year old boy than a regular grown up, Mike cleared his throat and went on;

"Look I'm not actually *working* at the moment so I can pretty much fit in around you and visiting times here, so I'll be in touch ok?"

"Oh, 'not working' eh?" said Carol, making quotation marks with her fingers, "As in *out-of-work* not working or just not working as in *choosing-not-to-work* or even *not-needing-to-work*?" she asked pointedly, she looked him up and down. Before Mike could respond, or even take offence at the cardinal sin of her making 'air-quotes', Carol continued;

"I had you down for a clichéd mature student working part-time in a second-hand record shop...or a music journalist because you look like someone who doesn't want to grow up, in a nice way of course. I do that you see, I picture the lives of people I meet and fill in the bits of their stories I don't already know. Now I've spoken to you a bit more I kind of see you as more of, maybe, a social worker perhaps. Well, at least a social-worker on a study sabbatical or something. You are into your music, cool t-shirt by the way, and you live alone with no-one but your dogs for company. You're not married but probably were once, and you have some kids somewhere, but you don't see much of them, which makes you sad. I reckon I'm usually quite good at this...so am I getting warm?"

Mike pondered what Carol had been saying. She wasn't a million miles away and yet she was still wrong on every single count except two; Mike really *did* love his music; and Mike felt sad. He looked at her; she was waiting excitedly for his affirmation of her skills. Her anticipation was palpable so, and as old habits die hard, Mike gave her what she wanted;

"Blimey, the dogs...I've been out all morning!" Mike exclaimed. " I'd better dash as they'll need to be let out but I'll call you when I know I'm coming back, I've held you up for long enough too," and he started to walk away. As he reached reception he turned to face Carol, he called out to her "And there's so much more I should tell you...that I have to tell you...but when we get the time, OK?"

"And, in case YOU were really wondering" said Carol in reply, "I know about Jeremy Kyle because it's always on in the Staff Room....and it's fucking SHAMEFUL!" and with her last word shouted loudly, she looked directly at the reception staff who in turn, looked away. Mike smiled at Carol and wished he was as brave as she was.

Carol raised an eyebrow and smiled broadly. She turned and walked to the door to the room

273

where Liam was being cared for; she knocked gently and walked in.

When Mike reached his car he opened the door and climbed in. Deep down he was still sad, sad enough that Carol had noticed it at least. Yet today, as unexpected and unlikely as it maybe had seemed possible earlier, today had turned into a good day.

And more importantly, Mike saw a glimmer of light and a possible way out of his personal gloom, for the first time.

I got a feeling inside of me,
It's kind of strange, like a stormy sea,
I don't know why, I don't know why,
I guess these things have got to be...

Chapter 28

As Sid downed the last of his drink and swirled the un-melted ice cubes around the bottom of the empty glass, Mike's mobile phone rang. It was a song that Sid knew that he knew, somewhere in the deepest and darkest recesses of his mind;

Who's that I see walking in these woods?
Why it's Little Red Riding Hood.
Hey there Little Red Riding Hood,
You sure are looking good,
You're everything a Big Bad Wolf...

Mike quickly picked his mobile up and answered it but it cut off as he did so;

"Christ the fucking signal in this place is complete shite!" he exclaimed sounding exasperated. "Look, I'll just go outside and call her back." and, as he moved to do so, his phone rang again.

Who's that I see walking in these woods?
Why it's Little Red Riding Hood.
Hey there Little Red...

Mike answered it quickly and stood up; in doing so he walked away from Sid and Amy who were still sitting in silence, staring at Mike with their mouths open. He went out of the pub's front door to ensure that he could maintain a strong enough mobile signal to complete the call this time. Meanwhile, unscrambling his senses inside the White Hart, Sid was still wrestling with faded memories of long forgotten punk records.

"Christ, anyone would think it was some kind of emergency!" said Amy, not realising how much she was helping Sid in his quest. An invisible light bulb lit above Sid's head, he turned to Amy;

"999, that's it, 999, their version of *Little Red Riding Hood*! I knew it, just couldn't drag it out of my dusty old brain for a moment that's all. Cheers Amy." Then he paused, "But why *that* tune? It's a good track I guess but why *that* tune for *this* girl? I wonder if she lives with her granny or something." Sid laughed, yet remained slightly confused.

Amy didn't much look like she'd ever be able to throw any light on the subject and simply shrugged her shoulders. Mike and Sid's taste in music had always left her a little cold. She had always been much more a fan of Duran Duran and Spandau Ballet. As Mike rejoined them at the table, he looked a little down in the mouth.

"She's going to be late," he said glumly, "Something's going on at work and she stopped on for a bit longer to help out. Only just leaving now by the sounds of it, so she'll be another three-quarters of an hour at least. Said she was still excited to meet you two though!" Mike's tone lifted slightly and he smiled, nervously.

"Sid wanted to know why *that* song as her ringtone Mike," said Amy, rather flatly. She was still privately re-living the *Rio* video in her head, temporarily transported back to her eighties heyday and enjoying the image of those beautiful men in their beautiful suits, sailing on their beautiful yacht in the bright sun.

"Yeah, I was. I have to say, that's a bit of a *blast-from-the-past* mate, 999? How come?" enquired Sid, shaking his still empty glass at Amy

276

and raising his eyebrows, indicating it was her turn to buy drinks. As she left her clear-blue eighties' sea fantasy behind, she pulled a face and stood up. Sid leant forward and handed her his wallet and smiled. Amy's face lit-up too and she went to order more drinks.

In answer to Sid's question Mike explained to him how, when he bumped into Carol at Queen Mary's she was wearing a theatre nurse's uniform, entirely made up of red clothing. He described how it matched her hair and fingernails too and that ever since, even though it wasn't the most flattering outfit she could have been wearing, he hadn't been able to get this picture out of his mind.

"I did have *Girl-U-Want* by Devo at first, well...for a few hours at least...but that vision of her in red just kept coming back!" he said, by way of further explanation.

Having bought the drinks to the table on a tray, Amy sat down beside her brother and handed him a pint of JLB and spilled a little on the table as she did so. She then slid a large Jack Daniels with ice across to Sid. Sid smiled, picked it up and inspected it; he took a sip as Amy wiped up the spillage with a tissue she pulled from her handbag. She had bought herself – with Sid's money of course – a bottle of rose wine which she placed on the table in a shiny chrome ice bucket. She also bought an extra-large bag of salt and vinegar crisps. As she tore open the packet and then carefully split each side of the bag to form a large rectangular foil platter of crisps for the middle of the table, she addressed her brother;

"Did he tell you why that song/ringtone thingy Sid?" she asked feigning interest in what was, in her mind at least, very much a dull - *boy* -

277

kind of thing. She helped herself to a large handful of crisps and sat back.

"Yeah, apparently it was because he didn't have any Chris De Burgh tunes on his phone playlist. A bit modern for you Mike eh? Well you could've had Neil Sedaka doing *Oh Carol* instead maybe!" Sid laughed, Amy was none the wiser. Mike appeared to be a little nervous and pulled a face;

"Look, it was also going to be *Red Hot* by Sam the Sham and the Pharaohs but I thought that might be a bit presumptuous, given the lyric content ok? Seeing as we've only just recently got together. Anyway, when she gets here, you don't need to be chatting to her about anything at all that makes me look weird or dangerous or anything like a nutcase. I guess I'm pleading with you, no, wait a minute, I'm bloody well *warning* you actually. You two can only say good things about me tonight, right?"

The truth was that neither Amy nor Sid had anything other than good things to say about Mike anyway. He was a trustworthy, caring and genuine soul who would do anything for his friends. He was intelligent, reasonable, mature and yet still a lot of fun to be around, when he wasn't depressed. He was also really easy to wind up.

"Yeah Amy, do you remember when Mike was seeing that *what's-her-name*, that girl who lived near us when we were growing up? The one he bumped into again later when she had loads of kids? What *was* her name?" Sid was grinning at Amy and Amy back at him. Mike knew what was coming.

"Oh yeah, Jackie!" exclaimed Amy, clapping her hands together as she recalled the girl who had lived in the same street as Sid when they were all kids.

"You always said she was rather *'generous with her affections'* when you were growing up and that she had a bad reputation. I always thought that was unkind Sid. Although she *did* have about a dozen kids when my dim brother here starting dating her!" Amy let out a dirty laugh, which in turn made Sid spit some Jack Daniels out in delight.

"Fuck me yeah! She *was* bloody easy wasn't she? I reckon we *all* probably lost our virginity to her!" said Sid, wiping the mist of bourbon whisky from his chin with his sleeve. Mike sprung to Jackie's defence;

"Actually, Jackie had a talent for self harm around the time we were kids as a result of how everyone saw her and treated her. She knew all about the taunts from complete bastards like you and it affected her pretty badly. *And* she only had three kids, albeit by three different fathers, and not a dozen when I met her again. She raised those kids with no help from anyone and also worked two jobs. I admired her but just didn't feel there was a connection between us or find her intellectually stimulating, that's all."

"Yeah, a ringtone of *Personality Crisis* by the New York Dolls wasn't it Mike?" retorted an indignant Sid, "You clearly weren't defending her honour back then like you are now mate! And what about that Mel bird then?" Sid was on a roll. Amy was transfixed; she loved it when Sid played with Mike like this.

"Yeah, she fucking hated me," said Amy with an over-theatrical look of sadness on her face.

"Not to worry Amy...she pretty much hated *all* of us, it wasn't just you!" said Sid. He was right

279

too. He qualified his judgment;

"I mean, man she had it all didn't she? She was beautiful, rich, posh but pretentious with it, well-educated and had expensive tastes. She was out of your league mate, she'd have been a perfect target for Tim but would've outclassed him too. She did look down on all of us and she used to patronise the shit out of you Mike."

"Can you actually *'patronise-the-shit'* out of someone Sid? Can you?" Mike pulled an enquiring face in his friend's direction and then paused to reminisce.

"Mel, I hadn't thought of her in ages," he said distractedly, "She was training to be a vet at Uni when I was with her wasn't she? We used to go to events at the local sailing club, cricket club and tennis club. And her family welcomed me into their home although I reckon they thought I was her *'bit of rough'* and secretly hoped it was a phase she was going through! Yeah, I first drank red wine with her family and..." Mike was enjoying the trip down memory lane for a moment, until Sid chipped in once again.

"Yeah I remember coming back from time to time in those days and seeing you go to all those fancy places. Problem was you couldn't sail, windsurf, ski, ride horses, turn out for the cricket team or play tennis. And all the time, she was popular with the other guys who were all richer, fitter, more tanned, sportier and far more successful than you. What happened in the end Mike? How did it end?"

Sid's question was greeted with a scowl from Mike and an answer from Amy;

"As soon as she qualified as a vet she went off to do conservation work in Africa with two university friends, male university friends!"

Amy laughed again and Sid joined her once more. Sensing that he would never win when being ganged up on by both his best friend and his sister, Mike laughed too. If he could manage to remain self-deprecating for a while longer, maybe he could bring this embarrassing topic to a close before Carol arrived. They had only seen each other a handful of times since their chance meeting at Queen Mary's. He really liked her and didn't want her being put off him too quickly.

"If mobile phones had been invented in those days, I would have given her a ringtone of *Money*, The Flying Lizards version of course," Mike offered, tentatively.

"Or *The Ruling Class* by The Monochrome Set!" added a smiling Sid.

"Or what about *Africa* by Toto?" floundered Amy, setting Mike and Sid off laughing again.

+   +   +   +   +   +

By the time Carol got to the pub, Sid and Amy had dragged a few more girlfriends out of the dim and distant woodwork for close examination and ridicule. The ones he chose to assign ringtones to attracting the greatest scrutiny. There was;

Marianne, who had *Princess of the Streets* by The Stranglers as her ringtone. She was *persona-non-grata* as far as Amy was concerned. Amy simply sneered and called her the 'Ring Collector'. Mike was engaged to Marianne in his late thirties. She had financially nearly ruined him as he spent all of his money on her whilst they were together. She, on the other hand, opened a savings account for her own wages and consequently never spent a penny whilst they were a couple. She also kept all of the presents they got for their engagement after

281

they split up. It later transpired she had been sleeping with two other men and a woman she worked with whilst engaged to Mike. He felt embarrassed and humiliated for a time and Mike was depressed for a while, but regained the ability to walk into the local branch of his bank without the anxiety of being pulled into an office to discuss his overdraft facility.

Rosie, had a tune by The Buzzcocks as her ringtone – *Boredom* – and was the polar opposite of Marianne. In fact Mike had met her on the rebound from Marianne and she was *so* nice, caring and loving that she never stood much of a chance given Mike's state of mind at the time. Although Mike's friends all liked her (she was something of a relief after Marianne) Rosie always seemed to know the relationship was doomed to failure and she understood that she lived in Mike's previous girlfriend's shadow. It was Mike's only relationship where he took advice from Sid on how to behave. It ended disastrously after Mike cheated on her by having a one-night-stand (the only one of his life) and if he could take his time over again, it was probably the only relationship where he would do things differently. He never had *really* strong feelings for Rosie, but he knew she deserved better.

Shelley, who looked like Marilyn Monroe and was the woman with whom Mike had the one-night-stand, was the first of his girlfriends that Sid ever fancied. Shelley had David Bowie's *Beauty and the Beast* as her ringtone, given to her as a tongue-in-cheek nod to the fact that Mike knew he was punching way above his weight. He once described her as the kind of girl a man would wolf-whistle at in the street but rarely take home to meet their mother. She was eventually offered a job in America and didn't think twice about leaving Mike and taking it. Secretly, Mike was relieved.

And finally, they talked about Clare. Her ringtone was – *and still is in fact* – the Undertones tune; *You've Got My Number, Why Don't You Use It?* Mike still gets the occasional text message from her at three in the morning on his birthday; on *her* birthday; and occasionally in the small hours of Christmas/New Year's morning. He also gets letters from companies saying that he owns a small part of The Moon or has had a new star named after him; or informing him that he is now a bona-fide Laird of somewhere unpronounceable and covered in pine trees in Scotland. He had even found anonymous greetings cards offering someone's undying love, tucked under the windscreen wipers of his old car. The purchase of the new Fiesta put paid to these incidents, although it was clear that these were always from Clare. Consequently, Sid always said her ringtone should have been *Psycho Killer* by Talking Heads and he swore that if ever Mike was found murdered, he would give Clare's details to the investigating officers immediately. She had been Mike's last girlfriend for a long while.

"Wow this sounds bloody fascinating, can anyone join in?" said a female voice behind them as they chuckled away, momentarily oblivious to their surroundings. Carol had arrived. As Mike stood to greet her he quickly noticed the pub had become somewhat brighter all of a sudden, as if someone had just opened the curtains on a sunny morning. He kissed her on the cheek and Carol started to explain why she had been delayed;

"Sorry I'm so flippin' late, was bit bleedin' hectic at work and then I couldn't find anywhere to friggin' park when I got here...I tried calling you again but it was going straight to voicemail...can't be much of a signal here I guess...Christ this place is busy...surely it's not the prospect of 'Burger Nite' that's brought them all in?"

Rather than introducing herself, Carol was already in full flow. She nervously filled the silence that had broken out since her arrival with lots of words, whilst simultaneously studying the sign written in white chalk above the pub fireplace for clues as to why the White Hart was seemingly packing customers in from far and wide. Being regulars themselves, Mike, Sid and Amy had rather ignored the signs that detailed the usual Tuesday evening fare that Nigel had to offer of course.

"Bloody Hell! Please tell me you don't teach English at the place where the sign writer in this pub studied do you?" asked Carol rhetorically with a bemused smile on her face. She continued;

"...Sounds interesting though and I'm *effing* starving, are we going to eat?" Carol asked, smiling and finally sitting down on the chair they had kept reserved for her whilst the pub was filling up. Mike hadn't said much as yet, but he had noticed that she was wearing a short black dress with white flowers around the edge of the square neckline. She was also wearing black tights and knee-high shiny black stiletto-heeled leather boots. Her shock of red hair shone, even in the dimly-lit White Hart. Carol certainly stood out amongst the usual White Hart crowd and, in short, Mike thought she looked terrific.

"You must be Carol, yeah? Come on Mike, do the fucking introduction thing then!" said Amy suddenly and rather rudely. She had by this stage, and on an empty stomach, consumed an entire bottle of rose wine save for the half-glass she had left in front of her. She was feeling somewhat relaxed.

"Er, yeah, this is Sid..." he gestured towards his friend and paused. Carol shook Sid's hand and said a polite "Pleased to meet you Sid, I've heard an awful lot about you." She smiled at him and Sid smiled back,

"Yeah, likewise..." said Sid, sounding a little less polite "...and all of it true I'm sure."

Mike frowned and turned to Amy; "...and this is my *delightful* little sister Amy," said Mike sarcastically, throwing a *behave-yourself-please* look at Amy. Before Carol could say anything, however, Amy chose to ignore her brother;

"My brother is completely loved-up about *you* y'know? He's had a lot of shit happen recently and then you turn up...with all your bloody gorgeousness and stuff..." she looked Carol up and down briefly and waved her hand up and down to emphasise her inspecting gaze before continuing; "...so you'd better be nice to him 'cos he's a bit soft ok? He's always been a bit fragile and needs someone to fucking look after him, or you'll have me to fucking answer to, ok?" Amy tapped the side of her nose twice and then pointed at Carol.

Carol kissed Amy on the cheek, put her arm around her shoulder and turned to Mike, who was looking on in dumbstruck horror at his sister's behaviour;

"Well, I bloody love *HER!*" exclaimed Carol, beaming at Mike and Sid before turning back to Amy; "We are going to get on like a friggin' house on fire we are!" and, seemingly to concur with her new best friend, Amy simply put her head on

Carol's shoulder and smiled a silly drunken smile.

After ordering food and getting Carol a drink – a Bloody Mary naturally – Mike wanted an update on Liam's progress. Carol got quite excited and explained that there had been some positive developments.

"When you last came to see him there hadn't been much to report, yeah?" said Carol.

Mike had been back to see Liam – and Carol - three times since that momentous day. The day when he met Liam for the first time since he was a baby and he met Carol for the first time since her meltdown at Mood Club. He was surprised that he felt little by way of nerves when in either one's company. He had spent years practising what he might say or how he might act when he met Liam and yet all of that had disappeared out of the window when it finally happened. True, this situation was very different from the many scenarios Mike had played out in his mind over the years, but it just seemed completely natural to chat together like they did now they had met. Liam had seemingly warmed to Mike immediately and was clearly happy to have him around.

Similarly, Carol made Mike feel like he had known her for years. He heard all about Carol's troublesome, yet seemingly typical, daughter Grace and how difficult she found being a single parent. In turn, Carol heard the truth about Mike's imaginary dogs, Malcolm and Vivienne. She thought it was weirdly hilarious that he happily shared completely made up canine adventures with the Mood Club rather than the real challenges around the Liam situation but understood completely. Mike also found it weirdly hilarious that he could tell Carol *anything* without fazing her or feeling remotely

286

embarrassed. All in all, it had been a weirdly wonderful couple of weeks.

"Yeah that's right. Liam was pretty stable and seemed a little bit stronger when I was last there, he spoke to me for quite a while actually, but his treatment was still pretty severe and I know it can take it out of you," replied Mike, a little despondently.

"I reckon he was on a bit of a high because of the iPod you brought him with your *'Everything Clash'* playlist on it but remember, hospital stays are tiring for anyone, let alone someone who has been through the wringer like Liam has. He bloody loved the present though; he spends more time listening to that thing than he does listening to his friggin' Mum and that funny Clive bloke I can tell you!" Carol turned to Sid, "It was your idea wasn't it? The iPod?"

"Me? Oh, yeah 'course" said Sid nervously trying to remain cool and nonchalant but failing miserably. "Wanted to put some of my stuff on there actually but Mike insisted we stick to The Clash and The Mescaleros, with a little bit of the 101-ers chucked in for good measure. He even insisted we get all the Mick Jones' sung songs on the list...the kid reckons they're better apparently. There's no accounting for taste but it turns out to be a bloody good playlist in the end."

"Well like I say, Liam loves it. We have to physically prise it from his hands when it comes to bed time!" Carol smiled at Sid and he shrugged his shoulders back at her in a *just-trying-to-help* kind of manner.

"I'm surprised the *Shavers'* stuff didn't make it on there eh Sid! Not like you to miss an opportunity to big up your own talents," said Mike a little unfairly. He was clearly still a bit nervous with his tipsy sister and uber-cool best friend there than he was when he was alone with Carol. "Nothing from any *Pop Factor* contestants either? You must be missing a trick!"

Sid scowled. He didn't like it when Mike attempted to score points and nothing pushed his buttons more, especially as he himself had been trying to stay on his best behaviour as instructed. Before he had chance to put Mike back in his place, however, Carol came to his rescue;

"I don't know much about *Pop Factor*, I friggin' hate all that Saturday night-shite on the TV but the *Shavers*? Do you mean Jonny Ronson's band? I fucking love them! Do you like them too Sid?"

"Like them? Listen love, I *AM* them!" announced Sid triumphantly. He went on to explain his relationship with the band and friendship with Jonny himself whilst Carol slowly and silently munched her way through a falafel burger (burger number 5). Mike, meanwhile, sweated his way through his chili burger (burger number 2) in sullen silence.

Carol was impressed with Sid's tales. She'd been a fan of the band's first album; the eponymously titled record Sid called *HIS* album, when introduced to it by an ex-boyfriend some years before. Much like Sid, she thought their latest offering *Pure Noise* was a tour-de-force. Sid was generous when recounting his earliest memories of Jonny by including Mike in the stories. Carol looked at Mike with a renewed sense of wonder and he, in turn, looked at Sid a little apologetically. Finally, offering to arrange a meet up with Jonny and the band the next time they were in the country, Sid reminded Carol that she was about to give them an update on Liam's condition.

"Oh yeah, of course, bugger me, we can go off at a bleedin' tangent can't we?" she said, with a big smile on her face. "You are something of an enigma though, aren't you Sid? I'm good at weighing people up but you...you're a bit of a tricky one."

"A leather wearing enigma, all wrapped up in a cliché!" interjected Amy cruelly, now drinking sparkling water and using a chicken breast burger (burger number 3) to soak up the bottle of wine she had fully consumed. Sid looked at her briefly and looked away again, choosing to ignore her rather than start an argument he had no chance of winning.

"I'm gonna pop out to use Nigel's *'smoking solution'* for a minute – that's a backyard covered in green tarpaulin to you Carol – and when I get back I wanna see a large JD on the rocks lined up here ready to go, ok mate?" he finished his sentence looking straight at Mike and Mike knew it was the least he could do. As Sid disappeared from view, Carol engaged a rapidly sobering Amy in deep conversation whilst Mike finished the beer in his glass and went back to the bar.

By the time Sid returned, Mike had just finished delivering a fresh glass of sparkling water to Amy, another Bloody Mary to Carol and a pint of JLB on a beer mat where he had been sitting. He handed Sid a large Jack Daniels with ice, accompanied with a quiet "thanks mate" and a smile. Sid nodded in acceptance and the pair sat down again. Carol started to relay the news from Queen Mary's to her now hushed and settled audience.

"It's quite exciting really, I don't know how you'll take it all though Mike..." she looked at

289

Mike sympathetically and paused before continuing; "...but it could mean a tremendous improvement for Liam and that's what counts at the end of the day isn't it?" The question hung in the air for a moment before Mike silently indicated that she was right and should continue with the news.

"Well, it's just that it seems that there *IS* a family member somewhere in the London area who has a really close tissue match and the same blood type as Liam after all. How exciting is *that*? All I know at the moment is that it's a male and he obviously lives close to the hospital as he's on a local blood donor list as well as being registered with the National Blood Service list as a donor at Queen Mary's. I mean, it's difficult to understand given the slim chances but it's true. We believe his dad is dead and we don't know of any uncles or cousins, but there *does* seem to be a *very* close relative somewhere nearby, so who knows. It's great yeah? Anyway, Irene in the Admin Team is trying to contact him right now. We don't know if this bloke could be a living donor, he might not even know he's got such a close relative of course. This might all be a bit weird. We're not allowed to get involved in such things as they're confidential of course but, by the time I get back tomorrow they *might* have something more to go on."

Mike's head was swimming with the combination of beer he had consumed and the news. Did it mean that he would be pushed away from Liam again, almost as soon as he had become closer to him after all these years? Was it still appropriate for him to be in the boy's life when he clearly had a new side to his family that he would need to be reunited with? And what would this news mean anyway? The relative would need to be contacted and informed and would certainly need to come to terms with the fact that he even had a family member he hadn't previously known of. There were no guarantees that they would even want to know about Liam, let alone meet him, much less help him in any way. There could be other ramifications for this person and whatever family *they* had now. They might be a willing blood donor but a living organ donor was quite a different thing to contemplate altogether. They shouldn't get ahead of themselves at Queen Mary's, Liam was still in need of a kidney and they had no actual donor as such, just someone who seemed to be a good match at some point in the future. Then, Mike's rumination was interrupted by Carol;

"You ok love?" she asked quietly. "It's a bit to take in I guess and it doesn't mean too much at this stage either does it? It's just that, well, it's a big development, that's all." She gently squeezed Mike's hand and rubbed the back of it with her thumb as she did so. Mike smiled at her. He couldn't help but feel that something like this would normally be the cue for him to start crying again. But somehow he felt stronger with Carol on his side this time, understanding how he must feel and supporting him. It was a warm feeling and he knew he liked it a great deal.

"You're right, of course" said Mike, his cheeks colouring slightly. "Frankly, I'm amazed Clive hasn't been on the phone telling me himself. He's not normally so slow to call!"

"Well he might have..." added Sid, "...but you know what the signal is like in this shit-hole. Even Clive's big boss Himself couldn't make a mobile ring in here without the aid of a signal booster and a whole host of angels!" and they all laughed.

291

+   +   +   +   +   +

As they said their goodbyes, Carol nudged Mike in the ribs and whispered in his ear;

"I can't drive home after all that booze...do you know anywhere local I could stay tonight?" and she smiled.

Mike, mentally scanning his house and finding only what he considered to be a minimum of dirt and untidiness, save for an un-made bed and some dirty dishes, rapidly replied; "Yeah, I reckon I know just the place. It's not far." and he smiled back at her. At that moment, Mike couldn't think of anywhere he'd rather have been or anyone with whom he would rather be in the company of. They put Amy and Sid in a taxi and started to walk towards Mike's house. As they did so, Mike's message tone sounded, telling him he had a voicemail waiting.

"Looks like I've got some signal back!" he said, pulling his phone from his pocket and looking at the screen. He instantly saw that he had missed three calls from Clive's mobile and two from the hospital number. He could also see that there was a voicemail message waiting for him. As he made to call his voicemail to retrieve Clive's message he looked at Carol;

"He must've been trying to call me for ages, from his phone AND the hospital reception phone as usual. He's so bloody predictable, thank heavens I heard the news from you first. Why doesn't he just send me a text like normal people eh? Then I could pick it up whenever it's convenient – to me - and get back to him. He wouldn't have to keep trying then. I s'pose it's progress that he's left me a voicemail message this time; he doesn't usually do that! I also s'pose I should let him know that *I know* already, he'll probably keep trying otherwise and we'll never get any peace..." but at that moment Mike's mobile rang yet again, interrupting the gentle tirade he was aiming at Clive.

This is, the Happy House,
We're happy here, in the Happy House,
Oh it's such...

Answering the call, and without pausing for Clive to speak first, Mike said,

"Hello Clive..." cheerfully, before increasing the level of condescension a little bit more; "...and thanks for your patience and persistence in trying to reach me. I've been in the pub and the signal there is bloody appalling mate. I was just about to call you bac...Oh, I'm sorry, who did you say you are?" Mike had been interrupted by an unfamiliar voice, it wasn't Clive at all. He stopped silently in his tracks and his face dropped as the voice explained who it was and why they were calling him;

"Hello Mr. Powell, I'm really sorry to be calling you this late in the evening but we've been trying to get hold of you repeatedly for a couple of hours. My name is Irene Harris and I work in the Admin office at Queen Mary's Hospital..."

If I was a haircut, would you wear a hat?
If I was a maid, could I clean your flat?
If I was a carpet, would you wipe your feet
In time to save me from mud off the street?
If you like me, if you love me, why don't you get
down on your knees and scrub me?
I'm a little grubby, from just being around.

Chapter 29

As Mike drove Carol into town to where she had
left her car the previous evening he couldn't wipe
the smile from his face. He turned to look at her
again, failing to believe that she was *still* with
him, *still* here, after staying the night at his house.
If he hadn't been driving he would have pinched
himself hard when he saw that she was *still* sitting
in the passenger seat where she had been twenty-
five seconds earlier – the last time he had checked
in fact – and wasn't a figment of his imagination.

"Well that was quite a night Mr. Powell..."
said Carol with a wink. "...in more ways than
one!" and she laughed a dirty laugh.

"Er, by '...*and in more ways than one*' I take it
you actually mean two ways last night and once
again this morning, right?" replied Mike,
sounding more like Sid and visibly swelling with
pride whilst reflecting on the exertions of the
previous few hours.

"Yeah alright Casanova...you were bloody
marvelous ok? The best ever!" said a grinning
Carol, "But you'd better start saving your strength
if you're going to go through with what we talked
about over breakfast."

Carol sounded serious for a moment and so

Mike stuck his bottom lip out and frowned. Sensing a typically fragile male ego, Carol qualified her previous statement; she didn't want to spoil the memory of the previous evening with a lecture this early in the morning, let alone this early in the relationship;

"I just want you to know that this isn't something to be taken lightly and there could be all sorts of reasons why it might not even be possible...and there will be all sorts of potential difficulties ahead too" and then, sensing it still wasn't enough to say just this, she added;

"I tell you what though; it's about the bloody bravest - and therefore the single most flamin' sexiest - thing I've ever known anyone to do. If it works out you know you'll be my hero for friggin' ever don't you?" and she smiled broadly again.

Mike tingled all over. Already, the thought of *'forever'* didn't scare him in the slightest when it was said by Carol. He could remember when previous girlfriends had mentioned things like *'...going on holiday together next year'* or hearing them ask questions like *'...and what would you like for Christmas?'* when it was only early March. He recoiled slightly at memories of making little discoveries like finding that an extra toothbrush had appeared in his bathroom after a regular girlfriend had stayed over a couple of times. Mike wasn't afraid of commitment, he was just fearful of getting stuck with someone who wasn't perfect for him. As well as being dumped somewhat regularly over the years, he could also recall starting a few of those *look-it's-not-you-it's-me* conversations himself when things got 'heavy' as Sid described it. He hated any situation where he had to demonstrate commitment in a relationship. It pretty much always freaked him out to the point that he needed to end it with the woman in question. This morning, however, *'forever'* felt warm and fuzzy. Today, *'forever'* felt like an un-worryingly comfortable concept for a change. Mike knew he had a long way to go in recovering from his fragile state of mind, but now he seemed to know that he *would* recover. It might take a while but, with Carol and Liam in his life, he felt a powerful sense of purpose for the first time in a very long time.

"For *'friggin ever'* sounds ok to me, I'm not sure I've got much on for the rest of my life anyway so you may be in luck, I reckon I could handle the undivided attention!" said Mike, summarising his thoughts without reasoning, worrying or ruminating in the slightest; "That is, if you're not too busy to hero worship me forever either?" he added, still grinning like a teenager. Carol smiled too.

As they arrived at their destination, Carol rummaged in her large shiny-black handbag and pulled her car keys from it. She leant across to Mike, took his hand and kissed him gently on the cheek. For a moment there was silence between them, although Mike could almost hear the urge inside of him to scream out with joy. He knew what he was about to do for Liam was huge; it was in fact bigger than anything he had ever known except for one thing. It wasn't bigger than what he felt for Carol at this precise moment. There were no words, there was no explanation and it was beyond comprehension. Carol looked him in the eye and spoke gently, almost too gently for Mike to hear her above the din in his head;

"So I'll let them know you'll be in today yeah? If you text when you're on your way I'll let them know what time to expect you." Then she added

"And don't worry about Liam or his mum and that. They know there's a match somewhere out here but they don't know who it is yet so they know nothing about how things have changed. It's only fair that they hear that from the person concerned rather than from someone in a lab coat carrying a clipboard." and with that she kissed Mike on the cheek again. Mike smiled and could feel himself welling up for the first time since he received the call last night. He was irritated that it was in front of Carol but needn't have worried as she was already climbing out of the car and heading towards the red Mazda MX5 across the street from the White Hart.

As Mike waved her off from the warm comfort of his car, he couldn't help but consider how the colour of Carol's Mazda seemed to match that of her hair, her nails and her uniform. He couldn't help also wondering why everyone seemed to have nicer cars than he did.

+   +   +   +   +   +

"How was *Lover Boy* then, did you have a nice night?" Grace wasn't living up to her name when Carol arrived home. "I got back from Nicki's an hour ago and thought you might be here but no, obviously you fancied a lie-in today for a change...a lie-in somewhere else!" and she sniggered like the fourteen-year-old that she in fact was.

"That's quite enough of *that* from you" said Carol as she dumped her handbag on the hall table and hung her car keys up on the hook by the door. "You've got exactly ten minutes before I leave if you want a lift, otherwise you're walking to school, ok?"

297

Grace poked her tongue out at her mother and picked up a small black bag, waving it at Carol to signify that she was, in fact, already equipped and prepared for the day. Within a few minutes Carol had changed into her work clothes and she and Grace were in the car on their way towards Grace's school. On the journey Carol described, without the post-pub/overnight details of course, much of what had happened the previous night. She explained Mike's story and what he had decided to do. For once Grace listened to her mother, only interrupting from time-to-time to exclaim the odd 'Wow!' or 'Blimey!' Carol also gave her daughter a set of instructions for something she wanted to do for Mike. She explained in detail the task in hand and what was required of Grace. By the end of their fifteen minute journey, Grace was won over as far as Mike was concerned and as they pulled up on the zigzag lines outside the school Carol pulled on the handbrake and then squeezed Grace's arm gently;

"So you know what I want yeah? Please don't do anything but find them for me at this stage, ok? You DO NOT have permission to use my credit card or anything, right?" Carol insisted with a serious expression on her face; "Just find them for me, exactly as I've described."

"No sweat Mum, ok? I know what to do and trust me, these places probably won't accept Visa anyway, I reckon it'll be cash all the way. Do you mind if I come in to see you after school? It'd be kinda nice to meet this one 'cos he sounds pretty different from some of the other knuckleheads you've dated for sure!" And with that Grace chuckled, kissed her dumbfounded mother and clambered out of the car.

Summer, Buddy Holly, the working folly,
Good Golly Miss Molly and boats,
Hammersmith Palais, the Bolshoi Ballet,
Jump back in the alley and nanny goats...

Chapter 30

"This could all take a couple of months Mr. Powell so you need to prepare yourself for a bit of a wait ok?" The nurse was starting to add a few notes to the clipboard she was holding. Realising the ambiguity of what she had just said, she qualified her previous statement;

"Not a couple of months *now* of course, I mean it could take a couple of months in total before any operation or transplant takes place. So, Mr. Powell, I know we have your blood type and we've already established that you are a good tissue match..."

"Mike, can you call me Mike please?" said Mike a little nervously.

"Of course I can Mike. I'm Sue by the way..." she said, before furtively adding "...and I'm a friend of Carol's" as if it was a mortal sin to know of her existence or of Carol's relationship with Mike

"Er sure, ok *Sue,*" said Mike, unsure what to do with this piece of information except store it away. "A couple of months you say? Why so? I'm a good match, Liam desperately needs a kidney, I have a spare one and I'm positive I want to go through with the procedure, so why so long?"

"Well often it can take maybe three months or even more, much depends on what tests you need, you know? Being a good match and your close family links are a great start as far as compatibility with Liam is concerned but there's more we need to know. It's nothing to worry about though, just about your level of fitness and general health so no fretting ok? We don't want to adversely affect your mental health do we? Ha, there's enough to consider with your physical health at the moment!" Sue chuckled to herself quietly and added,

"Apparently there's not much wrong with you physically...you appear to have passed all *those* tests already too...or so I'm *led to believe...*"

Mike wasn't sure what to make of Sue's last statement but the shock of hearing it in Carol's voice in his head saved him from potentially endless rumination. Then he thought briefly on the state of his mental health at that precise moment. It hadn't crossed his mind that the doctors may think him unsuitable due to his recent period of depression. The Mood Club seemed like a dim and distant memory to Mike these days.

"This is like something off *Eastenders* though isn't it? Your story with Liam I mean. Wow!" continued a still-impressed Sue. "It's not everyday you gain a teenage son and then lose a kidney as a result. I mean, I can understand a paternity test leading to the loss of the shirt off your back or even some blood, sweat and tears once the CSA gets involved...but a *kidney*?...that's a new one on me!"

Mike smiled, it was weird to say the least yet it also seemed such a natural thing for him to do for the sake of Liam's health and wellbeing. He appeared to be the only person who thought so, but he was certain he was right.

The rest of the morning and a fair proportion

of the afternoon went by in a flash. Various tests with a variety of doctors and nurses were followed by conversations about the procedure itself (keyhole surgery lasting two hours); the recuperation period (a week in hospital followed by up to twelve weeks recovering at home); the long term prognosis for Liam (96% success rate); long term prognosis for Mike (very good); could it be arranged for Mike speak to someone who had been through the procedure themselves (yes, the hospital would put him in touch with a living donor).

"You see Mr. Powell, Mike, do you mind if I call you Mike?" asked the third doctor Mike had spoken to and been examined by that morning, "You should call me Sayed by the way," he said when Mike agreed first name terms were acceptable.

"You see Mike; a living donor is an incredibly generous person who has put someone else's needs before their own. Parents do that everyday when it comes to comforts and food and suchlike, it is a completely natural thing of course. However giving up an organ is way over and above the *everyday*. What you are proposing to do is amazing. If this all goes according to plan or if it does not, the one thing I am certain of is that Liam is very lucky to have someone, a father as selfless and special as you, in his life."

As Dr. Sayed finished massaging his ego, Mike gazed into the middle distance, currently hidden by the pale blue curtains surrounding the bed that Mike was sitting on. He buttoned up his shirt as Carol came in.

"Did you hear that? Sayed here reckons I'm *special*," proudly announced Mike.

Carol looked at him, pushed her tongue

against the inside of her lower lip and crossed her eyes.

Mike laughed and Dr. Sayed stuttered;

"I-I-I'll, er leave you to it then Mike, hope it all goes well."

"Thanks Sayed!" called Mike after him as he disappeared through the blue curtains. A smiling Carol uncrossed her eyes and kissed Mike on the cheek;

"Well, all done here then?" she said, turning down the back of Mike's shirt collar and straightening it against his shoulders like a caring mother sending her five-year-old off to school.

"Yeah, for the mo anyway," replied Mike, quietly enjoying the little shiver down his spine from the attention Carol was giving him, "Although whilst you go in to see Liam, I have to go and see Maddie and Clive and I have to say, I'm not really looking forward to it. I know it's all turned out for the best but I could still strangle her without a second thought for what she's put Liam and me through."

"Look, we can't do anything about the past can we? We can't change what's already happened; we can only come to terms with the past yeah? You should remember that from the Mood Club." Carol sounded every inch the nursing professional for a moment rather than the all-too-freely-spoken whirlwind of a woman Mike had grown so fond of. Then she reverted to type, seemingly not to let him down;

"Anyway, we'll invite them to a Vicars and Tarts themed party at yours when you're both well enough to celebrate the success of the transplant, how's that sound?"

As they shared a laugh, Carol pulled a face again and Mike stood up. Carol fished in her pocket and pulled a mobile telephone out. It wasn't her normal one so Mike looked at her with his eyebrows raised. She handed it to him;

"Look, I know I'm in great danger of overstepping the mark here but this is for *you* to do with what you see fit ok? Y'know, maybe check it out with Maddie first...Anyway, it's my old mobile; I upgraded recently but this one's still quite good and works perfectly. I got a cheap pay-as-you-go SIM card for it and thought you could give it to Liam when you think the time's right. I've put your number and my number in it; he can sort out the rest himself I guess. If you call your phone you'll have his number, I've even assigned a special tune for your ringtone!"

Mike called his own number from Liam's new phone and then rang off. He had been waiting for this moment for a long time he thought, as he set up a contact profile for Liam and assigned *Kooks* by David Bowie as his son's signature tone. He then dialed Liam's number and heard it ring, with Carol's chosen ringtone, for the first time;

Fall is here, hear the yell,
Back to school, ring the bell,
Brand new shoes, walking blues,
Climb the fence, books and pens,
I can tell that we are gonna be friends...

"White Stripes eh? *Nice* touch. I'll have a think and chat to Maddie when Liam's feeling better," said Mike before kissing Carol full and deep on the lips.

+   +   +   +   +   +

"I've grown up a lot, a lot over these last few w-weeks Mike, I swear I have..." Maddie was crying and struggling to get her words out after hearing

303

the news, "...I don't think I'll...I'll ever be able to for-forgive myself for what I've put y-you and my darling Liam through..." and with that she broke down again. Clive put his arm around her shoulder and looked up at Mike. He too had tears in his eyes as he took up where Maddie had left off;

"This is the most selfless act imaginable Mike, especially given what you've been through at our hands recently. I pray that it goes as well as possible and that we are able to show you how much this means to all of us for the rest of our lives. I think that..."

"Look Clive..." interrupted Mike, getting a little impatient with the sermon being delivered to him in the corridor outside Liam's room rather than from the pulpit. "...much as it pains me to say it but I'm only doing this for my son. I'm certainly not doing it for you or Maddie ok? I'm a really good tissue match because, despite all the rumours to the contrary, Liam and I *are* closely related. I feel this is a small price to pay for getting my son back...I would have given anything you see?" Mike reached into his back pocket and pulled out a tattered brown leather wallet with an *Indian Motorcycles* logo on it. He opened it and pulled something from inside;

"Here, you'd better take this while we are at it" he said and held out a small folded piece of paper. Clive took it from him and unfolded it, recognising what it was immediately.

"I wondered why you never paid it into your bank," said Clive as he held the cheque for £30,000 he'd given Mike when they first met. He tore it in half and then in half again before continuing. "You must have great faith Mike, great faith indeed." and he looked heavenward again, this time for affirmation rather than the usual forgiveness.

"It's got nothing to do with faith; mine, yours or anyone else's. And it has nothing to do with your God, or anything like that for that matter. It was, well, it was only that, most of the time, I was too damned depressed to get my arse down to the bank. Simple as that. I suppose you could say I couldn't get myself motivated enough to give up on the situation as it just didn't seem right. Or that deep down, for some reason, something or some*one* was telling me I shouldn't be too hasty. But a 'higher force'? A God? Nah! I reckon it was just that I ruminated too much and liked watching *Cash in the Attic* more than the thought of walking down the High Street. Now, well I reckon I'd be taking money under false pretences, that's all."

Mike looked at Clive and then at Maddie and felt little for them at all. He knew he would need to form a relationship with them over time but, for the moment, at least, he didn't much want to do anything other than prepare himself for what was to come. He had Maddie's mobile phone number now (*Damaged Goods* – Gang of Four) and that was enough to be going along with. Mike spoke no more; he just turned and went into Liam's room.

"Hey, how's the patient doing nurse?" asked a smiling Mike, seeing Carol sitting and chatting with Liam.

"He's doing remarkably well considering the significant shock his system has been put through..." replied Carol winking at Liam, "...just imagine how you'd feel, getting hit by a car, suffering loads of injuries and then finding out the dead dad you'd never met turns out to be alive-

and-kicking and a college lecturer who still thinks and dresses like he's seventeen!" Carol and Liam laughed and Mike nearly burst with joy. Liam looked up and spoke, more like a mature twenty-five year old than a teenager;

"I always wanted a connection with someone, like a father. Mum always made out my dad was dead and so that was that. I got on just fine with the guys in Spain and France when we were travelling around so that was ok. Then I got back here and mum met Clive and he's nice. Not being funny but he was never the kind of dad I was going to have much in common with, not like the guys in Spain at any rate. Then I found all that stuff you kept for me over the years an' I thought, well, I thought that you might be as good as a dad, even if you weren't actually my dad. That's why I ran away, I wanted to meet you and find out why you did all that stuff for me. Now it turns out you *are* my dad and...well...it's like winning the lottery I guess."

Mike took a moment to absorb what Liam had just said. Managing, just, to compose himself he replied,

"Never mind all that mushy stuff, we've got a long way to go with all this..." Mike waved his hand around to emphasise that they were in a Renal Unit rather than at home planning a camping weekend together. "...and anyway, we need to get to know each other and become something more like a family. You need to meet your aunt Amy..."

"You're gonna bloody love *her!*" interjected Carol enthusiastically.

"Yeah...of course you are" said Mike, "...and my best mate Sid and my other friends and all that. Then there's Carol and Grace of course, we

306

mustn't forget them *and* we need to recover too. There's a lot to get through like I say and it might take a while...but it will be well worth it to see if we all get on together...."

"Talk of the devil..." said Carol as the door swung open and a young girl walked in wearing a grey blazer and a maroon school tie. "...This is *my* Grace everyone!"

"I'm not *her* Grace, I'm just, well, I'm Grace ok?" said Grace, her face colouring slightly as she raised an embarrassed eyebrow in the direction of her mother. Quickly regaining every ounce of her attitude riven teenage *joi-de-vivre* "You must be Liam and you..." she looked Mike up and down and then straight in the eye, "...you must be Mark?"

"Yes...er, no, well it's *Mike* actually. I'm Mike, and I'm very pleased to meet you Grace." Mike held out his hand rather formally and Grace fist-pumped it away. Mike looked at his hand rather quizzically for a moment, shook it slightly as if he had received a small electric shock and then looked back at Grace who had walked past him and towards Liam in the bed.

"Hey," she said softly.

"Yeah, hey," Liam replied. Neither said another word for a moment. Mike looked at Carol, shrugged his shoulders and mouthed the words "teenage telepathy?" at her but Carol just shrugged her shoulders back thinking Mike was announcing the title of a punk record by the Ramones - or someone similar - that he found befitted for the moment unfolding before their eyes..

"Did you manage to help me out Grace?" asked Carol. "Did you find what I needed at all?"

"Yeah..." said Grace nonchalantly; "...will

these do? I wasn't allowed to pay a deposit or anything...apparently you're supposed to be an *adult* or something to do *that*..." she pulled a *and-I-couldn't-care-less* face and handed her mother two photographs she produced from her school bag like a magician producing a white rabbit from a top hat.

Carol studied them, inspecting each in turn a number of times before putting her arms around her daughter and hugging her tightly. Grace squirmed and pulled a disgusted face in Liam's direction. Liam reddened and pulled a face back at her, smiling as he did so. Teenagers are so good at pulling faces. Turning to Mike, Carol said,

"Whilst you're being all schmaltzy about families and stuff, can I introduce you to Malcolm and Vivienne?" and she held out the photographs. Mike took them from her and fixed his gaze upon two of the sweetest looking puppy photographs he had ever seen.

"Of course, one's a Red Setter and one's a Lurcher so I guess you know which is which?" said a beaming Carol.

"Er, actually mum, I couldn't find a female Lurcher so they're both boys, they'll be ready for re-homing in a few weeks time if you definitely want 'em?" said an unapologetic Grace.

"Well how are we going to have a boy called Vivienne? That's not right is it?" Carol said, sounding both bemused and disappointed. A few moments went by before Mike spoke;

"Hang on, I know what! There was a male character in the *Young Ones* on TV with the same name wasn't there? We'll just have a male Vivian," he said, offering a simple compromise solution. Carol didn't seem enamoured;

"That's not the point though is it? They were

supposed to be named after Malcolm McLaren and Vivi..."

"Why Malcolm and Vivienne anyway?" asked Liam, interrupting Carol's flow whilst taking his turn at looking at the pictures. "If they're both boys, lets just call them *Topper* and *Jonesie* after the drummer and guitarist of the Clash? They're much cooler names anyway."

The End

Chapter headings;

1. *Boredom* – The Buzzcocks
2. *Looking After Number One* - Boomtown Rats
3. *Talking* - The Boys
4. *I Am Yours* – The Adicts
5. *Pale Blue Eyes* – The Velvet Underground
6. *Between the Wars* - Billy Bragg
7. *The Street Parade* – The Clash
8. *Quicksand* – David Bowie
9. *Lost in the Supermarket* – The Clash
10. *Anxiety* – The Ramones
11. *Doesn't Make it Alright* – The Specials
12. *The Card Cheat* – The Clash
13. *Isolation* – Joy Division
14. *Life* – Alternative TV
15. *Out of Mind* – The Cure
16. *Moods For Moderns* – Elvis Costello
17. *Candy Says* – The Velvet Underground
18. *Apollo 13* – The Tears
19. *No Fun* – The Stooges
20. *Psycho Killer* {English translation of middle-eight/bridge section} – Talking Heads
21. *Love Like Blood* – Killing Joke
22. *Novacaine* – Green Day
23. *A Song From Under the Floorboards* - Magazine
24. *Play For Today* – The Cure
25. *I'm Not Down* - The Clash
26. *The Midas Touch* – *The* Monochrome Set
27. *Enough Time* – The Stranglers
28. *New Rose* – The Damned
29. *Being Around* – The Lemonheads
30. *Reasons To Be Cheerful (Pt 3)* – Ian Dury & The Blockheads

+   +   +   +   +   +

About the author:

Originally from West London, Den Barry has lived on the South Coast for most of his life. He is 51 years of age, is married to Jane and they share their lives with three dogs and two cats.

As well as a husband, father and animal lover he has – at various points in his life (and in no particular order) – been (or still is) a drummer, a socialist and a pushover. Once a grocer he's also been a taxi driver, cheated on, flattered and spat at; he's been a role model, a performer, a grandfather and a Chairman; a singer, brother, father and historian. He's been described as a cynic, a punk rocker, social entrepreneur, music lover and even a Best Man. He's liberal, visually impaired and a QPR fan. He's also been a pacifist, a radio presenter and was once a catholic; he's been a housing manager, a film actor and skinny; a chauffeur, a confidante, a mature student and a cub scout; he has been a community development worker, a recording artist and clinically depressed. For some strange reason he wants to add the term "fiction writer" to this long, yet not exhaustive, list.

When he was a very young child, a neighbour used to chat to Den's mother whilst he sat on his Mum's hip listening to them. The neighbour, Edna Woodford, would watch Den quietly observing all around him whilst refusing to speak a word. Edna would say "He's taking it all in you know, he'll write a book one day he will, you just wait and see." Den's parents would repeat this rather dull anecdote over the years...to no avail.

In late 2011 Den started losing his sight unexpectedly and, following a series of operations, this resulted in permanently impaired vision. He continued to work for a while but was eventually forced to give up his career. Not enjoying the view from the scrapheap (due partly to his poor vision and partly because he felt he still had something to say) he was encouraged by Jane to start writing stories. Not only did it provide an outlet for his creativity, it was also a way to fill his time and it served as a form of therapy in lifting him out of frequent periods of low mood. Having no experience of creative writing he joined a creative writing group; spent time exploring his local literary scene and his first novel, *No Way Out* was finally completed at the end of 2015. Still receiving steadfast encouragement from the long-suffering Jane, his second – as yet untitled – novel is well underway and, as his friends and family will attest, Den *still* has plenty to say.

Maybe Edna Woodford was right all along...

Made in the USA
Charleston, SC
05 December 2016